LOVE&
OTHER
TRAIN
WRECKS

Also by Leah Konen
The Last Time We Were Us
The Romantics

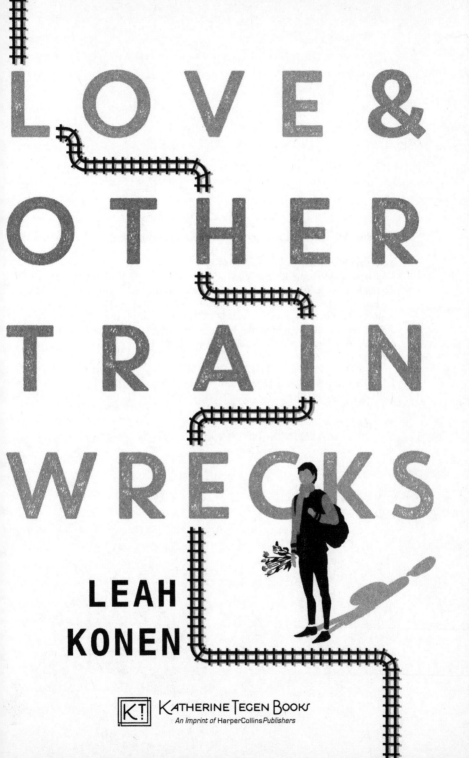

LOVE & OTHER TRAIN WRECKS

LEAH KONEN

KT KATHERINE TEGEN BOOKS
An Imprint of HarperCollins Publishers

Katherine Tegen Books is an imprint of HarperCollins Publishers.

Love and Other Train Wrecks
Copyright © 2018 by Leah Konen
All rights reserved. Printed in the United States of America.
No part of this book may be used or reproduced in any manner whatsoever without
written permission except in the case of brief quotations embodied in critical articles
and reviews. For information address HarperCollins Children's Books, a division of
HarperCollins Publishers, 195 Broadway, New York, NY 10007.
www.epicreads.com

Library of Congress Control Number: 2017938600
ISBN 978-0-06-240250-9

Typography by Carla Weise
17 18 19 20 21   PC/LSCH   10 9 8 7 6 5 4 3 2 1
❖
First Edition

FOR MY SISTER, KIMBERLY,
MY FIRST-EVER READER AND FAN

To:
North Pulaski

IN-TRANSIT FOR HOLD

From: SULZER
Date: Thursday, Sep 27
2018 12:19PM

Title: Love & other train
wrecks
Material type: Hardcover Book
Call number: FICTION
Item barcode: R0450915291
Assigned branch: Sulzer Regional

PART ONE

THE TRAIN

AMMY

THE TRAIN ISN'T AS ROMANTIC AS I THOUGHT IT WOULD BE.

I'm usually not that fanciful, but come on, it's a train. I'd imagined steel bar carts rolling down the aisle, people looking out the windows watching the country roll by, newspapers spread wide, and conductor hats tilted just so. Women in dresses and stockings and men in suits.

I guess I've watched too many movies.

And I've learned by now that nothing is like the movies. Especially nothing this year.

I'm currently on the Amtrak, a train that looks like a silver bullet but hardly moves like one, heading along the Eastern Seaboard. The seats are itchy blue polyester with a print that must have been designed before I was born, and there isn't

1

a bar cart in sight. I haven't even seen a place to get food, despite walking three cars up.

As I look out the window, all I see is a kajillion shades of gray. Patches of dirt and what should be grass. Slabs of concrete and factories that look like they came straight out of a Dickens novel—and Dickens isn't even my thing. An industrial wasteland. I touch my hand to the window. It's cold and icy, unlike the swelter in here from too many people wearing too many layers.

The train is crowded. There's a guy in a suit, a disheveled type who looks like he may have been off of work for a while but still wears his jacket, tie, and slacks like it's Miss Havisham's wedding dress. He's got a Rorschach print of sweat on the white button-down beneath his crumpled suit jacket.

And there are certainly no ladies in dresses and stockings like you'd see in an old movie, at least not that I can see. Mostly everyone is dressed like me—in jeans and a chunky sweater, with a pile of discarded scarves and hats and gloves, paraphernalia designed for the cold outside, not the heat in here.

Everyone is on their phones or tablets, and though the ticket taker *was* wearing a cool, flat-topped conductor hat, he had a decidedly gruff way of saying, "Tickets, please!" that made it clear to all within earshot that he'd like to be just about anywhere but here. It's all so far from quaint and romantic. But, then again, so is this whole stupid last-minute idea.

My phone rings, and I stand up to get it out of the overhead carrier, nearly hitting my head in the process. At five foot eight, I'm just tall enough to make the clearance tight. My red leather bag, a birthday gift from my dad, mailed express from Hudson, New York, three days *after* my birthday, is wedged in between my big rolling suitcase and three or four shiny plastic bags that read "Century 21." I tug at it with two hands, but in the process, my suitcase starts to come down, too. My red bag falls on the floor, but I manage to catch the suitcase before it does any major damage.

In front of me, I see a middle-aged man looking at me like I'm the most helpless thing on the planet. His wife stares intently at the plastic bags, as if I'm going to mess up whatever they have in there (sorry, not sorry). If those two hadn't put so much stuff overhead, I'd have had a little more wiggle room.

My phone stops ringing while I'm still holding the suitcase with two hands, and I shove at it a couple of times, but it doesn't seem to want to go back in with the plastic bags all tilted over now, so I lower it down slowly and plop it onto the seat next to mine. I know I'm probably not *supposed* to take up a whole seat just for my bag, but it's a five-hour train ride and I'm only in hour three and, to be honest, I'd like to avoid having a chatty neighbor at all costs.

I sit down and lean over to grab my red bag off of the floor when my phone starts ringing again.

"You going to get that?" The woman in front of me whips around. Lord knows what she had in those bags to make her so frustrated with me. Or maybe it's just the New York way.

I give her a shrug as I fish in my bag for my phone. Everyone on this train seems to know how to do the whole train thing a lot better than me.

But that's not quite my fault. I wasn't exactly planning on this trip. Until I called Kat, my almost-stepsister, last night, I had actually 100 percent decided against going. Something I'd decided months before.

Come. Stay with us for the week. You'll regret it if you don't. It will be easy.

This is not easy, not by a long shot.

I dig through the books and random stuff I shoved in my bag this morning as my phone continues to ring. My shoulders tense up, waiting for the woman to say something again, but finally I find it stuck between *Madame Bovary* and *Norwegian Wood*. As I suspected, it's Kat. I swear she's the only person our age who prefers calling to texting.

"Hey," I say, feeling the uptick in my pulse as soon as I answer.

It's not her that makes me nervous, but the whole situation.

Family isn't supposed to do that to you. But family is supposed to be a lot of things that, in the last year, I've realized it isn't.

"Tell me your text wasn't a lie. Tell me you're *actually* on the train." As usual, Kat's voice has that bubbly, uppity tone, like a Valley Girl who's had too much coffee.

"I am indeed on the train," I say. The woman in front of me again whips her head around, like I'm talking too loud, even though I'm talking at a totally normal volume level, IMHO.

Kat squeals, and I jerk the phone away from my ear instinctively. "Oh my God," she says. "I'm so excited. You're *literally* going to rescue me from the Dumpster fire that today promises to be."

Normally, I would take the opportunity to explain to her the difference between figuratively and literally, but I'm too preoccupied with my mom's words from this morning.

How could you leave me today of all days?

Whatever "Dumpster fire" Kat thinks she has on her hands, whatever's going on with Sophie's dress or Bea's hair, it's nothing compared to my last twenty-four hours.

"You know I'm not going to be all jumping up and down with glee for my dad and your mom, right?"

"I know," she says. "*Duh.* Me either. But still, your dad will be happy. He's been moping around all week. He misses you."

I roll my eyes and stifle a bitter laugh. I'm sure he does. I'm sure I'm the first thing on his mind right now. I'm sure it's all Ammy, Ammy, Ammy in his head. I mean, who wouldn't be thinking of the daughter they abandoned when they're about to marry a hot yoga instructor ten years their junior?

I'm an afterthought to him, a footnote on his new life, reminding him of his old one. I even found out about this stupid ceremony from Kat before I heard about it from him.

Kat doesn't wait for my reaction. "When do you get in?"

"One thirty," I say. "You can still pick me up, right?"

"'Course," Kat says. "At the Hudson station?"

"Yes."

"Sweet," she says. "P.S. I told Bea, but not anyone else."

I sigh. "You said you wouldn't tell anyone. It's supposed to be a surprise."

I can practically hear Kat roll her eyes through the phone. "She's my sister. And your soon-to-be stepsister. She won't tell. Plus, she's super excited."

Kat's words hit me harder than they should. *Soon-to-be stepsister.* This is really happening, even if, legally, it won't really count for anything. Bea and Kat all dressed up. Sophie, my soon-to-be stepmom, in some boho off-white outfit. My dad professing his love for a woman who is decidedly not my mom.

My eyes flit to the train doors ahead, and for a second, I wish I could run into the vestibule, pull the emergency brake, and tell them to turn the train around, take me back to Virginia, where I could give my mom a hug and tell her I'm sorry and that I'm still Team Mom, no matter what.

But I know at the same time that going back wouldn't be any better. That what my mom and I had is already lost, lost in a way that I never fully realized until last night.

"I'm excited to see *you guys*, at least," I say finally.

"All right, I gotta go help my mom steam her stupid dress. See you soon."

And in her Kat way, she hangs up before I have the chance to say anything else.

I stare at my phone, wishing we could talk longer, wishing I could tell her how scared I am that my mom won't forgive me for this, that I'm doing the completely wrong thing, that my dad doesn't even really want me to be there, that his new family is enough for him.

But I shake my head, forcing the thoughts aside. I refrain from opening up my messages, going into the rabbit hole that is the convo with my mom, which I muted about an hour ago out of mental health necessity.

Instead, I flip between all the social networks and scroll through photos of people gathered with their families doing family things for the holidays. Of Dara and her brother getting on the plane to Universal Studios. Of the smartest girl in my high school on a road trip back from South Carolina. I feel that familiar gut stab of jealousy I get every time I see a photo of an even somewhat nuclear family, and I bite my lip, trying to ignore it.

Deep down, I know my dad will be happy to see me. He wants me to be there. At least that's what he told me on the phone last month. But still, I know that if I didn't come, it would all go on just fine. I'm not his only family anymore. Mom's not even his family at all. We're second place. And that hurts.

I look out the window, seeking a distraction even in ugly industrial scenery, but it's totally dark, and I can only see subtle hints of graffiti against concrete tunnel walls.

We must have reached Penn Station, and I didn't even realize it. I lean my head against the glass, feel the cool, damp condensation, and tune out the sound of the doors opening, of the footsteps invading.

I want to sleep until I get there, not worry about any of this anymore. I want it to be tomorrow, I want this stupid day to be over, and I want to be sitting in Kat's room, watching *Friends* reruns and deciding what overpriced Hudson joint to hit up for brunch.

My eyes are fully closed when I hear the voice, urgent and impatient.

"Excuse me."

And then again, before I even have a chance to move.

"*Excuse* me. Can I get in here?"

NOAH

11:29 A.M.

You can always tell when someone hasn't been on the train before. Normally, I try to help them. I give them the old rundown, tell them you have to push the button to get the doors between the cars to open, let them know where the food station is located, and warn them to avoid the Santa Fe chicken wrap at all costs; it's kind of fun. Today, though, I'm too damn nervous to even care about it. I'm too preoccupied with Rina.

The train is weirdly packed for noon, when no one should really be commuting. I'm guessing a lot of people are still off for the holidays like me, even though it's January 3.

The girl looks half asleep; the condensation from the window has matted down her short, dark brown hair.

I point to her bag, the dead giveaway. It's the ultimate rookie mistake. "The train is full. So, uh, you need to move that."

"Oh," she says. "Yeah."

She stands up. She's tall, and I'm worried she's going to hit her head on the ledge, but she doesn't, just barely. Then she hoists the bag above her head.

I drop the flowers in the seat and go to help her, grabbing the edge of the bag for balance. I catch a faint scent of peppermint coming from her hair.

"I got it," she says sharply. She gives it a firm shove. It slides in like a puzzle piece.

"Thanks," I say. "Are these bags yours?" I ask, gesturing to a trio of Century 21 bags.

She shakes her head, and I'm not too surprised, because she doesn't exactly look like the type to be cruising cramped aisles for discount designer crap. I lean over her and give the bags a push forward, so they're not in our space. A lady in front of us gives me a look, but she knows train travel protocol well enough not to argue. I shove my backpack on top and grab the flowers before sitting down, setting them on my lap.

The girl glances a touch too long at the flowers, but she doesn't say anything.

I carefully examine the petals. Two of the flowers are ever so slightly smushed.

Will Rina notice? Yes.

Will she care? Hopefully not.

The girl's ticket is clutched in her hand. She's wearing a

thick, oversized hunter-green sweater and faded jeans. She's definitely the academic type, probably heading to a college tour of Bard, the liberal arts school near my town.

Rina used to go on about Bard students who'd come to the restaurant where she worked two summers ago. She said they were all special snowflakes going on about trigger warnings and all that. She hated the ultra-liberal, touchy-feely aspect of the school.

On the flip side, she loved the people who came up from the city, even though a lot of them were just as snowflake-y, if you ask me. It's half the reason why I added Hunter to my list last year. Why I decided, eventually, to go. Even though the Bard students never bothered me. Even though Rina and I once got into a long debate about whether or not trigger warnings should be a thing. She won, not because she was right, but because Rina is good at winning arguments.

Rina's a city girl at heart, even though she was raised in the country. She's got a no-bullshit way about her. It fits right in. She loves visiting her dad there. Loves getting lost looking for cheap handbags and sticky bao in Chinatown. Loves riding a Citi Bike over to Prospect Park. Loves dragging me through Century 21, filling up her own plastic bags with discount designer crap that, yes, I'll admit, does look good on her.

She was the one who came with me on my initial visits to Hunter, because that was when my folks were being completely self-involved and not at all on top of things. She was the one who convinced me that life could be pretty great on the Upper East Side of Manhattan.

I arrange one of the smushed petals so it doesn't look so smushed, review my handiwork, decide, or *hope*, that it's good enough.

I steal a glance at my seat partner, who's now reading Murakami. She's *definitely* a Bard girl.

Honestly, I think Rina's biggest issue with Bard is that it's so close to home. It would never be enough of a leap for her.

Apart from the stupid price tag, I probably would have been okay with staying close if it hadn't been for Rina. But unlike me, Rina needs adventure. Give her a month of really living there and she'd probably know the city better than I do. She's the type who'd turn down a street she didn't know and never look back.

I'm the type who looks back. It's how I lost her. But I'm going to fix that with this trip. I'm not going to doubt myself, or us, anymore.

I tuck the flowers into the seat pocket in front of me and shrug out of my jacket. Then I glance around. Across from us, there's a guy tapping away on a dinosaur of a laptop in a suit that's seen better days.

I pull my messenger bag, the one I use for class, onto my lap and retrieve my Kindle, then tuck the bag neatly beneath my seat. I've done this commute from my crappy, cramped dorm in the city to my parents' midcentury ranch in Lorenz Park, just past Hudson, three times now. But it's always been to visit my folks. Go home for fall break. Get laundry done. Snag a frozen casserole for my mini dorm freezer. The typical first-year-of-college drill.

I've never gone home for this reason.

I adjust the flowers ever so slightly, afraid they might get crushed even more if I'm not careful.

I try to focus on the words on the screen, but they blur before my eyes, melding together and jumbling around like ABC soup. I can't get Rina out of my head.

The girl next to me seems equally distracted. She's got a finger holding her place in her Murakami and is wriggling around and sighing loudly.

She looks like she's trying, unsuccessfully, to make the most of the foot or so of space between her knees and the seat in front of her.

She catches my eye briefly before looking away.

"Not quite the romantic train trip you imagined?" I ask.

She stops messing with the scarf at her feet and looks right at me. "Um, what?"

I was trying to make a joke. The train definitely wasn't what I expected the first time, what with the stale sweat around me and the uncomfortable seats.

She doesn't seem to take it that way.

Should I mumble never mind? Maybe.

Should I turn back to my Kindle and try to read? Probably.

But the thought of spending the next two hours wondering about how Rina will react to my arrival feels unbearable all of a sudden.

"First time on the Amtrak?" I ask, trying to sound cheerful.

She bites her lip and crosses her arms, her coat inching

into my space. Her eyes are wide, too far apart, like she's perpetually surprised, and her chin edges to an almost point, kind of like an angry heart. She is sharp everywhere that Rina is not; Rina with her wavy chestnut hair and her round face and that way she has of puffing her bottom lip out when she wants something.

"What's it to you?" the girl asks.

I laugh. It's like she's trying to go full New Yorker on me, even though her generic suburban accent—and her lack of understanding of the basic train rules—would have me guessing otherwise.

"Sorry," I say. "I was just trying to make conversation."

She rolls her eyes and turns away.

Oh well.

I glance back at my Kindle but still can't focus, so I tuck it in the pocket in front of me, retrieve my phone, and open up my messages.

I want to text Rina. So very badly. I want to talk to her again.

Of course, the problem remains of what to say:

Hey, I'm planning on coming by yours tonight for a grand gesture that will hopefully win you back. You around?

How's things? Been a while!

Do you think of me ever? I think about you ALL the time.

I close out of my messages. Anything I could say would come across as utterly ridiculous. That's why I have to talk to her in person. That's why I have to stick to my plan.

I'd love to stalk her on Facebook or Instagram. I'd love

to make sure she doesn't have a new boyfriend, even though Danny told me that Cassie told him that she didn't. I'd love to just see some recent photos of her, but she blocked me on everything last summer, as soon as we broke up. Rina clearly likes to make a clean break. I guess I can't totally blame her.

Apparently Cassie also said she thinks Rina misses me sometimes.

I check my feed, and there are my parents, in a selfie taken on the ship, Bermuda views behind them. I've tried to remain positive about this whole thing, but I'm still kind of mad at them for ditching me this year and leaving our house empty for Christmas break.

It's not like Christmas is that important to me. We're Jewish, for one thing, so it's not like it's ever been a huge deal for us. Still, I always enjoyed our sad fake tree and shiny tinsel. I'm glad that my dad moved back in and they called their trial separation quits, but as sweet as it is, I'm not sure that this "love renewal cruise" was entirely necessary. At least not a twelve-night one. I get nervous just thinking about how much they spent. Money was tight last semester, and that was with a small scholarship, my part-time job, and student loans. If they can't help me out with things like books and lodging, it's going to be tough.

I wasn't completely alone for the holidays, at least. My roommate at Hunter, Alex, did let me crash with him in his parents' ridiculous Dumbo loft for a few days. It was fun seeing the fancier side of the city. We had lox and capers on Christmas morning, and lobster and mussels on Christmas night.

Even so, I would have rather been back in Lorenz Park with my folks, unwrapping gifts under the tree and ordering buckets of Chinese takeout.

And with Rina.

I briefly glance out the window at the skyline getting farther and farther behind me, giving way to the ugly suburban sprawl that is Yonkers.

I guess I should thank my folks, really. It was their trip that made me realize just how much I missed Rina. It was their trip that reminded me that sometimes people can split up and still get back together.

That's what happens when two people love each other.

I glance back to my phone, flipping through my feed, but there's nothing interesting.

So I pull my Kindle back out because there's really nothing else to do.

"Damn it," I mutter under my breath. It's dead.

The girl turns her head and gives me a look, all of a sudden smug.

"You know, the funny thing about real books is that they don't need batteries."

AMMY

THE GUY NEXT TO ME GIVES ME THAT KIND OF DOOFY look that generically attractive guys always have. Like they've grown so used to their ultra-symmetrical faces pleasing the masses that they've never learned to manipulate their features in socially appropriate ways. I can't tell if he's surprised or angry or what, but I don't really care. I had to shoot something back after the (sexist?) comment about me not getting the romantic adventure I'd expected, which only made me angrier since, to be totally honest, he kind of hit the nail on the head.

But *he* doesn't have to know that.

I adjust myself in my itchy seat and take a quick look out the window. The industrial wasteland has turned to leaf-bare trees and pale gray sky, peppered occasionally with some ugly concrete graffitied buildings. I guess we're not to the truly beautiful parts just yet. Still, there is a river, and if I crane my head around, I can still see New York City in the background—which is kind of glorious, I'll admit it.

Then I look back at the guy, who's still giving me a blank look in response to my comment. His skin is olive-y, and his hair is curly. He's wearing a Steelers jersey, dark blue jeans, and has a bright orange puffy jacket tucked beneath a khaki messenger bag with a Taylor Swift pin on the flap—weird. He's probably in college, studying business or something.

A bunch of pink roses are tucked into the seat pocket in front of him, likely for whichever sorority girl is falling all over him this month.

"All I'm saying is, real books are much more reliable." I tap the front of *Norwegian Wood*. "You should try them sometime."

He laughs, and his blank look turns to a smile that takes up his whole face. "Oh, should I?"

I steal a look at the flowers again. Roses—so clichéd.

He's a classic bro: sporty, boring, basic. And a bro of the worst order, from the look of those flowers. You know, the kind who fancies himself a "good guy." He probably thinks that just because he follows the *Woman Wooing 101 Handbook* that it's all going to work out just splendidly. He's the type who doesn't realize that romance is pointless because everyone just ends up hurting each other anyway.

And I know this for a fact.

Even people you were 100 percent sure were going to be together forever.

Dara and Simone say I'm being too cynical. Dara reminded me that her parents split up, too, and she was still pretty much in love with the idea of love. Simone said it was natural to be cynical, but lots of children of divorce go on to have happy relationships.

But they don't get it. Because it wasn't just a normal split. I remember Dara's parents together. They were miserable all the time. Mine weren't. I swear the three of us had a thing that worked. Until it didn't. And when you get blindsided like that, well, it's hard to just bounce back.

Stranger McBro-erson is still smiling at me. Is he waiting for me to bat my lashes or something?

Then he cocks his head to the side and squirms in his seat, his feet ramming up against the bottom of the seat in front of him.

"Murakami?" he asks.

"Yeah," I say, maybe a little rudely. "You heard of him?"

"Ouch."

I shrug, and I'm not even entirely sure why I'm being so rude to this guy, but then I look at the flowers again, and they only serve to enrage me.

Sophie loves roses. There were these ugly little rose illustrations all over the stupid craft-paper invitation she sent. I make a split-second decision to double down instead of backing off, because I'm in that kind of mood, and I really didn't want to share my row with a chatty stranger anyway.

"What've you got on there, *The Da Vinci Code?*"

I wait with bated breath to see if he thinks this is an insult. Most would, but you really never know with these bro types. Just this year, a guy in my AP English class asked if he could do his classics project on James Patterson. Like, for real.

The guy flips the cover of his Kindle shut and puts it back in his bag. "There's really no need to be mean."

I laugh, but then I see that he's actually offended. I put a finger in my book. "Hey, you made assumptions about me. You thought I was a silly little girl looking for a fanciful train ride. Nothing wrong with me doing the same about you."

He tilts his head to the side, like he's trying to figure me out—and I *don't* want to be figured out right now. Then he crosses his arms, muscles bulging against his jersey, a move I'm sure he's well aware of. A couple of rows in front of us, a middle-aged man lets out a hacking cough, spreading I-don't-even-want-to-think-what-kind-of-vile-New-York-City germs everywhere.

Then the lady turns around and gives me her signature shushing look. Outside, the first spot of snow falls through the sky. I feel that familiar leap of my heart that always comes when I see snow, ever since I was a kid. But it disappears just as quickly, because I'm not a kid anymore, and nothing has the same magic as it used to. Not these days, anyway.

Besides, too much snow and Kat will have a hard time picking me up at the station.

The guy lets out a scoff.

"What?" I ask, unable to stop myself from engaging with Mr. Bro.

He grins. "You know, it doesn't make you an automatic genius just because you read Murakami. That's what everyone reads when they want to look smart. Plus, it's a little full of itself, anyway."

"*You've* read Murakami?"

He sighs, turns in his seat so he's facing me, and ticks off his big fingers. "*Norwegian Wood, Kafka on the Shore,* and *1Q84.*" He pauses, reading my reaction, and grins. "Don't look so shocked, okay? It's not that hard. One page after the next just like any other book."

I put the Murakami down and tap my fingers against my knee, ready to win this battle. "So what are you currently being prevented from reading? What's tucked away on the little Kindle that couldn't?"

His grin gets bigger. "*Mockingjay.* You know, book three of the Hunger Games."

I can't help it. I burst into laughter. "Murakami's overrated but the Hunger Games isn't? Jesus."

"You know, I said the same thing, until my g—"

He pauses, and it's like his smile disappears in a flash.

"My *ex*-girlfriend got me to read them," he says. "And they're great. You're only cheating yourself."

I look at the flowers again. What is he trying to do, win back a girl? Oh boy, this guy is a caricature of himself.

I steal another glance out the window. The speed of the

train makes the snow look epic, fast and zippy, like we're at the beginning of Space Mountain, the part before the roller coaster starts where all the stars whip by. The Hunger Games, I think bitterly. My dad was constantly trying to get me to read them last summer, inspired by his shiny new nuclear family. While my mom was popping Ativans to get through the afternoon, he was going on about how Kat was Team Gale but Bea was Team Peeta, and I needed to read them to break the tie.

Er, no thanks.

I look back at the guy and feel my stomach rumble. His face is that kind that rests in a smile instead of a frown, like Resting Bitch Face but Resting Happy Face instead. It's annoying. "Maybe that's why you love your Kindle so much? To hide away things like the Hunger Games?"

The guy's eyes narrow, and then his face falls, his emotions written all over it—Lord knows he would be horrible at poker. He taps his foot, his knee bouncing up and down.

"Yeah, and maybe you love not having one so you can show the world that you're a smart person who reads Murakami."

I bite my lip. I can see that I've upset him, and suddenly, taking out all my anger and sadness and frustration on a train stranger isn't fun anymore.

"Sorry, it's just that I'm hungry and I'm hot, and I've had the worst day. . . ."

But he doesn't listen. He gets up quickly, flipping around and walking as fast as he can down the aisle that leads to the back cars.

I turn, watching until he disappears behind the doors to the next car, and then I go back to my book. There's no law that you have to be friends with your train neighbor anyway, I remind myself. I'd bet a kajillion bucks that my book is about a kajillion times better than some whiny kids-are-killing-kids crap, anyway.

I don't care what anyone—especially not my dad, or some basic bro on a train—says.

But after a minute or so, I set my book down. It's impossible to read with everything bouncing around like pinballs in my head—what the wedding will be like, what my mom's doing right now, whether there will ever be a time when I feel normal again, when it feels like things have settled down.

The snow is coming down harder now, the weather getting all nasty. For the briefest of moments, I think about texting my mom. She loves snow more than a seven-year-old on Christmas morning.

But I don't know what to say.

And I don't want to see all of the things she's *already* said.

So I gaze out the window, and I watch as the weather gets worse and worse, and I pray that she'll find a way to forgive me.

That I've actually done the right thing.

NOAH

"WHAT'LL YOU HAVE?"

The woman has frazzled hair, deep laugh lines, and sounds like she's been smoking every day for about a thousand years. She's wearing the classic white-and-blue Amtrak uniform, and the buttons of her shirt tug and bulge, like her body is staging a coup, trying to break free.

The café car is the same crappy one they always have. It's only good for beer, according to pretty much everyone. Sometimes, the announcer guy even jokes about how bad the food is here. But it's all I've got right now in the way of sustenance.

"Can I get a turkey, gouda, and bacon wrap?" I ask. The

photo on the board behind her makes it look far more delicious than it actually is.

She nods. "Anything else?"

"A Coke," I say.

As she starts to ring me up, I think of my neighbor's words; she said she was hungry and that was why she decided to start a full-on argument with me over the Hunger Games. Which is kind of funny, now that I think of it.

"Make that two wraps," I say a little impulsively. I tell myself that I can always eat both if she doesn't want hers. Or if handing a stranger a sandwich comes off to her as creepy.

Karma's like a bank account; that's what I believe, at least. You have to constantly put stuff in it if you want to make a withdrawal later. And the thing is, I'm planning on attempting to make a rather large withdrawal this evening. It's the three-year anniversary of my first date with Rina. Or at least it would be, if I hadn't royally screwed everything up. I've got the flowers. I've got my apology speech. I've even got a handwritten poem. At seven tonight, I'll be at her door, ready to explain how big of an idiot I was, ready to take her to the place she was always begging me to take her to. I'm definitely going to need karma on my side.

The lady finishes ringing me up, and I pay twenty-one fifty, otherwise known as the equivalent of highway robbery, and head back toward my seat.

I walk through the café car, filled with men and women

25

doing business on their laptops while pounding bottles of Yuengling.

I tap at the button, and the metal doors start to slide, and I can already feel the cool winter air seeping in from the vestibule.

The car directly in front of the dining area is just as packed as ours. There's a din of old-man snoring, peppered with giggles and squeals from a trio of kids eating string cheese.

It's Saturday, and everyone is ready to get the hell out of the city and get a little peace.

I push the button again, breezing through to the next car, our car.

My neighbor is not even reading her book when I get back. No surprise there, really. I won't tell her this, but I only barely got through the three Murakami books I read. *Norwegian Wood* is the only one I actually read cover to cover. For some reason, everyone says he's the *best ever*, but I find it hard to agree. Now, the Hunger Games, on the other hand, with adventure and politics and a little romantic drama, is impossible not to like, even if it's not exactly the height of contemporary literature. But I read enough of those at school. A guy needs balance.

Instead of reading, she's staring out the window, which is frosted now from the weather outside, watching snow fall softly as the old brick smokestacks and the more rustic parts of New York State whip by. Once the brick buildings pass, all you can see are leafless trees and the Hudson. There's something magical about it, even though I've done it a few times now. It makes me feel free, like I could get lost in the woods and live my best life or something. . . .

I shake my head, realizing that I would never do anything like that. I would never let myself be impulsive enough to lose my way.

Rina's the type to go out of her way to get lost.

I'm not.

On the other side of the river, I see the top of one of the mansions up here that probably belonged to a Rockefeller. My neighbor seems to be warming up to this ride. Maybe the train *is* kind of romantic when you think about it. Not in the way the movies always show you, but in a different one, a better one, because it's more real.

I hope she's happy, and I hope she does enjoy Bard if that's where she's going.

I hope she gets all that she wants out of this trip.

I hope we both do.

I'm about to sit down when a little kid scurries by, kicking my shins as he does. The magic of the moment dissipates quickly. I look up to see a Brooklyn mom in loose, billowy clothes. She shrugs instead of apologizing, but I try not to let it get to me.

I sit down; watch as the kid's drooling little brother runs by. The cellophane around the sandwiches crinkles in my hand, and the girl is still looking out the window.

All of a sudden, I feel stupid for doing something so weirdly generous.

Rina's words flash through my head, the day before we broke up:

Why does everything have to be so difficult *with you?*

I briefly think about keeping both for myself, but that would shoot all my karma straight to hell, and so I clear my throat. "Uh, I hope you're not a vegetarian," I say.

"Huh?" She turns to me, stares at the wrap I'm holding out to her. She doesn't say anything, and I know that Rina was right. Giving someone a sandwich *shouldn't* be this difficult.

Why can't you ever just do something *without thinking of every possible outcome?*

Rina wasn't trying to change me, like Bryson was always insisting. Rina was trying to *help* me.

"I got you a wrap," I say, trying to infuse as much confidence into my voice as possible.

Her eyebrows arch, and her eyes seem to grow a size or two bigger. She looks for a second like that indie movie star with the brother. The brother who was in *Brokeback Mountain*, but not the actor who died. I'm horrible with names.

"You didn't have to do that," she says hesitantly.

My fingers tighten around the sandwich, crinkling the cellophane again. She doesn't want it. This is awkward. This is what I was afraid of.

"I'm sure it's not very good anyway, and if you don't want it, I can eat both. Take one for the team." I deliver my best smile, a forced laugh that I hope doesn't sound as weird to her as it does to me.

The girl takes a short breath, hesitating.

"It's for you, really. I would eat it if you really aren't hungry, or if you think someone you don't know buying you a sandwich is weird, but I got it for you. It's turkey and bacon." I push it farther toward her. "Here, just take it."

I'm so eager for her to just grab the damn wrap and put me out of my misery that my hand nearly shakes. I curse myself for being so awkward. For believing in things like karma, for getting on this damn train at all . . .

"Thank you, I'm starving," she says, interrupting my thoughts. She takes it, rips off the cellophane viciously, and shoves it in her mouth, taking an extra-large first bite. Relief washes over me like the first dip in a pool on a hot day, the feeling I always get when the pressure is off.

"Damn, you *were* hungry," I say.

Her cheeks get all chipmunky, but after a minute, she swallows. "I couldn't find food before."

"When did you get on the train?" I ask.

"Baltimore," she says, before taking another bite. "After driving an hour from Virginia." She points ahead. "I went three cars up, past the bathrooms and everything, but I didn't see anything. I was going to ask someone, but everyone looked so intent on their iPads. And then I didn't want to leave my suitcase alone for too long, so I came back. I figured maybe this train just didn't have food or something."

"You have to go two cars behind," I say. "The dining car is always in the back. The conductor is supposed to tell you, but sometimes they forget. You should have said something. I would have pointed you in the right direction."

She smiles and takes another bite. "I was too busy being in a bad mood."

That gets me laughing, really laughing this time.

I open my wrap, and for a few minutes, everything is simple. The sound of crinkling cellophane. The crunch of romaine. The taste of basic, no-frills turkey. The subtle vibrations of the train on the tracks. The vision of snow through the window. It's nice, almost. One of those little moments that people are always talking about in novels and movies and such. Perhaps this is one of the moments that changes the course of your life. Maybe this *is* the right thing to do to prove to the universe that Rina and I should be us again. Something about it feels *special*.

My seatmate crumples up her trash when she's done, forming it into a tight ball that she shoves into her purse. I do the same with mine, tucking it in the oversized pocket of my messenger bag, which is full of Altoids, extra-long CVS receipts, and that strip of pictures of me and Rina. The only pictures I have left.

I zip the bag shut and turn to my neighbor. "Uh, I'm Noah, by the way. Noah Adler." I stick out my hand.

She takes it, and hers is surprisingly cool, even though it's warm in here. "Ammy." She doesn't offer a last name, like she's some kind of one-name performer.

Or maybe I'm the weirdo for telling her both. Rina always said it was strange to be so formal with people.

"Ammy?" I ask. "Not Amy?"

She shakes her head, a hint of exasperation creeping its way onto her face. I'm willing to bet she's had this convo before. "Like Sammy without the S. It's short for Amarantha. It's from a poem or something. My parents are freaks."

"'Amarantha sweet and fair, ah, braid no more that shining hair!'" I recite it without thinking.

She narrows her eyes at me, and I pick at the skin around my thumb, worried I sound insane.

But after a second, she nods at me, kind of like she's impressed. "Not many people know that," she says.

I take a deep breath, steady my hand on the seat in front of me as the train goes around a slight curve. I feel that relief again. "I may or may not be studying comparative literature." I raise my hand to stop her. "I know what you're going to say: it's a *pointless* major."

She laughs. "Your words, not mine."

I stop picking at my thumb and decide to keep going. "I love Richard Lovelace. I think he's really underrated as a poet. He's not as famous as the Johns. You know, John Donne or John Keats—" I pause to make sure she's still listening. She is, her eyes locked right on mine. "—but I guess I don't have to tell that to your parents."

She breaks my gaze and shrugs. "Well, it's *still* a stupid name for a child. I don't think I've had a single teacher who's managed to get it right all the time. Not like Noah; that's easy."

"There was this little thing called an ark," I say with a smirk. "Most people know about it."

She looks down, fiddles in her bag. "Anyway, how much do I owe you?"

"It's my treat," I say.

"You don't have to do that."

I shrug. "I need some karma on my side. Believe me. You'll be doing me a favor."

She pauses for a second, then says thank you, acquiescing. She puts her bag down.

"Karma?" She raises an eyebrow. Behind her, I see an old school bus through the window, parked in a lot just in front of the woods. It's painted in bright colors, and there are peace signs on it, plus a light dusting of snow on top. It's always there at this part of the trip, the part where the train tracks don't hug the edge of the Hudson, where it quickly turns to only woods.

I look back at her, hesitating, though I don't know quite why. The Brooklyn kids from before are heading back down the aisle, and a guy in front of us launches into a coughing fit.

Is it weird to tell another girl about your plans to get your girlfriend back? Maybe. I'm not sure. I don't know the protocol on this one, because I've never tried to get someone back before.

I look out the window again, watching as the snow comes down, a little bit faster now. The painted bus is long gone. All I can see is woods.

Weird or not, I decide to go ahead and tell her. I adjust the petal of one of the flowers, then look at her.

"Does it have to do with those flowers?" she asks.

32

I tilt my head to the side. "Maybe."

"You're trying to get your ex back," she says with utmost confidence.

"Wow," I say. "You're good."

She smiles. "Lucky guess."

Maybe, but I decide she's good at reading people. She must be. "Tonight would be the three-year anniversary of our first date," I say.

"*Romantic*," she says, but she's got a bit of a smirk when she says it, and her voice is snarky. Like she doesn't really believe that *anything* is romantic. Not like that, at least.

I feel myself go red.

"So what did you do to screw it up?" she asks quickly, already completely sure that I'm the one who screwed it up.

She *is* good at reading people.

I take a deep breath, trying to think of the best way to explain, wondering if she could even give me some good advice, as we've still got over an hour together.

But I don't have a chance to get a word out because all of a sudden, I feel the train slowing. There's a screech of brakes on metal, and I watch as one of the little kids trips and falls, and before I can even jump up to help him, the car begins to shake back and forth, and the overhead lights go out.

The train comes to a full stop.

AMMY

I SWEAR, NO ONE ELSE ON THIS TRAIN IS FREAKING out as much as I am.

It's been almost an hour of this and still, nothing. The ceiling lights are off, and there have been no announcements for the last forty-five minutes or so—not even so much as a crackle on the intercom. The snow falls like it's its freaking job, covering the mass of trees—all we can really see where we're stopped—in a blanket of white that's bright and harsh against the dim in here.

There was lots of initial grumbling and pacing in the car, Noah quickly abandoning whatever he was about to say about his ex with a "crap" and "come on." You could hear a mom up front trying to calm her kid, the sweaty guy in the suit sighing loudly, and the lady in front of us going on about how their daughter-in-law is going to be pissed if she has to wait too long at the station to pick them up. But once the most recent announcement came on, the one that said they were looking into the "situation" and for everyone to "sit tight" and reminded people that "Amtrak employees have no additional information," a lot of people seem to have given up. Even the pacers have lost hope, with only a few stragglers leading the charge. Now we're all just sitting here . . . waiting.

I touch my hand to the glass, running my finger in circles through the frost, imagining that I'm cranking some kind of emergency generator that gets everything moving just right. The tips of my nails are ravaged from the last hour—from the last day—from the last year?—and I curse myself for my stupid anxious tic.

The wedding—or commitment ceremony, to be totally accurate, since my parents aren't even properly divorced yet—is at six. I still have time, theoretically, but I know that soon Kat will be helping Sophie do her makeup and all that jazz. Not to mention I have to do my makeup and my hair and iron the dress that's crumpled in my bag. I was supposed to be arriving in only a matter of minutes.

My phone buzzes, and I pull it out. It's Kat. I texted her when we first stopped to tell her I might not be getting in on time and that I'd text her when we were moving again.

Still nothing?

I send her a sad face, and I think about writing something else, but I realize I have nothing to say.

My mom didn't want me to go to this. She begged me not to "validate their infidelity" by attending. And I told her I wouldn't.

Until I started to wonder whether she was on my side at all.

Until I started to realize that if I didn't get away from her—even if it was just for a week—I might go crazy.

Until I started to ask myself if I was going to become just like her.

And so now, here I am, making this gesture that says I'm on Team Dad, hurting her in a way that I don't think I can take back, and now I'm not even sure if I'll make it?

It sucks.

My breathing quickens, and I bite at my pinkie nail, getting the last bit before the quick.

I stare through the spiral I've made in the frost, like there will somehow be an answer out there, but all I see are trees and snow. It's completely hopeless.

I look over at Noah. He's nervous, too, I can tell by the way he continues to pick at the skin around his thumbs, a different technique from the nail biting, but similar, no less—we have something in common, at least.

His eyes are locked on the seat in front of his, not a book or a phone or anything. He wants to get where he's going tonight. His wheels are turning, spinning out all the potential scenarios if he doesn't.

Just like me.

"Excuse me," I say to Noah suddenly, motioning to the

aisle, and he gets up quickly to make space for me. It's fairly dim in here without the glow of fluorescent lighting, but I head up the center aisle anyway, hoping a little walking will help me calm down.

I get to the end of the car, and a kid bops his little sister on the head with what looks like a rolled-up *New Yorker* magazine. An older woman in an expensive-looking full-length wool coat plays sudoku on her iPad. None of these people are trying to make their dad's stupid wedding non-wedding. None of these people even look like they're on a time crunch. Or maybe they're just better at accepting things than I am.

I reach the end of the car and turn back around, trying not to look like a total lunatic in the process. I walk back to my seat, hardly catching anyone's eyes, because it's New York, and just like Kat said, people seem to leave each other alone here—unless you're fiddling with your suitcase or letting your phone ring unanswered, that is.

The windows are getting frostier by the minute, and it's still bright out but a dreary bright, pale and white, like someone has laid a sheet of vellum over the bare trees. Or chosen a phone filter to make it look vintage and blurry.

Noah stands up to let me in. His eyes are wide open and eager, like a puppy dog's. "Are you all right?" he asks. He stares at his thumb again.

I scoot past him, his jersey swishing across the back of my wool sweater as I do, and sit down. I don't feel all right, not really. I don't feel all right at all.

"Yeah," I say as I mentally weigh the pros and cons of

examining my mom's barrage of text messages. "I just wish I knew how long this would take."

"You and the rest of us," Noah says, and when he sees that's the opposite of what I want to hear: "Delays are common, especially when the weather's bad. I'm sure we'll be moving soon. Whatever the issue is, it probably isn't *that* bad." He sounds like he's trying to convince himself more than anyone.

I let out a long sigh and pull my phone out of my pocket, but there's nothing new from Kat.

I look back out the window, at the condensation that is dripping down, turning my spiral creepy, like something out of a horror movie. I draw my name in the frost above it, then wipe off the moisture on my jeans, leaving a streak of dark on the faded denim.

I stare at the message icon on my phone. I muted my convo with my mom so I wouldn't get alerts, but still, the messages have been rolling in the whole trip, I can see by the tiny number over the icon that shows the amount of unread messages—it's up to twenty-eight now. It's stressing me out, now even more so since I have nothing to do but sit here.

I need to rip the Band-Aid off.

I know I have to.

It's going to drive me crazy if I don't.

I tap into my messages and click on the convo with my mom.

I feel my pulse start to quicken as I scroll up, seemingly endlessly.

Turn around

You better tell Dara to turn around

Call me

Call me

Call me

Damn it, Ammy, call me

Call me

How am I supposed to even know you're OK

Call me

Answer me!

And myriad variations of the above.

And then one, from just five minutes ago.

If you don't call me now, I'm calling your dad

It's not even that I care that much about whether it's a surprise, but it's just that I don't want to deal with the madness that would ensue if my mom called my dad, screamed at him in her anxious state on his commitment-ceremony day. I don't want to deal with the fact that Sophie would surely blame me, that maybe even Kat would start to wonder if I carry more drama with me than I'm worth. That my dad would probably blame me, too.

I want them all to like me; as much as I hate what he did, I want it.

In this strange way, I want to belong, even if it's only for a week.

Noah must hear my breaths get quicker, because he turns to me. "Are you okay?"

I nod. "I just need to make a phone call. Sorry."

"No worries," he says.

My mother answers on the first ring, like she had the cell phone in her hand. I'd bet a kajillion bucks that she actually did.

"Are you okay?" Her voice is shrill.

"I'm fine, Mom."

"Where are you?"

"I'm on the train," I say. "I'm almost there."

That's when she starts yelling. A big mess of words—*"you knew how much this would hurt me, you told me you weren't going to go, you were supposed to be on my side, we were going to watch* Gilmore Girls, *I had it all planned out"*—I can barely keep up with.

Her voice is loud and hoarse but sloshy, like she's been crying in between the yelling, and I can practically see the rings under her eyes, the grease in her hair, which hasn't been washed in days, the torn beds of her nails, which she destroys much worse than even I do.

I don't want to end up like her. That's why I had to go today. I was afraid if I spent another moment in that house I would start to become her. I was afraid I'd start to hate my dad even more than I already do.

I was afraid that her very essence would wrap me up like a burlap sack, a messed-up cocoon turning me into something different altogether. I was afraid I'd lose my dad completely, that he'd never forgive me for missing his ceremony, that I'd lose all chance at normalcy, even if it was fake normalcy created out of something really, *really* bad that he did.

But I can't tell her that.

"I'm going to get off the phone now, Mom," I say.

"*You can't do this; stop, Ammy, just stop—*"

"Mom, I'm okay, I really am, but I can't talk to you when you're like this."

"*Like what, like your father who left us and then had the nerve to do this—*"

"Mom, I'm going to hang up."

My voice is calm like that of the family therapist my dad said we should go to after he broke the news that he was leaving us for a woman he'd met on—I kid you not—an REI hiking trip to the Adirondacks. (As if you could pay for five sessions of family therapy and then everything would be okay.)

"*You can't just hang up on me, you can't just do that, you can't hang—*"

I end the call. The therapist told me, in one of our solo sessions, that when my mom's anxiety is through the roof, the best thing to do is to disengage.

Well, I didn't just disengage. I got on a train.

Noah is staring at me. He looks worried, his eyes are all crinkly at the edges, and then I see something even worse—pity.

I open my mouth to say something—*anything*—but I can't find my voice. All I feel is the bitter heat of tears coming on. I roll up the sleeves of my sweater, suddenly warm.

I don't want to cry, sitting here on a train in front of a total stranger.

I want to be up in Hudson, pretending to care about Sophie's dress, with Kat and Bea and the promise of regularness around me, my mom and everything that comes with her hundreds of miles away.

I know it's not fair to her—she's not the one who destroyed our family—but it's true.

"Uh, that sounded rough," Noah says.

And that's what does it. I feel the first tear begin to well. Shit.

I breathe deep, like I can make it all go away if I just get enough air. But the oxygen comes slow and shallow, like there's not enough to go around in this stuffy, stupid train.

I feel another tear come, and I wipe it away with the back of my hand.

"I need some air," I say suddenly, my breaths already starting to come in gasps. "I *really* need some air."

NOAH

1:31 P.M.

THEY TOLD US NOT TO LEAVE THE TRAIN.

That's what the first announcement said, at least.

Apparently even when the train is stopped like this, they won't let you go. It's some kind of liability thing. So it's not like we can up and go outside. But we can get close.

"Come with me," I say, standing up.

She gets up to follow. Her eyes are watery, and I look away, giving her a moment to wipe them again. Then I head down the aisle, turning to glance back once at the door to the next car to make sure she's still behind me. She's even taller than I thought, I realize, now that we're both standing up together. Almost as tall as I am. So much taller than Rina.

43

I push the button and head down the length of the car, push the button again and breeze through the dining car, too.

I push it one last time, and she follows me into the very back of the train. The doors shut behind us, closing us into this little metal room, the last car on the train, the caboose.

"It's cooler here, in the very back," I say. "It's not heated."

She nods. "Are we supposed to be back here, though?" She points to a sign that informs us, very clearly, that we are not.

"Probably not." I laugh, lean against the door, and try to stay calm and relaxed. When my dad would get upset after he and my mom split, it's what always worked best.

Ammy takes a deep breath, and I can see already that she's starting to calm down.

In seconds, there are goose bumps on her arms. She tugs on the cuffs of her sweater, pulling them down. We probably should have brought our coats, but after whatever kind of awful fight she just had with her mom, she obviously needed to get away from that car as quickly as she could. I wasn't really thinking about proper preparations.

Her breaths make frost in the air, and as her breathing slows, the clouds of frost get longer. Through the side windows, there is nothing but trees. Through the back, I see train tracks, stretching into the horizon. There's a sign—"Doors May Be Pulled Open Manually If Power Fails"—and I have that fleeting feeling again, of wanting to escape, get lost. The kind of feeling that Rina was always trying to get me to have.

The one that I only got after I lost her, when it was too late.

Ammy looks up at me. Her makeup is a little smudged. She doesn't say anything, just stares.

"I can get out of your hair . . . ," I say, my voice trailing off. I take a step back, toward the door.

She shrugs. "I'm sure you heard most of it. It doesn't really matter, anyway."

I shove my hands in my pockets. "Uh, do you want to talk about it?"

She shakes her head quickly. "No. I don't."

"Okay," I say, shifting my weight from foot to foot. I don't know quite what to say to make it better, but I don't want to leave her alone, either. I heard the way her mom was yelling at her. Neither of my parents have ever talked that way to me. I know she's just a stranger, and I have other things to worry about today, but still, she's a person. And whatever she's going through, it doesn't sound good.

She exhales. Her breath comes out long and slow like a plume of smoke. I realize that I'm pretty cold. Forget whatever they tell you about being a guy and grinning and bearing it; a penis doesn't make you magically warmer in situations like these.

But I don't move for the door. I don't want to leave her.

She steps back, away from the window, and runs her hands up the sides of her arms, staying warm. I step toward it, taking in the weirdly perfect view of snow, trees, and sky. It's like a painting, like this crappy old steel vestibule is our private museum.

"So what's your plan?" she asks, leaning back against the opposite wall.

"My plan?"

"To get your girlfriend back. Tell me you have some sort of plan besides just showing up with flowers."

I tug at the collar of my jersey. "The plan is flowers and a poem and to invite her to this restaurant she was always begging me to go to. I have reservations. . . ." I wait for a response, but she doesn't offer one.

After a moment, I say: "Pretty cheesy, huh?"

"I didn't say that."

She's not one to pour her heart out, that's for sure. She keeps it all in. Even something so small as her opinion on whether a stranger's plan to get his girlfriend back is up to snuff. Still, I can see in her eyes that she does think it's cheesy. That she probably thinks I'm pretty cheesy myself.

"So why are you on this train?" I ask.

She raises her eyebrows. "For the worst kind of drama."

"What's that?"

Ammy tugs at a peeling sticker on the closed window, then resticks it before looking back at me. "Family," she says, and her eyes go blank, like she's looking at a point in the distance, like she's remembering something not so great. It's not exactly shocking, given the little bits I overheard between her and her mom. "Let's just say that I really need to get to Hudson tonight is all," she says finally.

My ears perk at the sound of my hometown coming from her lips. So she's not going to Bard, after all. I wonder what she's got going on in Hudson. The area is small enough that I'm pretty sure I'd know her if she grew up there, that I would have seen her at Hudson High. "You're not from there, are you?" I ask.

She shakes her head.

"I'm going to Hudson, too," I say. "And I also have a time crunch. When do you need to be there?"

"Five," she says. "At the latest."

I nod. "Same for me." I step just the slightest bit closer to her, conserving our body heat in this freezing car. She does the same, and for a second, I think she's going to open up, tell me why she's going, what she needs to do there.

But then she looks back down at her feet, and we both hear a muffled voice overhead.

"An announcement," I say, momentarily forgetting about our respective destinations. I touch the door-open button as fast as I can and step into the next car, reveling in the instant splash of heat from inside. She follows.

". . . is not related to weather . . . a mechanical error causing delays . . . hope to be up and running as soon as possible, but it could be a few hours before the mechanic arrives . . . there are several other issues in the area . . . we appreciate your patience . . ."

"Did he just say *a few hours*?" she asks, looking at me frantically as grumbling and yelling erupt around us, as even the woman selling beers seems peeved.

Ammy looks at me like somehow I can change this.

I'm screwed. My reservation is at seven sharp, and I was

planning on getting to Rina's house by six, reading my poem and making my case, and still giving her enough time to get ready. Plus, I need to go to my house first and shower and change and all that. I can't very well show up to win back her heart in an old Steelers jersey that I know for a fact she hates. Another couple of hours' delay, and we could miss the reservation completely. I'd show up like an asshole in the dark with smushed flowers and a bunch of crappy explanations about how I had this all planned out, but none of it worked.

Why does everything you do have to be so difficult?

"This is not good," I say. "This is not good at all."

AMMY

NOAH IMMERSES HIMSELF IN HIS PHONE WHILE I DO the mental math and try to warm up from the brief jet into the windy vestibule sans coats. If it could be a few hours, it could be almost five o' freaking clock before we even start going. Which would put me in Hudson right in the middle of the ceremony, and there's no way Kat would be able to pick me up then. Even if I managed to get a cab, am I going to show up halfway into it, all *Surprise! I'm here*? Sophie chose this fancy Italian restaurant to have the ceremony in—I can't exactly arrive with my hair all a mess from traveling, in a dress that hasn't even been ironed. As Noah made clear, this is bad.

Everyone around us is freaking out, too. Calling the

49

people they were supposed to meet. Checking their phones as if there's an answer in there. Plaguing the poor Amtrak guy with questions he definitely can't answer.

I'm going to miss my dad's commitment ceremony. I'm going to break my mom's heart for nothing.

Noah looks up from his phone and turns to me. He's stuffed his arms into his puffy jacket, wearing the thing like a blanket instead of bothering to put it on properly. He looks like an electric-orange marshmallow man. "One of my hall mates was on a train that got stuck for nine hours once," he says quietly, almost like he's worried about freaking out the other passengers.

"Are you kidding me?"

He shakes his head.

"Do you really think that could happen?" I ask.

"I don't know," he says, and he turns back to his phone, where he's messing with the maps.

I look out the window. The snow continues to fall. Even if they do get the train running, by that time, what if the whole track is blocked? I take out my phone, pull up my maps. From here to Hudson, it's an hour and forty-five minutes by car. Even if Kat left right this moment, round-trip would put her well into the ceremony time. I really am screwed.

I open my messages to text Kat.

I'm not sure if I'm going to make it

As soon as I hit send, I see another text from my mom.

When do you get in? You let me know right now or I'm calling your dad.

I briefly think about telling her the truth, that we're stuck, but I know it will only make her more upset and anxious.

So I lie.

Already here

At Dad's now

Sorry

For a second, she doesn't say anything back, and I think maybe she'll let up now that she knows there's nothing she can do to stop me.

But then I see the dots that show she's typing.

The dots disappear. She has nothing to say to me.

In a flash, I see my mom last night, the half-drunk bottle of wine, the face she made when I told her I didn't want to talk about Dad anymore. That I was tired of *always complaining about Dad*.

Her eyes got bigger, and she looked at me as if I'd betrayed her just because I no longer wanted to bitch about my own father.

Her sentences had been looping around in circles for days. . . . "But can you believe he actually has the nerve to have a *ceremony* with her . . . after all I did for him . . . I can't believe he would do that to you, Ammy. Can you *believe* he would do that to you . . . to us?"

I push the thought aside, exit out of the convo with my mom, and check for any texts from Kat. Nothing.

I click into Kat's Facebook, seeing if there are any recent updates—any posts of them getting ready, but there's nothing. Just photos of Kat hiking and brunching and doing Kat things—all from a couple of days ago. There's nothing about the wedding non-wedding at all.

I wonder, for a second, if she really cares as much as she says she does whether I'm there or not. We've only been in each other's company for ten days, after all.

I was completely ready to hate Kat. Just like I hated Sophie, her mom, the woman who'd torn my family apart and could—according to my dad—do a very impressive head-stand in the yoga classes she led on weekday mornings. I was ready to hate Kat and Bea, these two blonde, tiny, sure-to-be insufferable stepsisters who were being pushed on me. I didn't even want to go visit my dad. In fact, I was just about ready to never talk to him again, which my mom was fully in support of. It was my best friends, Dara and Simone, who convinced me to take the trip. They said I could probably even squeeze in a couple of days in New York City before meeting my new "family."

My dad drove from Hudson down to the city to meet me, and we spent the weekend hitting up Times Square and the new World Trade Center building, shopping at Macy's and walking around Central Park, while I kept all conversation to one-word sentences and he shuffled around apologies. By the time we drove to his real home, in Hudson, I was fully dreading it. I didn't think I could handle another one of his weak apologies.

It was Kat who made it better. Kat who opened the front door to their old farmhouse in Hudson and embraced me with a bony-armed hug. I met Sophie only briefly before Kat dragged me out of the house to hit up her favorite brunch spot before picking up Bea from her community theater rehearsal.

We weren't in the car two minutes before Kat said, "I told my mom not to get involved with a married man, but she can be totally selfish when she wants to be. So that makes both of us the children of assholes. I guess we have that in common, at least."

I think I fell a little bit in love with her right then and there. Not in a weird, step-incesty sort of way. But I just loved how she could see things so clearly, how she was able to put into words what I didn't have the guts to, even when I'd watched my dad pack up his things and leave us. Even when I'd seethed with anger as I found out my mom was freaking *driving him to the airport*.

Through it all, I never had the nerve to really say what was constantly on my mind: that maybe he wasn't the person I thought he was. I knew that he'd abandoned us, that he'd fallen in "love" with another woman, that he'd messed up all we had, but I still couldn't manage to really see it in twenty-twenty or whatever. He'd been my dad for my entire life, after all.

And then Kat just said it. *Asshole.*

And it's a strange realization to have about someone you've loved all your life—that they're not that good of a person.

But what was stranger still was just how much I enjoyed that week and a half. I was still mad at my dad—I *am* still mad at my dad—but it was so much easier to be mad when we were eating Sophie's fresh kale salads and lemon-roasted chicken. When we were playing Boggle after dinner while Dad and Sophie split a bottle of Pinot Noir. It was infuriating, sure, that he'd been the one to screw everything up, and now he looked like he was having the time of his life.

But it was enchanting, all the same.

My family had never been like that, like a normal family.

I'd thought that made us special, but I started to wonder. I started to be just a little bit, teensy bit *jealous* of my dad.

Because he didn't have to hold my mom together anymore. That was left only to me.

I sigh, tapping out of Kat's Facebook, put my phone away, and look over at Noah. He's still messing around on his phone's maps.

"Finding us an alternate route?" I joke.

He pauses and looks my way. I notice freckles on the tip of his nose that I didn't see there before. He tugs at the collar of his jersey and shrugs out of his jacket.

"This is going to sound nuts . . ." He runs a hand through his hair, scratching his head like he's a cartoon character trying to solve a problem or something. *How will I trap the Road Runner this time?*

"Oh boy," I say.

"Hear me out." He raises a hand in protest, and he reminds me, just the tiniest bit, of Kat. It was her signature move when she was about to make a point. "There may or may not be a bus station only about a mile from here. See?" He points to the map.

"So?" I ask.

"Well, over fall break, all the economy Amtrak tickets sold out, and I had to take this bus line. It's random, I hadn't even heard of it before. It's called the Hudson Express. It goes right there. I live in a town just north of there, so I'll probably take a cab. Is your place in town?"

I shrug. "It's Hudson proper, I'm pretty sure. But it's just a little bit out of the main area."

"Perfect," he says. "We can split a cab if you want. It shouldn't even be that much slower. And there are buses every half hour. Which means we could definitely make the two-thirty. It's just that way through the woods." He points to the snowy frontier through the window.

"You're not serious?" I ask. "Go out there? Now? With all our stuff?"

He shrugs. "Three hours will have both of us missing what we need to do. You still haven't told me why you need to get where you're going"—he raises that hand again—"which is fine, given that we're still practically strangers and all, but I'd put money on the fact that you're not exactly willing to wait that long."

I pause, knowing that I should say no, that this is *insane*.

But feeling a flutter of hope all the same.

Realizing that some tiny part of me actually wants to see the ceremony. Actually wants to be part of this family, even if it's only for a week.

Part of me wonders if it could be longer. If I could put all that other stuff behind me and start new, just like my dad did, as awful as that sounds.

Noah must see my hesitation. "Believe me, I'm not the type of person who normally does stuff like this," he says. "But I can't see how this won't be shorter. Look at it this way: We just happened to sit down next to each other, two people going to the exact same stop? It's like we're supposed to do this, because we both need to get home."

I bite my lip and take him in. He looks like he knows what he's talking about. And something about what he said is right. Maybe he sat down next to me because whoever is sitting up there pulling the strings knows that we both need to get where we're going today.

"How long do you think it would be on the bus?" I ask cautiously.

"Not more than two hours, tops. Probably more like an hour and a half. Even with a twenty-minute walk to the bus station, we'd be to our respective locations just in time, methinks."

"Methinks?" I say. "Really?"

He just laughs, ignoring me. "Whatever. You'll get where you need to go."

I raise my eyebrows. That solves the problem of Kat, who still hasn't texted me back. If it's too close to the ceremony, I'll just split a cab with my new friend. The Italian restaurant is walkable from Sophie's house, so I can go in, get ready, and still be there in time.

I pause, thinking it over.

"But it's freezing out there," I finally say. The vestibule

alone was enough to raise goose bumps on just about every inch of my body.

He points to the mess of layers at my feet. "I think you're prepared. And it's only a mile. That's just twenty blocks."

"I'm from suburban Virginia, dude. I don't live in New York," I say, tucking an errant lock of hair behind my ear. I'm not trying to be cute or coy or flirty or whatever—*please*. But I hate the feeling of hair on my face, especially when I'm worried about something. It makes me anxious, and I don't like feeling anxious. Because that makes me worried that I'm going to turn into my mom. "Speak English," I say. "*Por favor.*"

He laughs. "It's like four laps around your high school track."

I nod. "Right."

"You can do it. *We* can do it."

I stare at him, at this guy I've only known for just over two hours. At this romantic bro-dude who just wants to make it home to get his soon-to-be-dumbstruck girlfriend back. It's cute, in its own little way. Even if it is clichéd.

Even if I've decided in the post–Dad-cheating-on-Mom world that romance is entirely a waste of time. It's still cute.

But that's not the point. There are reasons, surely, why I shouldn't just leave a train car to follow a stranger in the middle of freaking nowhere *and* in the middle of a freaking snowstorm. "You're not some kind of creepo sexual predator, are you?" I ask.

He laughs, but then his face goes serious. "Look, I get

why you have to ask that. But no, I'm not. I'm honestly just trying to get back to my ex to try to make my case. Perhaps"— he smiles genuinely—"you can even offer me a few pointers. And, look, if you don't want to sit with me when we get to the bus, I won't even be offended."

"It's only a mile?" I ask hesitantly.

He presents the phone to me. "Less. Point nine miles, to be exact. What could seriously go wrong in point nine miles?"

NOAH

AMMY HANDS THE PHONE BACK TO ME HESITANTLY, without saying a word. I shove it in my pocket. Then I adjust my flowers once again. They're still in relatively good shape, which will probably change after a mile in this snow. I know it's borderline nuts to go traipsing across the snowy wilderness with a bunch of hot-pink roses, but I don't care. I'll have to risk it.

Rina always wanted me to take risks.

This is a risk. And not because I'll probably have to replace the flowers I bought her.

It's a little bit crazy, the whole plan, even though I know from looking at the map that we'll be okay.

Which makes it way better than a poem or dinner reservations or anything.

Rina, I wanted to be with you so badly I literally walked a mile through a storm to get to you. . . .

Rina, for once, I didn't think about all the consequences. For once, I just did it.

I turn to Ammy. She's staring ahead, eyes locked on the seat in front of her. Her cheeks are still rosy from our visit to the vestibule. I'd bet money on the fact that when she answers, she's going to say no.

Can I still do this without her? Of course.

But am I adventurous enough to head into the great unknown during a storm with a half-dead phone and a bunch of roses? I'm not sure.

If Rina were here, there'd be no question. Rina would turn to me and say, her eyebrows raised eagerly, "Come on, let's get the hell outta here!"

In two and a half years of dating, Rina learned to weigh all the options for me, so I didn't have to. Bryson thought it was crappy. He thought I was "whipped." But I liked that about her. She was the one who urged me to apply to school in the city. Bryson said it was because she wanted to keep me close, because she wanted to go there, too. But I knew that it was also because she knew I'd love it. And I do love it, and I wouldn't have done it without her.

Rina was the one who told me it was okay to study comparative literature, even though both my parents thought the idea was preposterous. That was just about the one thing my parents could agree on in those days. Rina was the one who looked everything up on the internet, even these crazy stats from the Bureau of Labor Statistics. According to her, comp lit professors have quite the leg up on English ones.

Bryson was wrong, dead wrong. I liked that she pushed me. I still do.

The problem was only when she'd want me to do something that I *didn't* want to do. The problem was that sometimes she pushed me a little too hard.

Sometimes I wasn't quite ready to be the person she wanted me to be.

I think about that week at the lake, about standing on that ledge, looking down.

It's good for you to face your fears, babe. I'm here for you.

You know that she's obsessed with turning you into Mr. Perfect Boyfriend, right? She doesn't give a shit about you.

I look out the window. The snow is still coming down, but it looks like it's slowed. Or maybe that's just wishful thinking.

I want to get lost. The thought hits me again, just like it did when we were standing there, freezing in the back vestibule.

Screw Bryson. I want to face my fears. I want to have an adventure.

I want an adventure that leads me straight back to Rina.

She has to take me back. Once I explain and apologize and tell her the thought that's been running through my head all break: that she and I belong together. That nothing changes that.

That I can be exactly who she wants me to be.

I want that for myself now, too.

I see, for a second, a flash of Rina on my front lawn, three days after the phone call that put it all in motion, five days after the senior-year trip to Lake George that had gone so well until it hadn't. The welling of her eyes that she was unsuccessfully trying to keep under control. The anger as she demanded why I hadn't called her in days. The way she told me how much she hates me, how she absolutely can't believe it.

But you said we could do long distance. You said we could make it work. You said I was like a part of your family.

And I meant it, I think. Until I convinced myself that I didn't anymore.

How could you dump me over something so fucking stupid?

I don't know. I still don't.

I clear my throat, look over at Ammy again.

"So . . . ," I say. "What do you think?"

AMMY

So in one of our two solo sessions, the thera-pist my dad *graciously* footed the bill for after he destroyed our family told me that I should make pros and cons lists when I started to get sad or anxious, as they, in her words, "can provide a sense of control."

It was this whole big thing that she gave me photocopied workbook pages for, and I had to do it at home like she was my math tutor or something. You just wrote everything out, all the good stuff and the bad stuff, starting with the cons so you could get everything you're scared of out on the page and out of your head, and then you weighed it all up with a points system.

I kind of hated it, because the points system was totally

arbitrary, and the only person in control of it is you, so you can pretty much do whatever you want. I mean, who *wouldn't* want to do some stupid exercise to prove that they'd done the right thing, even when they knew 100 percent that they hadn't?

I imagined my dad's pros and cons list for leaving the family looked something like this:

Cons:

Destroying the family (5 points)

Ruining Ammy's junior and senior years and sense of security when it comes to family and love and trust and all that (10 points)

Sending wife into tailspin of anxiety (7 points)

Taking a financial hit at work to transfer up north (2 points)

Pros:

Getting with a hot yoga instructor who can somehow look past gray hair and obvious midlife crisis (5 million points)

Of course, therapist lady said that assigning the points yourself is the point because it helps you decide what *you* want to do, not what other people want you to do. It's, like, getting in touch with your inner self or your true desires or some other such bullshit. She made me do it when I was deciding whether to go up to see my dad that first time.

But anyway, despite my reservations, her tip is actually kind of useful. I tell Noah to chill a minute and pull out a pen and *Madame Bovary*, flipping to the back pages.

There it is, the pros and cons list that got me here in the first place. The one that I made last night, after my mom and I got in our huge blowout fight. After I called Dara, who didn't answer, because she was too busy getting ready for her stupidly perfect family trip to Harry Potter World. After I texted Kat instead, and Kat told me to get out for a little bit. To come to her. To do what I really wanted to do. To go to the wedding and pretend to be normal for just a little bit.

Cons:

Leaving Mom alone during "the worst day of her life" (10 points)

Knowing she'll probably get worse in one week without me (10 points)

Having to at least somewhat pretend to ooh and ahh over whatever stupid dress Sophie is wearing (10 points)

Dad probably thinking this counts as straight-up forgiveness, and it doesn't (10 points)

Mom never forgiving me (15 points)

Pros:

Having a week of fun with Kat (6 points)

Getting to hang out with Bea, too (4 points)

Being close to NYC, so we'll probably take one trip (3 points)

Not having to go through the emotional turmoil of watching my mom fall apart and get worse by the hour as the commitment ceremony looms (10 points)

Feeling like I'm part of a family again, even a bullshit one, even for just a week (1 million points)

See, I told you these things were morally ambiguous.

Noah glances over, but I turn to the window as I uncap my pen and start to write everything out, covering my work with my hand like I'm the star student in my second-grade class and worried about my neighbor copying.

I know this whole thing is pointless. I'm going to do what I want to do. But it helps, at least. And I'm not going to assign any kind of crazy point values this time. I'll keep 'em between 1 and 10, add it up, and see where I land.

Cons:

He's a total stranger (3 points)

Of course a train predator would insist that they're not a train predator (5 points)

It's cold as death outside (6 points)

My bag is heavy from all the books (2 points)

What if the bus doesn't come in this weather? (4 points)

Pros:

Noah doesn't seem like a predator, esp. since he's trying to get back with his ex (3 points)

It would be kind of a cool little adventure, street cred and all (3 points)

Kat would love the story (1 point)

The chance to get to Hudson on time, to be there for my dad (7 points)

I won't have to break my mom's heart for nothing (10 points)

NOAH
1:55 P.M.

AMMY'S GOT A HAND COVERING THE BOOK SHE'S WRIT-
ing in, and it looks as if she's doing some sort of calculus.
Scribbling numbers, adding things up. Is she calculating distance? Hours to home? Something else?

"What are you doing?" I ask.

She waves a hand. "Give me a second," she says.

I get out my phone and check the directions again. I only
have 27 percent, but I figure it's okay. It's a straight shot from
here. Point nine miles, as I mentioned before. And the bus
runs every thirty minutes. We have plenty of time to make
the two thirty.

I stare back out the window. The snow is still coming

down like the train car is our own personal bunker. It looks cold as all get-out.

Is it kind of a crazy plan? Yes.

But will we be fine? Also yes.

Will it be my chance to prove to Rina that I am the person she wants, once and for all? Most definitely yes.

Finally, Ammy looks up at me. She glances out the window and then back to me again. She closes her book. Then she gives me an almost mischievous look: her eyes narrow into slits; her head tilts to the side.

"If we're going to do this thing, we better go sooner rather than later. I don't have a ton of time to waste here."

It's all the answer I need. "Let's go, then," I say.

I help her pull her suitcase down from the ledge, and I offer to carry her books.

"What is this, *Leave It to Beaver*?" she asks me, laughing.

"Huh?" I ask, quite frankly a little surprised. Rina loved when I carried her books.

"Never mind," Ammy says. "Just know that it's not 1950, and I'll be just fine."

When we're ready, when Ammy has wrapped all of her myriad scarves around her neck and when I've tucked the flowers under my elbow, I lead the way down the center aisle, back to our vestibule.

Hardly anyone looks at us, even though we're carrying all our bags. People are too wrapped up in their own personal dramas, trying to figure out how they're going to cope with the delay. Luckily, there isn't an Amtrak employee in sight, since all the announcements made it clear that no one was to leave.

When we reach the back, I open the vestibule door and wait until Ammy is in, too. It shuts behind us, which is good, because no one will see us. It's not like I think they'll send the guards after us or anything, but even so, adventure doesn't exactly come naturally to me. I want as few hiccups as possible.

Ammy stares at the door and bites her lip. "You think you can just open it?" she asks.

I shrug. "It says you can do it manually if the power's out. And the lights are still off."

She crosses her arms in front of her. The edges of her chunky sweater poke out from her wool coat. For a second, she looks so cozy, all bundled up like that, that I almost don't want to lead her out into the cold. "Let's see you do it, then."

"Hold these a sec," I say. I hand her the flowers and shrug out of my backpack.

Then I take a deep breath. I'm all of a sudden as scared as I was when I was about to jump off that ledge, but this time I don't let it stop me.

"Here goes," I say, without turning to her.

I unslide the safety latch on the bottom. Then I grab the large handle in the middle. It turns under my weight, easier than it should be. The door opens, and there it is, the whole world in front of us.

Our adventure, beckoning.

"Well, that was easy," I say.

I grab my backpack and toss it out the back. It lands on the snowy tracks with a thud.

I'd guess it's probably about five feet down.

It's good for you to face your fears, babe. I know you can do it.

I turn back to Ammy. "Here goes nothing," I say as I take a step forward.

"Careful, Indiana Jones," Ammy says behind me.

I look down and, for a second, the ground seems to blur below me.

Just do it, it's not that big of a deal.

Before I can lose my nerve, I jump.

I land solidly in the snow, though I have to take a couple of steps forward to steady myself, and the jump sends a shock through the bottom of my feet. I'm thankful I wore my hiking shoes, because none of the snow can seep in.

I grab my backpack, dust off the snowflakes so they don't make everything wet, and turn to face her. Looking up at her, standing in the doorway of the caboose of a damn Amtrak train, I see, once again, just how crazy this plan is.

But I wanted my adventure, and now I certainly have it. Thanks, karma.

"You okay, there, slugger?" Ammy asks from above. She whispers it, like she's afraid of getting caught. It's kind of adorable, in its way.

"Hand me your suitcase," I say.

Slowly, she pushes it out the window and lets it hang there.

"You're going to have to drop it," I say. "Don't worry. I'll catch it."

Her face scrunches up a bit, like she doesn't quite trust me. Then she lets it go.

It lands in my arms hard, sending me back a couple of feet again, but I try not to let her see my grimace. I set it down on a slightly less snowy patch of gravel and step closer to the train. "You're all that's left," I say.

"One more thing," she says, and then she disappears from the window and returns with the flowers. She holds them out and drops them, right into my arms.

In all the excitement of the escape, I'd forgotten about them.

I set them carefully on top of my backpack, then return to her.

"All right, this is really it."

She nods, but she looks scared.

I hold out my hands. "Jump," I say. "I'll catch you."

And she does.

In moments, my hands are around her waist, holding her tight, softening her leap to the ground.

She looks up at me, and her brown eyes are wide and deep, and it's like time stops for a second. I have to remind myself to let go of her, to step back, to act normal.

I have to remind myself that this is all for Rina.

"You did it," I say.

She smirks. "I'm pretty sure *we* did it."

PART TWO
THE UNKNOWN

AMMY

MY FEET HURT FROM THE JUMP AND MY COAT IS ALL crunched up from where Noah caught me and held me for a second too long.

I almost would have thought that meant something, but I know his mind is on his ex-girlfriend. Not to mention, my mind isn't anywhere near romance. Even if there was no ex and it was just me and a cute (yes, cute, even if it's in a bro-y way) train stranger setting off on an adventure, I still wouldn't be down for any of that. Not after all the shit I saw transpire in the last year.

I honestly can't even believe I followed this guy. It's not like me—not at all. It's something Kat would do. Meet some

75

good-looking stranger on a train and set off on an adventure with him.

But it's not me.

My job is to hold my mom together, be pissed off at my dad, and count down the days until I'm off to college. Until last night, when all that changed.

I look to the left, almost in awe at the snow-sprinkled tracks rolling out in front of me. Slat after slat after slat laid out perfectly like one of those perspective exercises we did in Mrs. Efrom's freshman year art class. It seems to stretch endlessly into the horizon, almost asking me to drop everything and run down it. Freedom.

Freedom from what's back in Virginia. From my mom's constant discussion about how awful my dad is. From the uptick in my heart when I'm worried she's about to have a panic attack. From that fear that hits my bones when I wonder if I'm going to turn into her.

Freedom from all the anger that's taken over her the last year. Even if just for a second, or an hour, or a day, or a week.

Freedom, even, from the day-to-day, occasionally tiring gossip between me, Dara, and Simone, from listening to their stories and trying to pretend it doesn't feel like my whole world is falling apart.

Just me and the world and a train we're kissing good-bye.

And Noah, of course.

Noah, my fellow reluctant explorer.

I pull out my phone, shoot Kat a quick text.

Looks like I might be there on time after all. Don't worry about a ride.

"Come on," he says. "Let's get out of here before one of the train guys sees."

I nod, giving my rolling suitcase its first official tug. It gets caught a little bit in the rocks surrounding the train tracks, but it's not so bad.

"Do you need help with that?" Noah asks, turning back to me.

I shake my head, only mildly miffed that he thinks this weak little lady can't carry a suitcase one mile through snow. "I'm fine," I say.

Noah leads the way. It's only about twenty or thirty feet to the woods, and as we approach, my heart does a little leap again. Everything looks magical in the snow, like something straight out of a fantasy novel. I think about *The Lord of the Rings*, Harry Potter, this movie about teen witches I used to watch when I was a kid.

"It's like we're proper adventurers," I say as I follow him. "Like explorers. Or frontier people."

"*Frontier people?*" He doesn't turn back, but I hear a laugh in his voice. "I believe they're called, you know, *pioneers*."

In seconds we reach the woods. The snow lets up a little bit, the trees creating a canopy for us. The ground is packed down with frost-kissed fallen leaves that don't get swept away because there's no one here to do the sweeping. My suitcase starts to roll easier now that we're away from the blanket of snow.

I start to feel like maybe this was a great idea after all.

Luckily, the terrain continues to be fairly flat, and it's not so bad. As we walk, we make small talk, trading histories in little bite-sized nuggets, like we're on one of those blind-dating shows that used to play after school on MTV. Noah tells me that he grew up just outside of Hudson, in Lorenz Park. That he loves animals and that his parents regularly take in cats that lose their way, that now they have three. Snowball, Max, and Katniss, the last of which I give him total hell for, because he picked the name. He tells me that he wishes he had the guts to be a vegetarian because he hates all the environmental implications of eating meat but he likes the taste of burgers too much. And that his parents are professors who don't get to do much professor-ing anymore.

I tell him my cellophane-wrapped, bow-tied version of the truth, too. That I grew up in suburban Virginia and that we've always lived in the same house, this cookie-cutter model that at least ten other people in my neighborhood have, including Simone. I tell him that my dad is an accountant and my mom sells antiques on eBay, which doesn't sound like a real job, but it is.

Or at least it used to be—for her. I neglect to mention that she hasn't gone antiquing in ages. She actually spends hours on Facebook looking at my dad and his new life. She tells me it's okay, because the market is slow right now anyway. She's been saying that for months.

I neglect to mention that sometimes we all used to go antiquing together on the weekends, when Dad and I weren't hiking and I didn't have plans with Dara or Simone.

But I do tell him some things that are real as he walks ahead, leading the way, occasionally turning back to ask me once again if I need help with my suitcase.

I tell him how my dad and I used to go hiking together about once a month, how we'd spend hours in REI stocking up on all the latest gear. I tell Noah how the woods were special to us, a destination, not an everyday thing. How the sad little patch of woods in my backyard was nothing compared to this.

I tell him how I tried to be a vegetarian once after I watched this awful video on the internet and how I lasted only three weeks before I found myself at the Wendy's drive-through at eleven o'clock at night, ordering the Baconator from the passenger seat of Dara's Saab.

In fact we talk so much that I forget how much time has passed until we reach a clearing, a stretch of white ground and blue sky.

I pull my phone out of my pocket to check the time and stop short. It's been far more than twenty minutes.

"So I know I'm not, like, an official New Yorker or any-thing, but I would swear on my life that we've gone more than twenty blocks already."

Noah turns to me. His cheeks are red, and his lips are chapped.

I realize suddenly how cold I am, as the wind whips against my face.

He pulls out his phone. "It's been almost a half hour.

Maybe we're just walking slow?"

I feel that uptick in my heart again, because he's supposed to know how long twenty blocks is—Lord knows I don't. "Are you *sure* we're going the right way?" I ask. "We haven't seen anything like civilization in a while."

He taps at his phone. "I mean, I *think* I'm sure. The towns around here are small, so we might not see much until we're right on top of it, but yeah, I do feel like we should have been there by now." He taps some more. "I still don't have service. And the little dot is stuck back near the train tracks. You?"

I have to take my gloves off to unlock my phone, and the cold is biting, like tiny fishes nipping at my fingertips. I have a feeling that's not good. I load up my maps, but it still says I'm in the Bronx, which must have been the last time I had it loaded. "No service, either." I quickly shove my phone into my pocket, re-glove, and rub my hands together, warming them up. "You only *think* you're sure?" I ask, attempting to quell the anger that sits like a weight in my stomach. He'd made it sound so *easy*, back there on the train. We spent the last half hour shooting the shit. I had no idea I should be freaking out.

"You're not serious," I say. "You don't really think we could have gone the wrong way?" When I'd made the joke about not being a New Yorker, it was just that—a joke. I expected him to tell me to be quiet and stop complaining, like Dara does when we're on the fourth lap around the track.

It's definitely been more than four laps, I think. *Shit.*

Noah puts his phone away, too, and looks at me, a tinge of seriousness on his face, which he replaces fast as can be with a smile. I stop dragging my suitcase behind me. He points to another stretch of woods right in front of us. "Let me take your suitcase," he says.

I sigh loudly and it's easy to hear, too, because we're in the middle of nowhere, not a car, not even a *road* in sight. Earlier, we'd seen some side roads through the trees—hints of other humans, at least—but I haven't seen anything like that in the last ten minutes, maybe more.

My sigh creates a billow of frost in the air. "I don't *want* you to carry my suitcase. I *want* you to know where you're *going*!"

I'm yelling. Noah, almost instinctively, takes a step or three back, his jaw agape, the expression in his eyes quite obviously hurt.

I remind myself, suddenly, of my mom. It's an awful feeling. It sucks.

"I'm sorry," I say, and I feel like a child for flipping out like that, but also like an adult, too young and too old at the same time. I shouldn't have lost it, but I shouldn't have to deal with all of this, either. I shouldn't have learned to yell from my parents, the very people who are supposed to teach me to be a good, calm, levelheaded person. I should be concerning myself with Dara and Simone and the ins and outs of high school, what college I'm going to, not all of this.

Not my mom and my dad and all their mutual bullshit.

I want out, I think.

But more than that, I want it all to go back to the way it was before.

I feel my eyes start to well. I do not want to cry in front of this guy—*again*, but in the cold freaking wilderness this time. With my luck, my tears will probably freeze to my face, little trails of icicles ruining the little bit of blush and powder that are still left on there from this morning. It was enough to get all soppy-eyed back there on the train, and I really don't want to do it twice.

I turn away so he can't see me, and wipe the moisture from beneath my eyes before it has a chance to freeze.

Why do *I* have to be out here freezing my ass off just because my dad had to go and make a new family?

Why did the stupid train have to break down in the first place?

Why doesn't Noah know where we're even going?

And the worst part, the part that gets me more than anything.

Why do I have to be weak, just like her?

But when I turn back to Noah, his eyes are kind, even though I don't deserve it for snapping like that. He doesn't even seem to be asking for an apology.

And I appreciate it, this pass he's given me.

I appreciate it so much.

His voice is calm. "I *think* that if we just go through those woods right there, we'll be right where we need to be. Or I *hope*, at least."

I brush beneath my eyes again and smile weakly. "All right," I say.

Because I could use a little hope.

Right now, I could use a lot.

NOAH

I CAN HEAR HER FOOTSTEPS BEHIND ME, THE CHUG-chug of the suitcase dragging over exposed tree roots.

We're almost out of the woods.

Literally, at least.

But figuratively, I don't know.

This is why I thought before jumping, Rina. This is why I could never just go like you always could.

Ammy takes a deep breath behind me, and there's the tail end of a sigh as she exhales. "There better be a bus station on the other side of these woods," she says.

I'm praying that there is one.

That I didn't lead us on a wild-goose chase to prove a point.

And that I haven't ruined both of our nights with one stupid decision.

It's strange how quickly things moved from good to bad. We were going along, chatting about our lives.

I didn't tell her my parents almost split up last year, that they no longer have their professorships out of circumstance, not choice.

Or that I'm pretty sure they cashed in the last of their savings to take this damn "love renewal cruise."

Even so, it was nice to talk to someone.

Someone who had the patience to listen, who didn't rush me to just get on with it, say what I had to say, make a damn decision already. . . .

And then all of a sudden, the moment was over. We were back under the falling snow. Unsure of why it had taken us so long. Hoping against hope we weren't completely lost.

We can't be, I tell myself. There's no way. I looked at the map. It was only point nine miles.

I force a note of cheer into my voice. "I'm sure it will be," I say.

I see a patch of bright daylight and push through the last couple of feet of woods.

But that's when any hope I had gets dashed. Utterly. Completely.

"Shit." I stop in my tracks. I feel my stomach sink, guilt already washing over me.

Ammy doesn't stop quickly enough. She runs into me from behind.

I turn, and she must see in my eyes that this is not good news. She presses her lips together, waiting.

"I'm so sorry," I say.

"What do you mean? What is it?" she asks. She pushes past me. I follow.

We stare at it together. The back of a house. A little run-down, with peeling siding and a sagging roof that definitely needs an update.

The yard is overgrown, filled with kids' toys—fire trucks, plastic buggies—and there's a half-torn-up kiddie pool that's filling with snow.

Ammy stares straight ahead. "Tell me there's a bus station right past that house."

Despite her earlier anger, she's at least somewhat calm. Reserved, almost. It's a relief.

I see those five beautiful dots that indicate service, finally. But I don't need to look at the map. As it slowly loads, I fully take in what's behind the house:

The Hudson River. Icy. Stagnant. Probably filled with dead bodies if you followed it all the way down to New York City.

We've gone the wrong way. The completely wrong way.

I point to the map. She follows my hand to all the bad news. "We should have gone right out of the train. Not left."

"Are you serious?" she asks, her voice even. "You're sure?"

My heart is racing now, my breath getting shallow. "I think the map was flipped around." I touch the button that recenters it. "I'm so sorry."

But she still doesn't get mad. It's almost as if she knows

that if she does, I'll lose it, too.

Ammy stares at the house. She points to a gravel drive-way off to the side. "There are two cars. Someone's gotta be home. Maybe they can drive us? Or give us hot chocolate or something? Aren't country people supposed to be nice?"

But I shake my head, back up slowly as a chill creeps down my spine. One that, for once, isn't from the winter air. I gesture a few feet in front of us. Two signs I somehow didn't see before, because I was so concerned about the directions, about the river, about this *huge* hiccup in our plan.

There's one that says, in shaky Sharpie, "I ABIDE BY MY SECOND AMENDMENT RIGHTS TO PROTECT MY PROPERTY—NO TRESPASSING!!!"

And one that must have been ordered off the internet: "GUNS BEFORE BUNS," with a silhouette of a girl's ass and the outline of what I can only imagine is an AR-15.

"Oh shit," Ammy says softly. "I thought New Yorkers were, like, *antigun*?"

But I don't have time to explain to her that up here it's different, because that's when I hear a pop, a loud snapping *crack*.

It's true that I never shot a rifle myself, but I live in the country. I know that sound. My heart goes a million miles a minute, and I grab Ammy's suitcase, nod to the woods, and yell, "Run!"

And we do. As fast as we can.

AMMY

"JESUS CHRIST," I SAY. "JESUS H. CHRIST."

Noah still has my suitcase, and we're on the other side of the woods—finally. We ran so freaking fast I can barely breathe now, the icy air chilling my lungs from the inside.

"Do you really think those were gunshots?" I ask, more than a little alarmed. "Where the hell *are we?*"

Noah turns to me, his eyes jumpy, like he's scared, at least a little. "Honestly, I don't know if they were or not. I think they were, though. And I definitely didn't want to stay and find out if my gut was right."

"Yeah, me either," I say.

My jeans have gone from frayed to ripped at one of the knees—I guess a run through the woods is much harder on

88

your clothes than a walk—and the inch or so of exposed skin aches with chill. At least the running got us sweating. The rest of my body isn't quite as cold as it was before. For now, I think.

I look at Noah. The sleeve of his coat is also torn, and his face is red.

He catches my eyes, and for a second, we both just smile. Well, I force myself to smile because if I don't, I fear I might cry. I'd bet a kajillion bucks he's doing the same thing.

"Didn't think you'd be outrunning gunshots on your trip up to New York, did you?" he says.

I laugh weakly. "I definitely did not."

There's a pause, and he just looks at me, and I want to know what he's thinking, if he's as worried as I am. "So what do we do?" I ask finally.

He shows me the map. There's no service again—what is it with upstate New York, really?—but he has it pulled up from before. "We went *exactly* the wrong way," he says, his finger, which already has a bluish tint, pointing the way. "So we have to go toward the train to get back. Once we're there, if the train looks like it's at all ready to go, we can just get on. And if it's not, we walk to the actual bus. The next one was at three, and again at three thirty. You'll be late, but it's better than nothing."

I shrug. At least I'll have tried. And I can still toast my dad and Sophie without having to witness their sure-to-be-nauseating vows. It's not ideal, but it's something. "What else is there to do?"

He shakes his head. "I'm sorry."

I shrug again. "It's okay."

He leads the way back, and it's not really that hard to follow our tracks because we *were* in the middle of nowhere, and so we can see our footprints in the inch or so of snow in the clearing, already half covered up from the flakes that fell while we were pondering trespassing and potentially losing our lives. A tiny, quickly disappearing trail through the woods.

It's weird how you can make these tracks, and then it can all be near wiped out so quickly. *Undone.* I wish life were like that. I wish my dad's wanderings were just clunky footprints in the snow, ones that got filled in, erased, over time.

When we reach the second patch of woods, Noah, a gentleman (even if he's a gentleman who has no sense of direction, half-cocked travel ideas that could very well lead to frostbite or exposure, and a frustrating understanding of gender roles), insists on carrying my rolling suitcase, even though he has a decently large backpack on his back, too. This time, I don't protest, because although I do hate that gender norm, he kind of owes me, and it's too windy and cold out here to try and stand up for my ideals right now.

We keep a steady pace, because we have at least another twenty minutes or so of walking to get to the train and then another leg going in the opposite direction, which, Lord willing, will lead to the bus. We're quite obviously going to miss the three o'clock, but we should be fine for the three thirty—I hope.

"Should we play Questions?" I ask, needing something to pass the time, distract me from the bitter cold, from just how much my face already hurts.

"Questions?"

"It's this game that my friends and I used to play. It's really easy. I ask a question, and we both answer. And then you ask a question, and we both answer. That's it."

He laughs. "So, like a conversation?"

I huff. "If you want to put it that way, sure. But we don't have to think of any transitions or whatever. We just ask our questions and move on. It's fun, trust me. Like Truth or Dare. Without the dares. And we both have to answer every truth. Plus, we don't have anything else to do right now."

Plus plus, it always helped me feel better when I was upset. A round or two with Dara and Simone, and it's like I could step out of my own world, just for a little bit, and walk into theirs instead.

"All right, all right," he says. "You start, though."

"Okay, what do you like better, Twizzlers or Red Vines?"

Noah laughs. "*That's* your question?"

"I didn't say they had to be serious, end-of-the-world questions."

He raises his eyebrows. "Twizzlers, of course."

I shake my head. "You're missing out. Red Vines are so much better."

"Well, I'd kill for either of them right about now," he says.

I laugh. "Me too."

"All right," he says. "No more food questions. What's your

favorite book. You know, of all time?"

I take a big step and my foot lands in a mixture of snow-sludge and damp dirt. I shake it off and keep going. "Probably *Anna Karenina*. I like that it's like a soap opera and all dramatic and stuff but then totally smart, and Tolstoy makes all these awesome observations."

Noah smiles. "You gotta love *Anna*. Such a good book."

"Right?" I say. "Okay, what's yours? Dare I say *The Hunger Games*?"

"Hey now," Noah says as he gives my suitcase another big tug. "I am carrying your stuff. Be nice."

"Okay, okay," I say, laughing. "What is it, then?"

He turns to me and smiles. "*Beloved*. Best ghost story of all time and also probably just best story of all time."

And I have to hand it to him, though I don't hand it to him, not out loud at least—it's a good choice. A really good choice.

We keep walking, still protected from the majority of the snow by the canopy of trees.

"Do you have any brothers and sisters?" I ask.

"That's an easy one," Noah says. "Nope. Just me."

"Really?" I ask. "Me too. Did you like it growing up?"

Noah shakes his head. "I was always dying for a little brother. Someone to really drive nuts, you know?"

I don't know, because I always liked my lot in life. Our little family.

I always liked it until recently. Until my dad did what he did.

"Okay," he says, after a minute or so. "So when was your first kiss?"

I pause, heart beating fast, feeling myself turn red, and not from the wind chapping my skin, because my answer is embarrassing. Just last year, with one of Dara's cousins, who wasn't even that cute.

But he doesn't even wait for me to respond. "Mine was when I was eight with this girl named Cora who lived down the block. But she kissed another boy the same day, and then I felt kind of shitty."

That sends me laughing. And when I don't offer my own answer, Noah doesn't push. I think he gets it—in this game, you're not supposed to push. That's the whole point.

As the snow continues to fall, eking its way through the canopy of trees, and I try to keep Kat's room in my mind, the promise of *Friends* reruns and a full dishing session about everything that went on today, the conversation changes, and the questions get a tad more serious.

He asks me where I see myself in ten years. I tell him that I have no earthly idea, because I don't.

I tell him that that's a really weird question for an eighteen-year-old to ask.

I don't tell him that right now I'm only worried about getting through this year. That I refuse to think that far ahead because I refuse to believe, ever again, that everything will just "work out." Ten years is a long way off, and so much can happen between then and now. So much has happened even in the last year for me. So much that I never thought possible—and not in a good way.

He expands on his comparative lit tenure-track plan, and it's laughable how much detail he's thought out. He's so different from me in every way. I don't even know what colleges I'm going to apply to—though I'm going to have to pick a few soon—much less what I'm going to study, what the hell I want to do.

There's a pause in our conversation, and that's when I ask him what Dara and Simone and I always used to ask one another: "What's your biggest regret?"

He stops for a second, turning to me. There are snowflakes in his hair, and we're in a tiny clearing—a half clearing, if you will, not big like the one from before—and for a second, it's like a whole little world, just for us. "I don't believe in regrets."

I laugh. "Come on," I say. "Everyone has regrets."

"I really don't think it's good to dwell in the past."

I narrow my eyes. "Thanks, Mr. Hallmark." I shrug. "You don't have to answer if you don't want to. But no need to get all *philosophical* on me."

He turns away then, stepping out of our mini world. But even though he projects his voice forward, like he's talking to the trees, I can still hear him.

"Fine," he says. "I don't believe in regrets. I really don't. I think it's a crappy way to live, thinking like that. Can I say something I wish I'd done differently?"

I laugh. "Er, that's the same exact thing, dude."

"It's not, though. Regret is all about sadness and

mourning. It doesn't *do* anything. Wishing you hadn't done something—that's about learning." He pauses. Then: "I wish I hadn't broken up with Rina."

He walks a bit faster, and I pick up the pace.

"Was it all your fault?" I ask.

He turns his head to me. "That's two questions."

My mind starts to spin, trying to fill in the gaps, wondering what exactly happened between them, but I don't have time, because Noah stops then, turns to me, head tilted to the side. "So what's yours? What do you wish you hadn't done?"

My lips part, and suddenly I'm at a loss for words. It's something about the way he puts it. It's so direct. When I played this game before, I never had a *real* biggest regret. I said I regretted not quitting gymnastics when I was eight. Or I wished I'd signed up for AP art class instead of computer science. But none of that stuff mattered. I have a real regret now, in the truest sense of the word. I believe, deep down, that if I'd done things differently last Thanksgiving—who knows, maybe I wouldn't be here.

"Mine's a true regret, even if you don't believe in them. Sometimes it's impossible not to dwell in the past," I say. "No matter how much you want to argue about semantics."

He shrugs, but he seems to take me more seriously than he did before. Like he can see I'm sharing the raw, naked truth.

"So what is it, then?" he asks, and his words are suddenly soft.

I take a few large steps ahead, giving myself a little space.

"I'm going to skip that one for now."

His long legs shorten the space I've created between us in seconds—I may be tall, but he's taller. "Can you do that?"

I shrug. "It's my game, not yours."

He laughs at that, but he keeps pushing. "Tell me something else, then. Tell me the reason why you're going to Hudson. I told you mine."

I turn to him, and he's grinning, one side of his mouth turned up farther than the other. He's got a goofy smile, for sure. His teeth are all crooked, I realize, and a little too spaced out. His lips pull back too far and show his gums. It's a physical flaw that looks strange against his strong jaw and deep-set eyes.

But then his smile disappears, and I'm not sure quite what I've done, but obviously one of my certainly-not-so-perfect features has given me away. He can see that this isn't just about a high school breakup. I curse myself for being so freaking easy to read.

"Sorry," he says immediately. "If you don't feel comfortable, you don't have to tell me anything. *Really.*"

I bite my lip, and then I turn forward and pick up the pace again.

Noah's obviously still waiting for my answer. "It's not a sob story or anything, okay?" I snap. "No one's, like, dying of cancer or heart failure."

He's quiet. He doesn't ask me anything more.

We reach another tiny clearing, and he leads the way.

I turn back for a minute, looking at the circle of white in

the absence of trees, the way the snow falls, still so delicately. It's not hard or angry, like you'd expect from a storm. It's gentle, slight, more like dandelion seeds. My mom always said it was her favorite kind of snow. You know, the soft kind, just like this. I reach out my gloved hand and catch a few flakes, and there's something about the way they scatter on my glove, and suddenly, it's like I'm back there, in my yard on my birthday when I was seven. It was two days before Thanksgiving. I'd been telling my mom and dad that all I wanted for my birthday was snow, but my parents had been adamant—in our part of Virginia, at least, snow before Christmas was a rarity.

But I got my wish.

At 7:00 a.m., it started falling. Slowly and softly but steadily, just like this. I abandoned my Eggo waffle and ran to the window. My dad took one look at my face and pulled out his phone, calling in sick to work.

I threw a jacket over my pajamas, an extra pair of my mom's warmest gloves on my hands, and snow boots over my bare feet—I couldn't even bother with finding clean socks, and I had blisters for a week after. The three of us were outside for, I don't know, *hours*. Watching it fall. Dancing around the backyard. We'd zip in for hot chocolate when we got too cold, throw our wet clothes in the dryer (eventually I did put on socks), and repeat. In the quiet moments, while we were waiting for the chocolate to warm or the drying to finish, my dad would laugh, pinch the red of my nose, and tell me I looked like Rudolph—and he would kiss my mom on the lips.

We were all so very . . . *happy.*

What the hell happened to that? To us?

"You coming?" Noah asks.

I nod, following him. He doesn't ask any more questions—my cancer comment put him off, I guess. I was being dramatic, sure. And yet I think about what my therapist said. Divorce is like death. The way you grieve for it, at least.

But I think about two years ago, when Simone's dad got cancer. And when, six months later, he died. I remember how Simone stopped getting her monthly relaxers, because she couldn't even stand to do something as normal as make a hair appointment. I remember how Simone's mom lost weight, first a couple of pounds and then close to ten or fifteen, how she looped a tiny hair tie around the back of her wedding ring so it wouldn't fall off. I remember how Cary, Simone's older brother, who was at Vanderbilt, threw himself into classes and went from coming home every two weeks or so to hardly at all. I remember how their house became almost like a museum, the *TV Guide* that her dad had flipped through still sitting, dog-eared, on the end table in the family room.

I've seen death, and this wasn't it. *My dad* is still here. A not-so-short train ride away. What I said to Noah was true. It's *not* like anyone has cancer or heart failure.

And yet why does it *still* feel so bad, then?

We reach the end of the woods, and I try to push it all out of my mind, get my head on straight.

We're almost to the edge, and soon we'll be at the train, and maybe, just maybe, it will all be fixed. Maybe I'll even make it to the ceremony almost in time.

I follow Noah out into the sun.

But that's when my hopeful mood drops.

"You've got to be kidding me," I say as I look straight ahead.

At the slats of the tracks.

At the train, crawling away.

Crawling away from us.

I break into a run, leaving Noah behind.

NOAH

3:18 P.M.

SHE BOLTS, RUNNING FAST AND FURIOUS, BUT IT'S not nearly fast enough.

I watch in horror and disappointment and what feels like as many stupid emotions as there are snowflakes in the sky as the train pulls away. It chugs along like nothing was ever wrong with it.

Leaving us out in the cold. Literally.

Quickly turning my plans with Rina to murky slush.

By the time Ammy stops running, the train is a small dot on the horizon. In seconds, it's gone.

She turns to me. She's too far away for me to see the look on her face, but it doesn't take much creativity to imagine it.

Her suitcase sits beside me in the snow, abandoned like

100

a child at the mall who got separated from its parents. I grab it, give it a tug. It somehow feels heavier than it did a minute ago.

She doesn't move to meet me, and the wind slaps at me brutally as I walk the fifty feet or so toward her. The snow falls fiercely now.

This is why I wasn't ever adventurous, Rina. Because things never work out.

I approach, and her hands move to her hips.

She stares at me, waiting, but I don't stop walking. There's nothing else to do.

By the time I reach her, she's white with anger.

"I'm sorry," I say.

She shakes her head, her short hair whipping against her cheek. "You told me about your friend," she says. "Who got stuck for hours." Her voice cracks, and her eyes glisten. I have the strangest desire to let go of her suitcase, toss my backpack to the ground, and wrap her in the biggest, longest hug. Solve every single one of her problems, even though she won't tell me what they are.

"I'm sorry," I say again.

She takes a deep breath. Her voice doesn't falter when she answers. "I was supposed to—" and for a second I think she's going to tell me why she needed to be in Hudson by five sharp. I find myself wondering who she's meeting. Why it matters so much. What's making her so upset. Who hurt her so bad.

The thought of someone hurting her—boyfriend,

girlfriend, friend, family, whatever—makes me weirdly furious. For a second, I forget that I'm screwed, too. That all my plans with Rina will most likely be shot.

She bites her lip, and she doesn't say anything. The moment passes.

I look around me, taking it all in. The empty train track. The stretch of snow-dappled steel. The trees on either side and a big bunch of nothing in both directions. It's not even a proper stop, so it's not like we can cut our losses and wait here for the next train. Any train that does come, if trains are still even running in this weather, will whip right by the two teenagers idiotic enough to hop off a broken-down Amtrak to set off for the bus.

I try to focus. I get out my phone and check the time. It's almost three thirty. If we catch the four o'clock, I'll definitely be rushed getting ready, and I probably won't have time to get new, better flowers, but it will be better than nothing. Plus, what other option do we have?

"We have to get the bus," I say. "That's what we came back for anyway. It's no different than if the train had still been here, not moving. That was our plan. We can still catch the four."

"It *is* different," she says. "Because if you hadn't had your stupid idea, we'd be going exactly where we need to go right now."

In a flash, I see Rina, wonder what she's doing tonight. Wonder if I even stand a chance anyway. If she'll love my story or think it's too little, too late.

102

When I don't say anything right away, Ammy reaches for her suitcase, grabs it, and starts walking, whipping it over the desolate steel tracks. I make sure there's no train barreling down the tracks and follow. "Ammy," I say. "Come on. We're in this together."

She turns. "In this *together*? I'm only in this because *you* completely misled me!" Her voice falters for a second, but she seems to call the anger back.

"You don't even know where you're going," I protest.

"I can use maps just as well as you," she says bitterly, without looking back. "Probably a kajillion times better, actually. Because anyone who has a brain knows that the train was going north, so if we came out of the back of the train and took a right, *obviously* we'd be going the wrong way."

Her words hurt. She's right. It's so clear, I should have known. I run ahead, turn, and stop her before the next patch of trees.

"So why didn't you tell me?" I ask.

She sighs. "Because I didn't know where in the world we were going! I didn't know we were supposed to go away from the river."

"I got confused by the map," I say. "I'm sorry."

"Whatever," she says. "Just move." She's so much taller than Rina is. I have almost a foot on Rina, but only a few inches on her. We're practically eye to eye, and hers are puffy and tired. Outwardly, she's angry, with her clenched fists and her deliberate walk and her raised voice. But when I look at her big brown eyes, all I see is hurt and disappointment.

And something else . . . fear?

She doesn't know how this is going to turn out, and it's not only because we missed the train. I'd bet everything on it.

The eyes are a window to the soul, that's what the overly used proverb says, but I've always preferred Alfred, Lord Tennyson's version: "Her eyes are homes of silent prayer."

Never has the line been so apt as it is now, I think as I look at Ammy.

I put my hands on her shoulders. "I messed up," I say. "And I get it. I'm so sorry. I was only trying to help." I feel her shoulders relax the tiniest bit, and her eyes flit briefly to the ground. I drop my arms to my sides. "I thought it would work. I thought we'd beat everyone else to Hudson. I wouldn't have asked you to come with me if I didn't."

She shrugs away from my grasp, but she doesn't say anything.

All I want in the whole world is to get Rina back. That's why I'm here. But I want to help Ammy along the way. I do. And it's not just because of karma. It's because she's the kind of person who seems like she would never ask for help. And that's always the kind of person who's most likely to need it. I know that because I'm that way, too.

"We're in this together now, and it's not a good idea for us to split up." I venture a small smile. "We're not in a bad horror movie."

She lets out the smallest of laughs.

My smile grows wider.

She stifles her laugh quickly. "I'm still mad at you," she says.

I shrug and reach for her suitcase, determined to make the four o'clock bus if it kills me.

Surprisingly, she lets me.

AMMY

WE WALK STEADILY, NOAH LEADING THE WAY. WE *must* be going the right way this time, because I have service, even if it's spotty, and I can actually see a bus station on the map and our little blue dot moving toward it. Not to mention, we're walking east—you know, *away* from the river. Which is just basic logic, and I know he knows I'm right on that one. I felt bad seeing how hurt and embarrassed he was when I called him out on it, but still.

The woods are sparser on this side, and Noah moves faster, his long legs stretching out in front of him, like he's on a mission—which he is, I guess. I have to walk pretty fast to keep up, but I'm okay with it, because time isn't exactly on our side right now.

He doesn't say anything, and for that I'm grateful. Because he's the kind of person you could totally find yourself opening up to, telling all your secrets if you're not careful. It's his stupid eyes. A sweet little animal's eyes on a big bro-y guy. All round and *I only want to help you* kind of eyes, the ones that crease at the corners and practically invite you in. It's downright unnerving.

And I don't want to tell him everything. Because I know what happens when I start talking about my parents. People pity me, at least people who aren't Dara and Simone. It's humiliating.

And then I inevitably cry. Which is even worse.

And I'm *not* the kind of girl who goes crying to the big strong guy when shit goes wrong.

I steal a glance at my suitcase, which Noah pulls swiftly behind him.

At least I'm really trying not to be.

I feel a buzz in my pocket, and I realize I haven't given Kat the updates since I told her I'd be on time. I pull out my phone. There are two messages.

I look at my mom's first.

I never meant for it to turn out this way

I don't say anything back, then open Kat's, a weight already sitting in my stomach. I hate to disappoint her.

Arriving soon?

I text back right away.

No, back to being late. Crazy storm.

We left the train and now we're headed to the bus.

107

Umm, girl, who is we ;)

No one. He has a girlfriend, anyway.

Which is kind of a lie, but it also kind of isn't.

So is there any way you're going to make it for the ceremony? I

neeeeeeeeeeeeeeed you

Doing my best

Ok keep me posted, pleeeeeaaaaaaaassseeee make it!!!

P.S. Mom is freaking out about her dress but if you need a ride I'll

try to steal away

OK, will keep you posted

Peace, sis

The word hits me right in the heart, and I feel this tug, like a magnet drawing me up to that stupid farmhouse and my stupid new family.

When I came back to Virginia after my trip here last summer, Mom insisted that I go through every single detail of every single moment, and I found myself pretending that it had been just horrible, even though it wasn't. Because I was Team Mom.

And I still am, I tell myself.

It's only that Team Dad just feels so much easier sometimes.

Especially when it makes me a sister, even if I'm a fake one.

Noah turns to me then, so quickly that I almost run right into him, and for a second our faces are only inches apart. I remedy that right away, taking three quick steps back.

"Everything okay?" he asks.

I nod, shifting my weight from foot to foot. Realizing for the first time that after walking *more than* point nine miles, *twice*, in inch after inch of snow, my shoes are damp.

There's protection in here, with the trees as cover, but all it takes is one look up to see that the snow isn't thinking about stopping anytime soon.

"Well, good," he says, though he doesn't seem to quite believe me. "Because I'm pretty sure we've reached civilization." He smiles, like God's just sent us down manna from heaven. Or one of those parachute packages from the *Hunger Games* movie. (Yes, I watched the movies, and they were just okay.)

He takes a few quick steps ahead, and I follow him out into an open field.

And there it is.

"A road!" I say. "Actual freaking asphalt." I run up to it, leaping onto it. It's slushy and gross from where cars have driven past, and jumping in it makes my shoes even damper, but I don't care one bit. The yellow line that cuts it in half is like the most beautiful thing I've ever seen in my life.

"God," Noah says behind me. "Get out of the road. It's a blind curve."

I step back, and I turn to look at him. "Sorry," I say.

He just shakes his head.

He's one of those people who's always looking out for others, who's always worrying about stuff. How does he even know I wasn't looking? (I wasn't.)

Still, something about it is nice.

He looks back and forth and then crosses, and I follow him. We walk along the shoulder for about fifty feet or so, and then we turn onto a smaller road.

With a sidewalk. And a 7-freaking-Eleven. Praise the Lord. I don't think I've ever been so happy to see one of those, the green-and-orange sign, the dingy glass like a beacon guiding the way.

Noah follows my eyes. "What, do they not have 7-Elevens in Roanoke?" he asks. "You look like you've just seen the face of God."

I laugh. "Right now, it might as well be."

And then I try not to think about how he remembered not just where I'm from but the exact name of my city, which I mentioned when we first started walking. I try not to think about how, for some reason, that makes me happy.

"Fancy a corn dog?" he asks.

I shake my head vehemently. "I don't want to do anything to risk us not getting on that bus."

"I know," he says. "I kid. I kid." He swerves my suitcase past a pile of trash bags on the sidewalk. "Who knows, maybe we'll laugh about this one day? That's what people always say, isn't it?"

I raise an eyebrow, reach out my hand to take my suitcase back now that the road is smoother, now that we have a magical thing called cement sidewalks, but he shoos my hand away.

"I'll hold the laughter until I'm on that bus, thanks," I say.

"Fair," he says. There's a liquor store awning above us and it gives us a brief, welcome break from the snowfall. "But don't tell me you won't log this one away to tell Ammy Jr. That time you wandered out into the snow with a stranger, got lost, nearly got shot by some guy in the country, and still found your way home. It's almost romantic, like an old movie or something. . . ." His voice trails off as we cross the street.

And I think about what I thought going onto the train. How it would be romantic.

In a weird way, I guess it is.

Noah is a total romantic, I realize. I mean, I knew he was sappy—*hello*, cheesy flowers—but this is a different kind of romance. The desire for the world to be magical all around you. Not everyone's like that.

My mom's always been that way. Half the time I think it's what makes her life so difficult, her anxiety so bad.

Because she could never be happy with the actual world she had. She never really wanted it until after she lost it.

"Come on," he says, not letting the subject drop. "You've got to agree."

I look to the right, and I see hints of a cute main drag, the kinds of things you'd imagine in a small town in the Northeast. Brick storefronts. Vintage signage. A movie theater that looks like it's been turned into some kind of bar or music venue.

He's right (though I won't tell him that). And for a second, I can't help it. I think of the way his hands felt on my shoulders, the way his hazel eyes caught mine as he steadied me, trying to calm me down, the way I was close enough to see a smattering of freckles on his eyelids, cracked skin at the edges of his pale lips. The way the fleece hat sat lopsided on his head, revealing only a tiny bit of his face behind bundles of Gore-Tex and nylon.

Stop it, I think, cursing myself for thinking of him that way at all. The cold must really be getting to my head.

But I can't help it—I think of that movie, the one my mom loved to watch with me: *It Happened One Night*. This thirties film by Frank Capra about this rich heiress who is fleeing a bad marriage or something and meets this guy on a bus, and the bus breaks down, and they set off together, and then—*well*—you can imagine the rest.

But that's all beside the point, because romance is off-limits.

Dara and Simone and everyone else might think I'm crazy, but I am not about to go there.

I'm not going to be like my mom. With the obsessive questions, the insistence that I tell her everything about my dad's new life. The absolute refusal to let him go. The way she still has pictures of the two of them strewn around the house, even though her new passion is telling me round the clock just how much she hates him.

The yelling at me when I suggest ever so subtly that maybe she should talk about something else for a while, when her anxiety gets the best of her.

It's not her fault that she is the way she is sometimes. But it doesn't make it any easier for me. It doesn't change the fact that I wish sometimes she could just be more of a mom.

But the thing is, I'm not going to be like my dad, either. Telling myself that love conquers all like a freaking twelve-year-old.

Because everything's been a mess since my dad "fell in love" with Sophie.

He lost his marriage.

My mom lost her mind.

And I, well, I lost them both.

Noah's words about this being all romantic are hanging in the air, and so I make sure to shut them down. "It's actually more like a Lifetime movie," I shoot back, even though it's been too long for the joke to really stick. I force a laugh. "You know, where a guy takes advantage of a nice girl and leads her off into her eventual demise. . . ."

He smiles and stops at the next crosswalk, waiting for a car to pass. There's that lopsided grin again. He's gotta be the only person in the world who could make waterproof Gore-Tex fabric look good.

"We're almost there," he says. "Are you still going to sit with me, or have you grown altogether weary of my presence?"

I keep my eyes locked ahead, waiting for our walk sign. "Again, all discussion will happen once we are on the bus and safe." I steal a look to the side, and he looks a little hurt, like he thinks I'm serious. "Don't worry," I say. "I won't leave you alone on the bus."

"Phew," he says dramatically, as the light turns and we cross. "I was worried. Especially since my Kindle is dead." He winks. He's such a nerd—a bro nerd, but a nerd all the same.

"What time is it?" I ask.

"Three forty-nine," he says. "Plenty of time. We're only a couple of blocks away."

"Do we have to get tickets?" I ask.

Noah nods, maneuvering my suitcase safely over a patch of ice on the sidewalk. "Don't worry. I'll get yours. I owe you, after all."

"Oh, I wasn't asking. . . ."

He turns to me and smiles, and the snowflakes on his eyelashes glisten in the winter sun. "I wasn't asking, either."

And I roll my eyes—because you have to roll your eyes at something like that.

But inside, I'm smiling. Just a little.

NOAH

3:50 P.M.

I'VE NEVER FELT THIS WAY ABOUT AN EYE ROLL before, but for some reason, it's amazing. It's like she puts me in my place but makes me feel all warm inside at once. It's something about the way she does it. Like she's making fun of me but is somehow on my team all the same.

God, I need to stop analyzing eye rolls.

Rina, I remind myself. *Rina, Rina, Rina.*

When Rina disagreed with me, it never felt like we were on the same team.

But that's because they were bigger disagreements. I wasn't ready to be the guy she needed. Not then.

But I am now.

Hell, I just trekked through miles of wilderness with a

stranger. I dare her to tell me I can never just *go.*

I check my phone again. "That's it," I say. "Up ahead there. That sign."

"Time check?" Ammy asks.

"Three fifty-one. We're good."

A snowflake lands on her lips, and she presses them together, like she can taste it.

She smiles, and I notice for the first time that her mouth is quite small, her lips not thin but not thick, either. She's got the kind of mouth that some idiot doctor in Beverly Hills would suggest plumping up with collagen injections. The kind of mouth that's perfect the way it is.

I turn away.

There's a brick building up ahead, past a stretch of crappy delis and gas stations, with a tall sign that's cracked and blank from this side. It says Hudson Bus Lines on the other, I'm sure of it.

We're almost there.

A car whips by, going too fast for this weather, leaving tracks in the icy snow. It's one of the few vehicles on the road. People, normal people, the kind who *don't* decide to travel up to Hudson to make a grand gesture in the middle of a huge-ass winter storm, are inside now. They're with their families, watching *The Twilight Zone* on Netflix. Breaking their New Year's resolutions. Trying to figure out if anyone will deliver pizza in this weather.

I wonder what Rina is doing right now. I imagine her up in her room, on the wrought-iron bed that looked like it belonged to a Victorian princess. God, that bed creaked awfully. Made it exceedingly difficult to fool around.

Is she reading? She certainly wouldn't be one to touch Murakami, more like a book of monologues. Rina wants to be an actress, and she's got it, the presence, the expressions, that way she has of making her voice carry.

Is she looking up acting programs, deciding where she wants to go next year?

Or is she relaxing? Taking one of her super-long naps? I think about that last week together at Lake George, right after graduation; sometimes I'd come in from the beach and she'd just be conked out in bed in the middle of the day. In the sun leaking in through the windows, it was all there right in front of me. All of her. The minuscule scar on her chin from where she fell into a coffee table when she was little. The bud of a pimple from slathering on sunscreen every day. The way her eyelashes looked more blonde than black when she wasn't wearing mascara.

The way her face when she slept looked downright angelic.

Bryson told me she wasn't good for me early on. I'd taken us a back way to the movie theater, because I thought it would be faster. We got there late, no seats left but the very front row. Rina huffed and sighed through one and a half hours of superhero action.

Bryson cornered me afterward, while she was in the bathroom, asked me what I was doing, shared some choice words about her behavior. It smelled like stale popcorn and chemical fake butter, and there were the sounds of a Pokémon pinball machine drifting in from the corner. And I felt like I had to choose between my best friend and my girlfriend.

The choice was easy.

I didn't hang out with Bryson much the rest of sophomore year. But eventually, he saw that things weren't going to change. By junior year, we were all friends again.

He was happy when I broke up with her. Ecstatic. Only three days later, he made me come with him to the basement of this idiot guy who was a year older than us but still hanging around town. I had three beers that night, which was a lot for me. . . .

Sometimes I still think it would have all gone down differently if I hadn't stayed friends with Bryson.

"*Hello,*" Ammy says.

I turn to her as we walk. She's staring at me.

"I asked where you think the ticket machine is."

"Damn, you really are worried," I say.

She knits her eyebrows together as we pass a deli that's closing up early. "Hey, it's my last chance to get there at a remotely reasonable hour. I don't want to screw it up."

"Sorry," I say, and I feel the ache of guilt again. She wouldn't be in this situation if not for me. "I think there should be a kiosk, in addition to the guy at the window, but you never know at smaller stations. We have time."

She nods, and we cut through a parking lot, beeline for the brick building. A bus comes into view. A large one. Ahh, sweet glory.

"I never thought I'd be so happy to see a bus," Ammy says, walking faster.

"Me either."

"Time check?"

"Three fifty-three."

"Perfect. I hate being rushed for stuff like this."

"Me too."

There is no kiosk, so we head into the line, which is empty. The ticket seller is standing up, his back to us.

There's a sign on the window.

"All Evening Buses Canceled Due to Weather."

And then there's a grumbling roar of an engine.

"Oh Jesus, no," I hear behind me.

I turn to see Ammy, breaking into that same desperate, pointless run I had to witness when she chased the train. The bus is well across the parking lot, pulling away. She doesn't go more than twenty feet before she turns back, an awful, defeated look on her face.

"Tell me that wasn't our bus," she says, out of breath.

"It couldn't be," I say. I check my phone again, which is about to die. Three fifty-four. There's no way.

"Excuse me," I say, knocking on the glass. "Excuse me." The man in the booth turns to me, taps on the glass right back, pointing to the sign.

Ammy's breaths quicken behind me. "It's okay," I say, turning toward her. "We'll work this out. Don't worry."

I tap on the glass again. The man looks like he's in his late fifties, slightly rotund, and exhausted. He rolls his eyes and sits down, leans up to the microphone in front of the gap in the window. "Can I *help* you, sir?"

His name tag says Chet. Of *course* it says Chet.

"That bus wasn't the four o'clock bus, was it?"

The man shakes his head, and my heart soars with relief. "That was the three-thirty. It was held up due to the weather."

I turn to Ammy, give her my best smile. "It wasn't the four o'clock!"

Her eyes light up, and the thought hits me, strong and impossible to ignore: she's so beautiful when she's happy.

"So can we have two tickets for the four, please?"

The man points at the sign again, almost smugly, with a touch of *this generation couldn't survive ten minutes without their precious phones.* "Sir, that bus is *canceled. All* the rest of the buses are canceled for the storm. The snow is supposed to go all night. That's why the sign's up."

It feels like my heart falls from my chest to the bottom of my stomach.

"Is there another bus after that?" I ask.

"Can you read, sir?"

"I'm just asking!" My voice is rising.

He clears his throat, and I swear all the frustration that the guy's ever felt in his fifty-odd years is written on his face. "I'm going home now, *sir.*"

I stare at him, watching him pack up, hardly able to believe it.

We're fucked.

Totally, utterly fucked.

There are no other buses. The train left forever ago. There probably aren't even cabs on the road, even if we could get a cab in whatever small town we're currently occupying.

I won't get to Rina tonight. We'll miss the reservation. The anniversary. All of it.

I'll get there tomorrow on a day that means *nothing* with a sad excuse about getting held up last night, and she'll probably slam the door in my face.

And Ammy—wherever she's going, I've ruined it now.

Karma. So much for goddamn karma.

I turn around, ready for the fight, the outburst, the anger, all directed at me. Knowing I deserve it.

But she's laughing.

Keeled over, one hand on her suitcase handle, the other on her stomach.

She's shaking with laughter. Giddy, uncontrollable laughter.

I look back to the man, and he takes a moment from his hurried packing up to shrug, giving me that look that guys sometimes give each other when a girl does something nutty. I look back to her. "Are you okay?"

She can barely stop laughing enough to nod, but then finally, she speaks. "Yeah," she says. "I'm okay."

"But . . . we're screwed."

She starts laughing again. "Oh, I know."

"But—"

She puts a hand on her hip. "Look," she says, interrupting me. "I've run after two modes of transportation now, missing them by only minutes each time." She holds her hands out. "And it's still fucking snowing, and it doesn't look like it's going to stop. I'm stuck with someone I've known all of five minutes in the middle of nowhere. If I can't laugh about that, Lord help me."

I let out a deep breath, but her humorous mood doesn't make me feel all that much better. "I don't know what to do."

She crosses her arms in front of her. "I only have ten percent battery left on my phone. You?"

I check mine. "Just one," I say.

She nods. "I figured. There's gotta be a diner or coffee shop or something around here, right? Let's go charge our phones, and make a new plan."

I shrug. "All right, I guess. But every plan I've had today has been an utter Dumpster fire."

She laughs again. "Well, you're not going to get rid of me now, so let's just try to at least make a plan that's *not* a Dumpster fire, okay?"

"Okay," I manage.

"Come on," she says, and she starts to head out of the parking lot.

She doesn't know where she's going. Neither of us do. And my phone is this close to conking out completely.

But at least she's doing *something*, I remind myself.

At least it's not like all the pressure is on me.

It's almost like we're on a team now, and she's going to act as captain for a little bit.

She may have only known me for "all of five minutes," but she knows enough to know that I need some help.

And I'm thankful for that. I really am.

AMMY

I ONLY GET AS FAR AS THE EDGE OF THE PARKING LOT before it all hits me, before my laughter, my forced attempt at positivity to cheer up Noah, all feels just . . . stupid.

Because I'm going to miss my dad's wedding.

Well, my dad's fake wedding. But still.

Even if we could somehow miraculously pull a plan together, there's just no way I'll get there in time. There's no way.

Noah sidles up to me. "Do you know where you're going?" he asks.

I shake my head, and so we stand there at the edge of the parking lot while I search for something close by. It doesn't

124

take long to find the Main Street Café, on—you guessed it—Main Street, the road we walked on much more hopefully only a few minutes ago.

We retrace our steps to the main drag. The streets are empty. People are huddled in their homes in preparation for the storm.

"Is it open, you think?" he asks.

I shrug. "It says that it's open until nine p.m., but yeah, I don't really know. It's worth a shot, though."

We turn right onto Main Street, passing a closed coffee and sandwich place on the way—which sends me into a mini panic—but I keep walking anyway.

I pick up the pace a little, and just as I do, my foot slides beneath me, slipping on a patch of ice. Before I even realize it, Noah is behind me, catching me, holding me, hands around me like he can protect me from everything.

"Are you okay?" he asks. His voice is deep, coming from behind, close to my ear. "That's black ice."

"I'm fine," I say, feeling that jolt of electricity again, the same one I felt back when he caught me jumping down from the train. I take a deep breath, pulling myself together. Willing my voice not to betray me.

"Uh, I think it's up there," I say. There's a blue awning over an older storefront with antiqued yellow siding. There's no "Open" sign on the door, but I'm hoping that's just a fluke.

My heartbeats have calmed a bit by the time we get in front of the door, and I pull on it quickly, feeling instant joy as it opens, as I hear the ding of a bell.

It's dim inside, which doesn't give me too much hope, and it's empty. Shit.

"Excuse me," I call into what looks like an abyss. "Are you open?"

There's nothing—not a sound, not a movement. I look back to Noah, and I know the fear on my face has to be showing now.

And then I wonder, for a second, what it would be like to have his arms around me again.

But that's when I hear a clash of pans, and a waitress whooshes through the double doors to the kitchen. She cocks her hip to the side. "Two?" she says.

I nod, relieved that they're open. Relieved that my stupid thoughts about Noah were interrupted. "Please."

She sighs, walking around the counter and grabbing two menus that look like they could use a good cleaning. She's young, probably only a few years older than us, with red hair, freckled skin, and a scowl that looks like it's been permanently etched into her face. She tosses the menus down on the table and doesn't say anything else.

I take a seat and Noah follows. Immediately, he crouches down, looking under the table.

He pops up. "Well, good news is, there are plugs down here."

"Thank the Lord," I say, fishing my phone and charger out of my bag and tossing them to him. I nod at the flowers, tucked into the top of his backpack, wet and wilted and totally destroyed. "I think you're going to have to get a new bunch of flowers," I say.

"You think?" he says bitterly. And then: "Sorry. I'm just stressed out."

"I know," I say. "Me too."

Noah ducks back under the table to plug our phones in. When he comes up, he ventures a small smile. "Props on finding the diner," he says. "I think I was ready to lie down in that parking lot and let the snow cover me up."

I laugh. "Someone had to pull it together. And you'd been doing it for me all day."

I cringe internally as I remember the way I yelled at him before, and I'm thankful that the bus debacle sent me into laughter instead. It gives me a tiny hope that I can escape my fate—that I won't turn into my mom after all.

The waitress comes back over, and the glint of her sparkly blue eye shadow catches in the lamplight from overhead. "You guys want coffees?" she asks, holding two chipped white cups and a steaming carafe.

"How'd you guess?" I ask.

She doesn't smile or laugh, just sets the mugs down— not very gently—pours the coffee, and nods to a container of creamers and sugars on the table. "I'll be back with real milk," she says. "Do you know what you want?" She doesn't bother with a pen or paper.

We exchange a glance, and Noah's eyes survey the menu, because she *definitely* doesn't look like the type you'd ask to "just give us five more minutes, please." After a quick look, he orders a double cheeseburger, and I get a double, too—because at this point, why not?

As she walks away, he grins. "A double," he says as he pours not one but four sugars into his cup. "Nice."

I add a little creamer to mine and narrow my eyes. "Are you trying to call me fat or something? You don't have to be six feet tall and a dude to order a double, you know."

He laughs for a second, but then sees that I'm at least somewhat serious. Any high school guy worth his salt should know that you *don't* joke about a girl's weight. You just don't. "Oh, God, no. I mean, you look great. *Obviously*. . . . Sorry," he says. "It was a dumb thing to say."

But I barely hear his sorry, because all I can focus on is that lovely little *obviously* thrown in after he said I look great. I feel my face start to go hot, and I practically dive into my coffee.

He sips on his, too. And then we both look up at the same time, catching each other's eyes. I'm positive my face is red.

And it's so strange, because we are strangers, and we both have very different reasons for being here, and I meant it when I said that romance was off-limits, and he's taken, anyway, with his soon-to-be-former ex. . . .

But still, if I didn't know better, it would feel almost like a . . .

Well.

Like a date.

I've never been on a real date before.

He's still looking at me, and I stare down at my hands,

at my chipped nail polish that I was going to fix before the wedding, back when I thought I'd be in Hudson with plenty of time to spare.

I look back up, and thankfully—disappointingly?—he's no longer looking at me. Instead, he's flipping through a tiny machine on the table.

"Is that a jukebox?" I ask.

He looks at me, smirks. "You've never seen a mini diner jukebox before?"

I shake my head.

He goes back to flipping, but I don't take my eyes off of him. I don't know why I'm suddenly feeling . . . different.

It's something about the restaurant, the way the booth seats are so close together, the yellow paint on the walls and the kitschy signs about how "Children Left Unattended Will Be Towed Away at Owner's Expense" that makes it feel quaint, homey—intimate.

Or maybe it's from before, from the way he looked at me when I started laughing. With relief. Appreciation. We'd known each other for such a short time, and already it was like we could communicate without words.

Stop it, Ammy, I think. Stop it.

I remind myself that *all guys* are off-limits, that he is *especially* off-limits because he's hung up on another girl, but then he does something stupid—he settles on "Suspicious Minds."

My heart stops for just the tiniest of seconds.

Because if this really were a date, I'd be swooning.

"You like Elvis?" I ask.

He shrugs. "My mom was always playing his stuff when I was little."

"This is my favorite song," I say.

"Really?"

I nod.

"Like your *favorite* favorite song? Of all the songs in the world?"

"His voice is so . . . I don't know, oaky."

"Oaky?" he laughs. "That's what my parents are always saying about wine."

I feel myself start to blush and bite my lip. "Do you know what I mean, though? Like, so rich. Warm, I guess." I feel stupid, suddenly. Ridiculous.

But it's okay because that's when the waitress brings two very quickly cooked burgers, and the spotlight is off of me for a moment, as Elvis sings the last verse.

She sets them down a little roughly and plops a bottle of Heinz in the middle. "Need anything else?"

I shake my head. My burger may look lackluster, but I would expect nothing more from a place like this.

She walks away, and I lean in a little toward Noah.

"Do you think there's another bus or train?" I ask.

He shakes his head. "There's definitely no other bus line that goes to Hudson. And the closest train stop is like twenty miles away. Remember, we didn't get off at a real stop."

"I know," I say.

"And even if we could get to that stop, I wouldn't count on it running in this weather."

I drum my fingers on the counter, wondering what on earth we're supposed to do. Minutes ago, I was worried about not making it to my dad's wedding in time. But now?

I'm worried about everything. I can't ask Kat for a ride when the wedding is in less than two hours. I can't call my mom and give her the pleasure of knowing that my whole plan has failed—as far as she knows, I'm already at my dad's. I can't ask my dad to abandon Sophie at the Italian restaurant altar or whatever to come out and save us. We're stuck.

I look over to the waitress, who's wiping down the counters with a dirty-looking rag. "Is there a cab company around here?" I ask. I know it would be, like, super-duper expensive, but at this point, I'm desperate. I have a credit card with a five-hundred-dollar limit, so that's something, at least.

She laughs. Not a good sign.

Noah and I exchange a glance.

She raises her eyebrows. "It's not really a cab kind of place."

"Thanks anyway," I say weakly, and then I turn back to Noah. "What are we going to do?"

He shoves his burger in his mouth, buying himself time to answer.

I do the same. It didn't look that appetizing a second ago, but it tastes good, really good. Especially after being in the cold.

Burgers and coffee, I think. Burgers and coffee between strangers. Well, *former* strangers.

I put my burger down and look at him seriously. Behind

him, a burly man comes inside and hangs up his winter hat on the coat stand at the door, scuffing his shoes on the mat. At least we're not the only customers anymore. Maybe the waitress will hate us less.

I steal a glance at her, but she's rolling her eyes while the man isn't looking.

Maybe not.

"Really. What are we going to do?" I ask again. "No cabs. No bus. No train. And I don't exactly think we can sleep in this diner until your random bus company starts up again."

"I don't know," he says, popping a fry into his mouth.

"We have to do *something*," I say.

He nods and pulls his phone out from under the table. "Lyft?" he asks, tapping at his phone. It's still hooked into the outlet, tethered to this place—just like us.

"You think they'll have *Lyft*?" I take another bite of my burger. It's half gone already. I pop a fry in my mouth and watch him.

"It can't hurt to check," he says. "What else are we going to do?"

The snow continues to fall outside, and I devour the rest of my burger while he taps away. Through the window, I can see that it's starting to get dark.

I finish the rest of my fries and pray that he has some luck.

Because we are quickly running out of options.

NOAH

THERE'S A SMALL TV MOUNTED ABOVE THE MAIN counter. The kind that was probably manufactured ages ago, a cube that's fat and clunky, with a rounded screen. There's no sound, but the waitress keeps looking up at it, between glances at her watch. I don't need sound to know it's not good news. There's a guy in a gray suit waving his hands around the map, showing us the Doppler. From the looks of it, this isn't going to let up tonight.

I glance back down at my phone, checking Lyft.

Ammy stares at me eagerly, like all the answers lie in this one little app, and I'm the gatekeeper.

It's refreshing endlessly, moving lines that show me it's working, except I know that it's not.

Bingo.

"It says there are no cars," I say.

"Should you try it again?" she asks.

"I've tried it probably five times already," I say. "And Uber, too. We may have to rent a car."

Ammy is done with her burger already, and I take a huge bite of mine, then follow it up with three fat fries. The waitress leans against the counter, avoiding any glance at us, looking put out. There are only three customers in here: us and the guy who walked in a few minutes ago. Ammy's coffee is empty.

"Do you want more?" I ask, pointing to her cup.

She shrugs. "I think the waitress hates us. I've been trying to get her attention, but no luck."

"Excuse me," I say, waving my hand back and forth like I'm looking for someone at a concert, not like I'm trying to flag down practically the only other person in the room.

The waitress looks alarmed, so I tone it down a bit. "Could we possibly get some more coffee, please?" I gesture to both our cups. She grabs the carafe and slowly walks toward us, pours some sludge.

The coffee is hotter than before, steam rising off of it. Thank God, because I'm not sure when we're going to be this warm again. Ammy pours in a bunch of milk, grabs her cup, takes a sip.

"You're funny, you know," she says when she puts it down.

"What do you mean?" I take a sip as well.

She shrugs. "You just are." Then she pushes her plate

away and leans back in the booth. She drums her fingernails on the table. They're painted red and chipped around the edges. She flakes a bit of polish off and looks at me with that look I've already come to know quite well—a questioning one: *Are you sure about that?* "So don't you have to be, like, twenty-five to rent a car? That's what my dad always says."

I attempt to get more ketchup out of the glass bottle, banging on the bottom to no avail. Ammy doesn't ask if I want help, just grabs it from me and gives it a quick karate chop to the middle of the neck. It slides out smoothly.

"Thanks," I say. I pop another fistful of fries into my mouth, eating them fast and wiping my mouth with a napkin so cheap you can practically see through it. "You only have to be eighteen," I say. "It just costs more."

She starts drumming her fingers against the table again.

I shrug. "I have an emergency credit card from my parents. I'm pretty sure this counts as an emergency."

Her eyebrows knit together. "Won't they be mad? Should you call them to check first?"

I scoff. "They're in the Caribbean on their cruise. I can't call them."

I stare down at my plate, dunk another fry in ketchup.

Quite frankly, even if I could call them, I don't think I'd want to. The cruise was a luxury, with money they don't really have, because my dad read on some blog that you have to "invest in your marriage." They took it quite literally. Ever since they've gotten back together, they've been doing lots of stuff like this. Fancy dinners out. Couples' cooking classes.

A spa weekend in the Adirondacks. It's good. I'm glad that they're connecting with each other again. But I'm worried about them, too. Between all the student loans I'm taking, and the fact that I'm majoring in comparative lit, I'm not going to be able to help them if they need me. They'd give me the money if I asked, sure, but I'm worried that pretty soon they won't have it. That there will be no safety net—for me or for them.

What will probably happen is I'll put it on the credit card, and then I'll pay it off with a good chunk of the money I saved from weekends as a busboy at the fancy Upper East Side French spot. It was the money I was planning on using for my own love-renewal trip, the money I was going to invest in me and Rina.

The reservations tonight, the ones I probably won't even be there for now, were at the New American, a restaurant by one of the chefs that had a TV show a few years back. It's supposed to be good. Really good. You have to book a couple of weeks in advance. Rina bugged me to go all through our relationship. She just wanted us to get all dressed up and go to this foodie spot that she'd read about in the *New York Times* and *New York* magazine and all the other publications with the words New York in them.

I always said no, that we could get ten dates out of the money we'd spend that night.

You worry too much. Sometimes, you have to just do something.

It was easy for her to say that, though. Her mom's house was all paid off. She didn't have to worry about things of that nature.

I look up. Ammy is staring at me like I'm an alien.

"We lost you there for a second," she says.

I shove one last fry into my mouth. It's soggy. Ammy's plate is already empty.

"Did you hear anything I said?" she asks.

I shake my head.

"I said I can pay for part of it. The car rental."

"You don't have to. . . . I mean, it's my fault."

She shrugs. "You were only trying to help. And it's not your fault, really. I should have looked at the map before we left. And we're here now. I have some money saved up from babysitting these three little brats all summer. It's fine."

"Really?" I ask.

She laughs. "Yes, really. It's just babysitting money. And I need to get back, too."

Not for the first time, I wonder why. What, who she's going back to. But I push it out of my mind and focus on the good. That she's forgiven me for leading her in the wrong direction. At least a little bit. It means a lot. From the look on her face, I think she can see it.

The waitress comes back and sets the check down. It's twenty-one dollars. We both throw two twenties in.

While we're waiting for change, Ammy doodles on her napkin. Little spirals that are weirdly mesmerizing.

"So how bad is it if you don't get there in time?" I ask.

Her doodling stops abruptly. She looks up.

"You know you still haven't told me where you're going," I say, unable to resist.

"I don't really want to talk about it," she says, almost on autopilot.

I shrug. "Why? I'm a good listener, promise."

Her lips form a thin line. All the friendliness that was in her face a second ago leaks out just like that.

"Sorry," I say. "I only thought that—"

She interrupts me. "You know, you still haven't told me why you and your ex broke up anyway." Her eyes are on the napkin, and she starts doodling again.

I shrug. "People break up."

"Yeah," she says, without looking at me. "And they don't get back together."

The waitress comes over with a tray of crumpled bills and change.

Ammy still doesn't look up. "You didn't, like, cheat on her, did you?"

I nearly spit out my coffee, and my heart begins to race. "What kind of question is that?"

Her eyes meet mine, and she shrugs again. They're captivating, those eyes. They practically dare you to look away, like a Renaissance painting.

Her eyes widen. "Wait, did you? Really?"

I take a sip of coffee. Caffeine has a weird, calming effect on me. It's counterintuitive, but it always has. I look down, then back at her. "No. I really didn't."

Ammy breaks my gaze, abandons the spirals, and starts writing out her name in swirly letters, just like Rina used to. She keeps her eyes locked on her napkin. "So you just freaked out and broke up with her, the *perfect girl for you*, as you yourself said on the way here. For, like, no reason at all? And *that's* your biggest regret?"

"I'm trying to go home and fix things," I say. "That's why I'm here, remember?"

"I'm just asking, what is there to fix?"

"None of your business." I practically spit the words out.

She shrugs, her eyes still avoiding mine. "Well, then don't get all up in my business, okay?"

I shake my head, my heart racing faster, my face burning. "You know what? I need to go to the bathroom," I say brusquely.

I get up and walk to the back without another word.

The bathroom is empty, the stall doors open, the three dingy sinks free, the trough of black-and-white-tile urinals abandoned.

Thank God.

I head to the middle sink and turn on the water, let it run cold. I cup some in my hands and splash it on my face.

I reach for a paper towel, but the damn thing is empty, and I end up drying off with the bottom of my shirt.

I stare at myself in the mirror.

I didn't cheat, I remind myself. We weren't even together then.

But I look at myself again, and I realize that everything hurts: my head, my bones, the chapped skin around my eyes.

I didn't cheat.

But that's not the only way to fuck something up.

AMMY

I watch him walk away, instantly feeling guilty.

I wanted to get back at him for asking me why I'm going to Hudson when I'd made it good and clear that I didn't want to talk about it.

And the thing is, it looks like I succeeded.

The waitress gives me a look, raising her eyebrows just a tiny bit like we're some high school sweetheart couple who's just had their first fight. I look away, fiddling with the change instead. I set aside her tip and then divide the bills and change between us, arranging Noah's in a neat little pile on his side of the booth.

Then I pull out my phone, load up my maps, and look

for the closest car rental place. It's nearly three-quarters of a mile. I tap their phone number, because maybe they can pick us up—don't some of them do that?—and it rings six times before someone answers.

"Hello." The man's voice is gruff. Whatever corporate message he's supposed to say probably went out the window a long time ago. In the background, I hear voices. They're busy.

"Uh, I'm calling about a rental car. We're about a half mile away," I say, rounding down in the hopes that they'll be more inclined to help us. "Is there any way someone can pick us up?"

"Not in this weather," he says. "We're slammed over here."

"But you do have cars?"

"We do have cars, yes," he says.

"Should I—"

But the line goes dead. The dude's hung up, just like that.

I put my phone back in my bag, begin wrapping my scarf around my neck, preparing for the brutality that awaits us outside.

I didn't mean to be mean; really, I didn't. I just never expected Noah to give me that look. That *but how did you know?* kind of look. It was the same look Dara gave me when I jokingly asked if she liked Steven, the ultra-nerdy guy in our AP bio class, because she'd been talking about him so much. I didn't really, until I saw that look.

He said he didn't cheat, but regardless, even if he didn't, he did something he feels really bad about. He wouldn't have given me that look if he hadn't.

Not that it matters, I remind myself. He's a stranger. Someone I'm stuck with and absolutely nothing more. Because even if I wanted there to be something more, well, I have my promise to myself not to get involved with anyone.

Not to mention, his heart is pretty much completely spoken for anyway. I glance at the ruined pink roses, and I have to stop myself from rolling my eyes just thinking about why anyone would ever choose pink freaking roses.

I force myself to stop, to consider the matter at hand instead of Noah's bad taste in flowers. I mentally run through the pros and cons of going to the car rental place.

I start with the cons:

It's cold out there (5 points)

Scratch that, it's *freezing* out there (another 5 points)

It's three-quarters of a mile, which is almost the same length as the evil point nine miles that got us into this mess (10 points)

Noah and I aren't even really getting along right now, so it will probably feel longer (5 points)

It's gonna get dark soon (10 points)

Then I think of the pros:

We don't have a single other option, not one that I can think of, at least (a thousand points)

There's no need for math this time, that's for sure.

The door to the bathroom opens, and Noah walks back to the booth briskly.

His face is pale, and there are tiny droplets of water on his temples.

"I'm sorry," I say. "I didn't mean to upset you."

He doesn't meet my eyes, just crumples up my neat little pile of money and shoves it all in the pocket of his jeans like I haven't even said a word.

"There's a car rental place three-quarters of a mile away. They can't pick us up but they say they have cars. I guess we'll just walk?"

He nods, still avoiding my eyes. "Let's get going, then."

Noah shrugs into his coat quickly, and I do the same. In seconds, we've got all our things. We manage an unenthusiastic thank-you to the waitress, and then we're back out in the cold unknown—the unknown that is swiftly getting darker and darker—the bell dinging behind us. Reminding us not so subtly that we're leaving our warm little hideaway, even if it wasn't the most hospitable place on earth.

"It's just up Main," I say. "It's not that far."

Noah nods and then steps ahead, leading the way.

At the corner, he drops the wet, messed-up flowers in the trash can. He doesn't turn around to check that I'm behind him. When the light tells us to go, he just walks.

It's not five blocks before Main Street morphs from cute little drag with sidewalks to two-lane road with a gravelly shoulder, woods on either side. Thankfully, there are LED streetlights. Otherwise, we'd be screwed even more than we are.

Of course, we are pretty screwed anyway. Because it's the dead of freaking winter, we are walking directly into the wind, and it's cold as balls.

It's just three laps around the high school track, I remind myself.

Just three laps. That's, like, nothing.

I'm extremely tempted to stick out my thumb and hitchhike—or show a little leg like they always do in the movies. But there aren't that many cars anyway. And I'd risk them not seeing me and hitting me on the side of the road or something.

Besides, that kind of thing only worked a long-ass time ago, when you weren't worried that every passing car was some kind of maniac killer.

After ten minutes or twenty—it's hard to tell in this weather—I pull out my phone to see how far we've gone.

We're going the right way, but we've only gone a quarter of a mile so far—*shit*.

There's a text from Kat.

Any word, girl?

Are you okay?

I'm cursing the gods of public transportation right now, by the way

I laugh weakly and then text her back.

I'm okay but I'm not gonna make it in time

Keep cursing the gods for me, plz

Kat always knows how to make me laugh—it's one of the many things I like about her. She's not anything like her younger sister, Bea, who's sweet and soft-spoken, who doesn't have a snarky bone in her whole entire body. The two fit the older-younger sister pattern almost perfectly. Kat is outgoing, popular—a little bossy. Bea is quiet and reserved but with a rebellious streak, like a girl James Dean.

Bea is by all accounts nicer and easier to get along with, sure, but Kat was the one who welcomed me that week I stayed with them.

After brunch that first day, before we picked Bea up, we walked around, hitting all the thrift stores in the main downtown area.

Kat joked about her mom's overpriced chakra crystals and how now my dad believes every stupid word she says about "healing energy." She said it was downright hilarious that someone who read all these books about Buddhism and karma and putting good out in the world felt A-OK breaking up a marriage.

At brunch, Kat asked for the check when I still had half my sandwich left, because she wanted to go, and she wanted to go right then.

Because of that, Simone said she sounded a little controlling when I FaceTimed with her and Dara that night.

But there was something nice about it. That whole week and a half, I was just along for the ride. Kat made all the plans. Kat called all the shots.

Since my dad left, since my mom's anxiety took over, it had felt like all the responsibility rested on me. Lord knows my mom wasn't the one deciding what we were going to have for dinner while trolling Sophie's Instagram feed full of inverted-yoga-pose photos. I was the one expected to hold it all together.

I wanted someone else to take charge, to say her way or the highway—and to truly mean it. I wanted an older sister. And even though she was only a week older than me, those were the roles we fell into, even if it was for such a short time. She made fun of me for reading too much. She gave me tips on properly plucking my eyebrows. She borrowed my jewelry without asking and didn't apologize when I caught her.

I'd never had a sister. Or a sibling, for that matter.

It had always been my mom, my dad, and me.

And I didn't have one—not yet—but on that visit, I saw what could be.

I saw what my dad saw in all of them. And though I hate to even think this way, though it makes me ill to think this way, I saw why he would choose them over us.

It broke my heart. And I hated myself for how much I wanted to be a part of it.

I open the message chain with my mom, but there's nothing new, which means she's probably opened the wine and will begin texting again in a little bit.

And I have a crazy thought—what if I stay for more than a week? What if I *never* go back?

What if Kat and I really get a chance to be sisters?

Because as much as I want things to go back to the way they were, before my dad left us, as much as I want that with all my heart and more, it's still hard to imagine being an only child ever again.

NOAH

I HEAR A SPLASH, AND I TURN BEHIND ME TO CHECK on Ammy.

In the glow of the streetlights above, I can see that her right foot is completely submerged in a puddle. In the darkness, the slush looks almost dangerous. Murky and black. She must be freezing.

"Serves me right for walking and texting," she says bitterly.

"God," I say. "Are you okay?" I'm half talking about her foot and half talking about whatever conversation she was just involved in.

But she just shakes it off and keeps walking. "I'm fine," she says. "Carry on."

And so I do, walking forward, into the wind, head locked down.

I'm not mad at her. Maybe she thinks I am because of the way I acted back at the diner.

But I'm not—I have no reason to be mad at her. I'm mad at myself. I raise a hand in front of my face, shielding myself from the wind and the snow, which is still falling, only falling diagonally now. For a second, I close my eyes, and I see myself at the lake on that cliff, looking over, Rina down at the bottom, yelling at me to just . . .

Jump.

But every time my toes got so much as a foot from the edge, my palms started to sweat. I stepped back, my stomach doing somersaults.

She didn't know that I could hear her, down there talking with Cassie. She didn't realize how much the sound echoed up to us.

"He can't do *anything* without freaking out about it. It's *chronic.*"

Cassie said something about it just being a cliff, about it not being a big deal.

"I know," Rina said. "And it shouldn't be. But he's like this with everything. No one wants to be with a guy who's scared and worried about the whole entire world."

No one wants to be with a guy.

Her words were piercing and shrill, like one of those high-pitched sounds that only dogs are supposed to hear. I stepped away from the ledge. Bryson hadn't heard her, and he yelled at me to get out of the way before jumping in himself.

How different would things have been if I'd just had the courage to jump?

What would have happened if I hadn't let her words get to me like they did?

Where would I be if I hadn't gone to that stupid party three days after we broke up?

I take a deep breath, look around me. The sun has set, but there's still a dusky blue hint to the sky near the horizon. Pretty soon, it will be completely dark. We have to get to the car rental place before then. I glance at Ammy, but she's trudging along, avoiding my eyes.

I wasn't even trying to rebound. Honestly, I wasn't.

We were broken up, properly. There was none of that on-a-break stuff, the stuff Bryson was always pulling with Cassie because he claimed they weren't "official."

We were indeed done. We'd had our fight at the lake. Then we'd had the fight at my house. It was over. We hadn't spoken in three days. We'd gone from texting just about every hour, her telling me all the ins and outs of everything, from what she was watching on TV to family drama, which had been particularly difficult of late. It was a weird adjustment, being on my own for the first time in years. Bryson said I needed to come out with him, get my mind off of her. Bryson reminded me of every negative word Rina had ever said to me.

His cousin Chloe was pretty. She was wearing a polka-dot halter dress and her hair was in a ponytail that sat on the top of her head, and she had something on her lips that made them perpetually shiny. She was smart, too. She was in college at Bard, studying political science. She had all these ideas on socialism that I hadn't heard before.

I had three beers, which was probably three beers too many, and pretty soon we were sitting close together on the couch in Bryson's basement. Bryson and Daniel were busy messing with the Xbox.

We kissed.

And then we went back to the spare bedroom in Bryson's basement, and we did more.

It was so fast, and it was so meaningless, and as soon as it was over, all I felt was a punch to the stomach. Chloe, who was indeed smart, saw right through me. "You look miserable," she said.

"No," I said. "Really."

And then: "I'm sorry."

She smiled weakly. "Bryson told me you just came out of a bad breakup."

She waited for me to say something, but I didn't. All I could think was that that's what two and a half years of me and Rina had turned into—"a bad breakup." The thought made me feel even worse.

"All right, I'm going to go now," Chloe said, readjusting the top of her dress.

I managed another apology as she walked out the door, leaving me alone.

And I lay in that bed, and all I could think about was how much I'd messed it up. Rina would find out. Bryson would tell Cassie, and Cassie would tell her. And she'd never forgive me.

I can't get her back now, I thought. Over and over and over.

It's done.

I had no idea just how much I wanted to fix everything with Rina until it was too late to do so. What was I going to do? Call her and tell her I'm sorry I broke up with her for a stupid reason three days before, and after hooking up with someone else, it's now all of a sudden clear to me that we should be together?

The sound of my name breaks my train of thought, and I turn around. Ammy is standing ten feet back, her purple wool coat and red knit cap and red bag illuminated by the streetlight, the only colors in a sea of white and dark sky. I have the weirdest desire to take her picture right now—*Ammy in Winter in a Wool Coat at Sundown*—and set it on the edge of my desk in the dorm, look at it every day.

"Are you okay?" I ask, walking back to her, careful to avoid a chunk of ice on the side of the road. "What happened?"

She shrugs. "I think so. It's just that my feet are soaked and I can't really feel my toes. Is that bad?"

I walk closer and stare down at her feet. Her jeans are wet about five inches past her ankles, probably from where she stepped in that puddle when we first started walking.

My heart beats a bit faster. My mom used to tell me all about how her sister got frostnip, gave me lecture after lecture when I started snowboarding.

It's unlikely, even though we've been out for hours. It takes longer than that. But I don't like the look of her fully submerged foot.

Plus—and this part is hard to just brush off—if anything did happen, it would be completely my fault. I couldn't handle that.

I cross my arms. "What do you mean? You *literally* can't feel them?" I ask. "Or figuratively?"

She purses her lips, thinking, her small mouth getting even smaller. "I don't know. It's hard to say. Is that bad?"

Aunt Arden's fingers still tingle from frostnip, even twenty years later. I don't want to do that to Ammy, a girl who'd be well on her way to her destination if not for me. *God.* I double-check the distance on my phone.

"We're still a half mile out," I say. "At our pace, it could take us another half hour, at least. Damn it."

She bounces from foot to foot. "I'm sure it's fine," she says. She starts walking again, taking the lead.

I zoom out on the map a bit. "Wait a second, I've been here," I say.

She stops and turns, puts a hand on her hip. "On this desolate stretch of highway?" she asks.

"No," I say. I push my phone at her. "The Atwood. It's an art museum. I went here once on a field trip in high school."

She just stares at me, nonplussed.

Finally: "You *do* know that we're not, like, in *Ferris Bueller's Day Off*, right?"

"What?"

153

"Never mind," she says. "Why in the *world* would you want to go look at art right now? Have you lost your mind?"

Her words are clipped, but it doesn't matter. I step ever so slightly closer to her. "I'm worried about you," I say. "My aunt got frostnip from skiing. It's not as bad as frostbite, you don't lose your fingers or toes or anything, but hers still tingle years later. I don't know, I just couldn't deal with it if something happened like that because of me. We should warm up."

She scoffs. "I mean, it's not like you would *know* about it—if I did get frostnip or frostbite or whatever."

I shake my head at her. "That's cynical."

She presses her lips together. I want her to smile again, like she did before. I want it so badly it's strange. I want to tug her red knit cap down on her head and rest my hands on her cheeks. I want to leave them like that for a moment, until she looks at me and smiles. Until our eyes adjust to each other's in the ever-growing dark. Until we're the only light that we can see.

Rina, I remind myself. I'm supposed to be thinking about Rina.

"I guess I'm just in a cynical mood," Ammy says finally, her voice rising slightly at the end.

She's angry, and for a second, I feel that fear of messing up. I remember this time I suggested to Rina that we go get Thai food. The way she yelled that she'd told me a hundred times that she hated Thai because she'd gotten food poisoning from it when she was ten. How she told me she couldn't count on me to remember anything she said. I got in the car and drove away, but when I tried to call her, she didn't answer. We didn't talk for seven and a half hours, and I sat in my bedroom, worrying, wondering if the love of my life was going to cut me out over greasy noodles. Rina always wanted me to think less, to do things without overanalyzing the outcomes. But sometimes she made it really hard to live like that. If you messed up, she wasn't having it.

But Ammy doesn't take it any further. Ammy just crosses her arms, waiting for me to say something else. It's an instant relief.

I point up ahead. "It looks like it's just up there. Let's go in, warm up. Who knows, maybe one of the docents can give us a ride? It's not *that* far."

She stares at me, and hardly thinking, I step closer, rest my hands on her arms, and rub up and down quickly, trying to warm her up.

Her eyes catch mine: alarmed, but not necessarily unhappy.

I drop my arms and step back. "Come on. The place will warm you up much better than I can." I force myself to laugh.

She rolls her eyes, but there's the smallest hint of a smile there, and she follows behind me anyway.

AMMY

THE GUY AT THE TICKET DESK LOOKS AT US LIKE WE'RE totally, 100 percent insane.

I catch my reflection in the glimmering ultra-modern, ultra-reflective glass wall that separates the lobby from the coat check. I look a mess. My nose is red and my lips are chapped and errant hairs are stuck to my forehead like I pasted them there with the glue you used to use in kindergarten. My hat is even lopsided.

I feel a mess, too. I wasn't kidding when I said I couldn't feel my toes. I really can't.

Maybe that's why I didn't object when Noah came up with this crazy idea. Because as much as I want to get to Hudson at a somewhat reasonable time, I honestly can't imagine

156

walking even another tenth of a mile in this weather, much less another half.

In fact, the thought of going out there—after even thirty seconds in the warmth of this place—is hell.

"Are you still open?" Noah asks.

The guy, probably in his midtwenties, with thick nerdy glasses and slightly greasy hair that flops across his face, just laughs.

"Is that a yes?" Noah asks.

He must realize we're serious, because he clears his throat, stands up straighter, and puts on a proper museum voice. "Yes, sir, we are open for forty-five more minutes. Two?" he asks.

Noah surveys the admission board. "Two students," he says. "Please."

The guy runs Noah's card and prints us two tickets. He goes to hand us a map, but Noah is already off, into the next room.

"Thanks," I say, taking the map, which immediately warps in the snow still stuck to my gloves.

I follow Noah, through one room and then the next, until he stops in front of one with a bench in the middle. It's oversized, with black tufted leather and shiny chrome legs. It looks like freaking heaven right now.

I stand my suitcase up against the bench and plop down next to Noah, who's dropped his backpack, taken off his gloves, and is leaning back on his hands.

I peel off my gloves and then kick off my shoes without

even bothering to untie them, hardly able to take the coldness anymore, squirming out.

Yes, I know that it's totally ridiculous to change your nasty, winter-worn shoes in the middle of a freaking art museum, but there's no one else in eyesight—no one but Noah, at least—oh, and also, at this point, I don't care anymore.

My socks, hot-pink ones with poodles on them that I borrowed from Kat last summer and never gave back, are wet. I peel them off, bundle them up, and stuff them in the front zipper of my suitcase.

Noah watches me, an eyebrow raised. "What?" I ask.

He shakes his head quickly, but there's an odd look on his face, his eyes scrunched up, his lips pressed together. I can't place it.

"Nothing," he says.

I just shrug. "I know it's gross, but honestly, you should change your socks, too. It will keep your feet warmer."

He kicks his feet out proudly. "My shoes are waterproof."

I look them over. An ankle-high pair of Keens. I've got a similar pair I wore when I used to go on hikes with my dad. Key phrase: *used to*. "You wore hiking shoes on a train ride? Were you *planning* on the train breaking down?"

He laughs. "They're more comfortable, really."

"Nerd," I say, and I pull out another pair of socks, the warmest ones I have, Smartwool hiking socks my dad bought me the last Christmas before he left.

"Let me see your feet," Noah says as I start to pull them on.

"Seriously?" I ask.

"Come on," he says.

Reluctantly, I kick them out. They're wet and gross, and my toenails aren't painted, and it feels altogether too intimate.

"Satisfied?" I ask.

He reaches out and pinches my big toe. "Ouch," I say, reflexively whipping my foot back. "What, do you have a foot fetish or something?"

He laughs. "No, but at least I don't have to worry about maiming you for the rest of your life. You're fine. If you can feel that, you're totally fine. Especially with those warm socks."

"Great," I say.

"I really am sorry," he says. "And I'm sorry I got upset in the diner."

I shrug, pulling the socks on and lacing up my shoes. I appreciate that he's trying to be cool about everything, but to be honest, his frequent sorrys are starting to annoy me. "I don't want sorrys," I say. "I want a solution."

Noah just shrugs and looks down at his feet. "You said we were in this together," he says. "Back in the diner. You said it wasn't all my fault. I didn't force you to come."

And he's right. I did say that. He didn't force me.

But still—it's hard not to think about what could have happened if I hadn't agreed to go with him.

And then I have a crazy thought:

If I could do it over again, I would.

I shake my head, trying to push it away, and look down at

my feet, too. At those stupid Smartwool socks, the last present I got from my dad when we were still a family.

I know we probably weren't that happy at that point. But still. My grandma drove in, and we had a twenty-pound turkey for four people, and we watched *It's a Wonderful Life* and *National Lampoon's Christmas Vacation*, in that order—always in that order.

It wasn't perfect, not by any means. There was still an easy-to-miss but hard-to-forget dent in the wall by the front door. I'd developed a habit of taking the shortest of breaths before walking into the kitchen, as if preparing. My stressed-out phone calls to Dara had gotten a little more frequent since my seventeenth birthday.

But we were still a family then. Forget all the other bullshit. We had that. It was very much *before*.

Noah is still looking dejected, so finally, I speak. "It's okay. I know we are. And I know that I chose to come with you. It's not your fault—I meant it when I said that. But I can't help but think . . ." My voice drops for a second. "Well, what are we going to do?"

He sighs, leaning back on his elbows and staring at the ceiling. "Do you think you can go back out there if we warm up a bit? Do you think we can walk the rest of the way to the car rental place?"

I look around me at the all-white walls and sharp angles. It looks like a museum on TV, cold and modern. But the air, on the other hand, is warm. Radiators cranking with that kind of steamy heat you only really find in the Northeast. My dad kept going on about how nice the heating systems were up here, as if I cared at all. All that's to say, it's warm in here. Very warm. And it's hard to imagine leaving this place in anything colder than a car that's had the heat cranking for at least ten minutes.

I raise an eyebrow. "Do you?"

He kicks at my suitcase. "Maybe if you drop the Murakami."

I laugh weakly, because I'm not really in the mood for jokes.

It's silent for a minute between us. Finally, Noah lifts his hand up, pointing in front of us. "So, what do you think? Scale of one to ten?"

"Noah, I really don't want to talk about art right now."

"Come on," he says, delivering a grin that I just know is at least partially forced. "We have to warm up a little bit, before we can even think about going out there again."

I roll my eyes but decide to play along, hardly knowing what else to do. "It's a Pollock, right?" I ask. I'm pretty sure. Bea is obsessed with him.

Noah breaks into a grin, which is at least partially genuine this time. He hops up, dashing over to the little white card on the big white wall. He turns back to me. "Of *course* it's a Pollock," he says. "*Number 13*, to be exact. Come look at it with me."

"Seriously?" I ask, an eyebrow raised.

"Come on." He gestures at me with an outstretched hand.

"Are you *sure* you haven't seen *Ferris Bueller*?"

His eyebrows scrunch up, which tells me he hasn't, but I stand up anyway, leaving our bags in the middle, only just now realizing how much my bones ache, from the cold, from the bitter disappointment, etc., etc. Noah is standing only about two feet away from the painting, so close, like he wants to absorb every brushstroke, crawl right in. I stand next to him.

"Really, what do you think?"

I cross my arms, suss it out. "I think if I got paid millions of dollars for splashing paint on a canvas, I'd be one happy girl."

He laughs. "You think you could do it?"

I shrug. "Couldn't anyone? I know he was the *first* to do it and all, but still."

He points at the painting, hand moving from one corner to another like we're surveying some kind of perfect natural landscape. "The colors. And the textures. And the way it's chaotic but also harmonious. I definitely don't think *I* could do it."

I follow his hand, and—yeah—I guess he kind of has a point, but it still doesn't make my heart sing. It still looks more like chaos than harmony to me.

And I don't like chaos.

"Who wants to see chaos in art?" I ask. "Don't we have enough of that already? Show me a beautiful landscape. Give me a Monet or a Van Gogh. Make me smile."

He turns to me, smirks. "And yet you don't necessarily read the happiest of books."

"That's different," I say.

"How? Aren't they both art?"

"Paintings are supposed to be pretty," I argue. "They're *supposed* to wow you. Books are supposed to remind you that life is hard for everyone. That other people have it even worse than you. I know you know that, because you love reading as much as I do."

He smiles. "You know, I couldn't get my ex to read a book besides *The Hunger Games* to save her life."

I smirk right back. "I thought you liked *The Hunger Games.*"

He tilts his head a little bit to the side. "I do. But it's not the same. No matter what argument I made however many hours ago. You know that."

I feel a heat rise from the bottom of my toes all the way up to my face. And it's not from the radiator this time.

"I do," I say, not dropping his gaze.

His eyes don't leave mine, and I want him to say something so badly—anything—just to break this up. Because I'm not sure what is about to happen, and I can't stand it.

Then, finally: "Why won't you tell me why you're going where you're going?"

And that does it. That splits the moment right in two.

"Because you're a stranger."

"Am I?" he asks. "Really?" His face looks hurt, like this is some kind of long bonding exercise instead of what it is, now that I'm thinking clearly again—two of us trapped out in the middle of nowhere just trying to get home.

I'm stuck, and I have no one to turn to. I can't call my dad or Kat or Bea for help. The wedding starts in less than an hour. I can't call my mom, because I already lied to her. I can't even call Dara, who's probably drinking Butterbeer as we speak. Or Simone, who I know for a fact is getting ready for her third date with Nora tonight.

And even if I could, how could they help me? There are no cabs; there are hardly even any cars on the road. Even if we could get a hotel room or something, how would we freaking get there?

All I have is this guy, a stranger. And he's more concerned about talking about *art* than making an actual plan that gets us out of here.

I'm not just worried about making it to my dad's in time for the wedding. I'm worried about making it anywhere at all.

Noah is still looking at me, obviously hurt. But I don't have time to placate him. I don't have time to stare at paintings and trade life stories and pretend that this is fun. I'm not going to woo a high school sweetheart back. I'm going for my family, for something that's not supposed to be missed.

"Yeah," I say, nodding and avoiding his eyes. "You are."

NOAH

IT'S WEIRD HOW MUCH HER WORDS HURT ME.

I know we're strangers, of course we're strangers, since we've only known each other a matter of hours. But quite frankly, it feels like we're not.

Ammy heads back to the bench. She sits down and fiddles with the zippers of her suitcase, avoiding me.

I shift my feet. The room is wide and open, but it seems, all of a sudden, like it's too small for both of us. "I'll be right back," I say, leaving her to watch my backpack.

She doesn't even look up.

I head through the galleries toward the entrance. My mind turns as I walk. Why did she shut me down back there? Why did she call me a stranger?

Why do I care so much?

When I reach the lobby, the guy is messing around on his phone. I hesitate, halfway between one room and the other. I don't know what to say. How to beg this guy for a ride without sounding like a lunatic.

I hear Rina's voice in my head.

Don't think so much. Just go.

No one wants to be with a guy who's scared and worried about the whole entire world.

In an instant, it's like I'm at the lake again, backing off of that ledge, watching Bryson run easily past, feeling the ache of sadness in my stomach at the casual way Rina could put me down.

At the way she wasn't on my team at all.

I would never be here if I'd just jumped off that cliff.

Or if I hadn't told Bryson what she said. If he hadn't insisted I call her on it.

Or if I hadn't exploded at her in our room on our last night at Lake George—detailing every negative thing she'd said or done to me over the course of our relationship.

I wouldn't be here if I hadn't broken up with her over a jump off a cliff at a lake.

If I'd done it all differently, everything wouldn't be such a train wreck.

But then again, I never would have met Ammy.

I shake my head. Why do I keep having weird thoughts like this? It's not the point. Right now, I *have* to do something to fix this.

I take a deep breath, push all my hesitations aside. Not because of Rina's demanding. But because *I* know I need to.

"Excuse me," I say, forcing some confidence into my voice as I walk up to the counter.

"Yes, sir," the guy says. His eyes look less than enthused to be talking to me. They don't match his voice at all.

I ease in slowly. "I was wondering if you could help me. Do you know if there are cab companies around here?" I ask.

I already know the answer, but it seems like the best way to start off the conversation.

He narrows his eyes, then shakes his head. "Not really. And I don't think many people are out on the road in this weather."

"Or Uber or Lyft or something?"

"This isn't exactly New York City." He scrunches up his mouth like he doesn't like the taste of my questions. "You guys didn't drive here?"

I shake my head solemnly. "We walked from the Hudson Bus Lines station. We missed the last bus. We're only trying to get to Enterprise to rent a car, about a half a mile north, but we got worried that my friend was getting frostbite in her toes, so we decided to stop in here."

What the hell? I think. Might as well lay it on thick.

"Oh shit," the guy says, his smooth museum voice easily giving way to a less formal one. He sounds like he's from the country, probably a little farther north than Hudson. In my experience, the farther you get away from the city, the thicker the accent becomes. "Are you okay?" he asks. "I mean, should

I call the hospital or something?"

Crap. Too thick, I realize. Definitely too thick.

"No, she changed her socks, and I think she's fine. It's just that . . . well . . . we're just a little worried about going out there and walking again, especially now that it's dark out."

The guy's voice gets a tad gruffer, a tad defensive. "You want a ride, that's what you're asking?"

"Well . . ."

The guy sighs. "Look, I didn't even drive here. As soon as we close, in about twenty minutes, I'm shutting down and walking home. I live across the parking lot. It's half the reason I took this job, even though it pays just about nothing for someone with a degree—it comes with its own apartment."

My face falls. Damn it. Crap. Blast. Shit. For the umpteenth time, shit shit shitty shit shit.

"Well, thanks, anyway," I say, turning away. Feeling that same ache of failure, the one I felt when I walked off that cliff.

I head back toward the gallery, racking my brain for something to tell Ammy. Something that's not, *Hey, remember how you couldn't feel your toes a minute ago? Get ready for that feeling again! We're going right back out!*

I stop for a minute, breathe deeply, and clench my fists together.

It's hopeless. We'll never get to the end of this trip.

Rina will definitely not take me back.

My fate is as doomed as those flowers, sitting soggy in the bottom of a trash can somewhere.

"Hold on," I hear behind me.

I turn on my heel. "What?" I ask. I'm back to the counter in three big strides.

"I just don't want to send you guys out into that," he says. "You're *sure* it's only a half mile? You're not under-exaggerating? Or, you know, whatever the real word for the opposite of over-exaggerating is. . . ."

The thing is, *over*exaggerating isn't even a proper word. It's redundant. Exaggerating covers the sentiment on its own. Ammy would be internally laughing right along with me if she heard him say that.

But I don't tell him that. I don't think it would help my case. *Our* case.

I nod eagerly. "I promise. It's *really* just a half mile."

He takes a deep breath. "Go get your friend. And let me call my wife. She should be getting out of work soon."

"Oh my God, are you serious?" I ask.

He nods, shooing me away with one hand as he pulls out his cell phone with the other. "Go, quickly, before I change my mind. I'm risking a night on the couch just to ask her this."

I turn, bolting through the galleries back to Ammy. She's sitting on the bench, reading her Murakami.

If I didn't know all I did, if I hadn't spent the last several hours with her, if I simply saw her like this, I'd think she was a girl, here for the afternoon, taking a break to read a book.

I'd think she was beautiful, sitting there like that, with

her legs crossed at the ankles, with her head tilted down, bangs covering her eyes. With her hands delicately flipping each page.

I'd want to talk to her, that's for sure.

I'd want to talk to her for a long time.

I take a step forward, clear my throat so she notices me.

She looks up immediately, closing the book without marking her page.

"This is going to sound crazy," I say, "but I have good news."

AMMY

WE STAND OUTSIDE THE MUSEUM, IN THE BITTEREST cold, easily the coldest it's been all day, staring at an empty, desolate parking lot. It's dark out now, the only light coming from three sad streetlamps that only really serve to remind us that, yes, it is still snowing, the flakes glistening in the dim cones of light.

"You're sure someone's coming?" I ask again.

"I'm sure," Noah says, rubbing his hands together to keep warm.

"You're sure the guy didn't just tell you that so we'd leave and he could close up the place early? He really looked like he didn't want to be there, if you ask me."

"I'm sure," he says again.

I'm about to say that he was sure about a lot of things that didn't quite pan out, but then he steps closer, wrapping me in a side hug, running his hand up and down along my arm like he did before. Except now I can feel the whole side of his body against mine. Now my heart is beating so loud I'm sure he can hear it through my wool coat.

"There," he says, pointing across the parking lot as a boxy car pulls in and makes its way straight toward us, its headlights blinding against everything else.

Instantly, Noah drops his hand and takes a step away from me. Like the car shocked him out of whatever that was. Like it reminded him that this whole trip is just a pit stop on the way to our real lives.

And I hate to admit it, but I wish she'd given us just one more minute.

I wish his arm was still around mine.

The car turns, pulling up so it's parallel to the curb where we're standing.

I notice the red hair before I notice the put-out expression.

"Why am I not surprised that it's you two?"

Shockingly—or not so shockingly, given that we are in a tiny-ass town whose name I don't even know—it's none other than the waitress from the Main Street Café.

Noah breaks into a grin. "Sorry to drag you out here . . . did you miss us?"

I smile, trying to be polite. "Thank you *so much* for doing this."

The waitress's sour look dissipates. "No problem," she says matter-of-factly. "Now get in before you freeze your asses off."

Noah takes the backseat and leaves me the front. I can't decide if he's being chivalrous or if he's defying traditional gender roles by encouraging me to sit up front.

Her car is a forest-green old Mercedes with tan leather interior and a Jack Russell terrier bobblehead on the dash. She flips through the radio stations, settling on some kind of hip-hop.

Before I do anything else, I grab the bar beneath the seat and give it a tug, scooching it up as far as I can while still being somewhat comfortable.

"That enough space?" I ask Noah.

"You're the best," he says.

My heart flutters, and I curse myself for being so freaking cheesy about everything.

"Where are you guys going?" the waitress asks. "Bobby said it wouldn't be more than five minutes?"

Noah leans forward, taking charge. "The Enterprise, just up the road?"

"I know it," she says, nodding. She turns the music up slightly louder and pulls slowly out of the museum parking lot. "I'm Selena, by the way."

"I'm Ammy," I say.

"Amy?" she asks.

"Like Sammy without the S. My parents are weird."

Noah laughs from the backseat.

"This is Noah," I say.

Selena nods, and she looks significantly less pissed off outside the restaurant, without the apron, with her hair let down. "So why in the world are you guys stuck out in the cold and bouncing from crappy diner to snobby museum?"

I turn to Noah, and he smiles sheepishly. Then I turn back to Selena. "It's kind of a long story," I say.

"Well, you've got a couple of minutes," she says. "I'm all ears."

We take turns recounting parts of the story, and she laughs, and she laughs, and then she laughs some more. But it's not nervous, hysterical laughter like what came over me at the bus station. It's just laughter—pure and simple—at the absurdity of it all. At us hopping off the train. At the guy with all the guns. At the just-missed train. Followed by the just-missed bus. At the fact that we huddled in her diner mainly to charge our phones. And the fact that we went to an art museum to avoid what probably wasn't even remotely close to frostbite—or frostnip—or whatever.

She asks us how we know each other, and the honest answer gets her laughing even more.

"You guys seriously should have told me that when I waited on you," she says. "It's just like that movie."

"What movie?" I ask.

"*It Happened One Night*," she says. "With Dreamy McDreamFace and the actress with the big eyes."

"Claudette Colbert," I offer.

Selena laughs, raising her eyebrows. "The story would have brightened my whole mood, that's for sure. And I *definitely* would have offered you a ride."

I bite my lip. "Oh, well, we—"

"Didn't want to ask me anything because I had my bitch face on?" she asks.

"No, I mean . . ." I scramble at the words.

She waves her hand, dismissing me. "It's okay, really. You wouldn't believe the creepy men who come in there, try and flirt with me—try and grab my ass if they've had one too many beers at the bar down the street. It grates on you. I have a degree in biology, and Bobby has one in art history. We're doing our best to get by until I can save enough money for grad school and he can figure out what the heck to do with a degree in art history. People look at me, and they see a young redhead in a diner, and I swear, they assume I can barely read. One time, an older guy asked me—I'm not joking—if I knew how to subtract. That's the main reason for the bitch face. Also, I was pretty sure that you guys weren't going to tip."

I laugh, glad that I was generous back there. Not that I wouldn't be. But still.

"Not because I thought you were assholes or anything," she adds. "Just because you're young. Anyway," she says, running a hand through her hair, turning the music down and tapping her hand on the wheel. "Where are you guys off to? After getting the rental car?" She pulls up to a light and stops.

"Hudson," Noah says. "Well, she is. I'm technically going to Lorenz Park."

Selena smirks. "Maybe you two should consider going to the same place."

Noah laughs awkwardly from the backseat as the light turns green. "She won't even tell me *why* she's going where she's going."

"Oh, won't she?" Selena asks, looking at me with a genuinely friendly smile and playful eyes, like we aren't telling her the whole story.

I shrug. "He doesn't need to know everything. Not to mention, *he's* going to win his ex-girlfriend back. He *really* doesn't need to concern himself with my problems."

Selena looks surprised for a second, but then her smile grows. She alternates between looking at me and catching Noah's eyes in the rearview mirror. "You know, it took me and Bobby two whole years to tell each other we liked each other. Back in college. We met freshman year, but we couldn't get it together until we were juniors."

"Well, it worked out, didn't it?" I ask.

She doesn't answer, just pulls around, right up to the Enterprise. "Here we are."

"Thank you so much," I say.

"Seriously, you saved our asses," Noah says.

"It's really okay," she says. "Glad I could help. And *be careful* out there. Drive slow, pull over if you need to. Be safe."

"We will," Noah says, and I know that he means it.

I've only known him for, like, five minutes, but I already know that he would never do anything to intentionally put me—or anyone—in harm's way.

176

Noah grabs my suitcase in the backseat, and I reach for the door.

"Oh, and about me and Bobby, *of course* it worked out," she says. "Only if I could do it all over again, I certainly wouldn't have waited those two years."

NOAH

WE WALK TOWARD THE ENTERPRISE, AND I BEG THE gods of karma that this works out for her. I'm hoping we'll get a lucky streak. That there will be a car, and I'll get her home at a reasonable hour that's not midnight. That everything will be all right.

Of course, even if it is, it won't be all right for me. I know that.

My reservations are in just over an hour. My plan is shot. What I wanted to happen is not going to happen, at least not in the way I planned.

I have the wildest thought all the same.

I think—only for a second—that I wouldn't change this if I could. These few hours together have been something special. An adventure I will tell my kids about one day.

Something I don't want to give up.

It doesn't mean I shouldn't be with Rina. Or that I shouldn't still go see her tonight, if it's not too late.

But it doesn't mean I'm a total robot, either.

We walk through the front door, and I catch Ammy's eye. There's hope there, with a touch of happiness.

A robot wouldn't notice how beautiful she is. Wouldn't care about whatever happened that she refuses to talk about. Or give a damn about her icy feet or the way she looked when she was sitting there reading Murakami in the gallery.

I'm no robot.

The inside is exactly what you'd expect of a car rental office, a fluorescent-lit, linoleum-floored building probably hastily put together in the eighties. There's a sad, dingy front desk, and two guys sitting behind it.

We step up to the line. There are only two people in front of us, an older couple. From the way the guy at the desk is typing, it looks like they still have cars. They have to.

I don't know what we'll do if they don't.

But I know, in some weird way, that whatever happens, we're in this together.

I smile at Ammy, trying to be reassuring.

"You think they'll have cars?" she asks, almost reading my mind.

"Yeah," I say. "After the day we've had, they've *got* to."

She smiles at that, but weakly. The kind of smile Rina gave me when she came to bed that night at Lake George.

She asked me what was up. She asked me why I'd been so quiet all evening. At first, I stuck to my story.

Nothing. Everything is fine.

The older guy puts his arm around his wife while they wait for the paperwork. They're both wearing matching puffy red coats. When she leans into him, they fit together in a way that seems right. My parents look like that sometimes; not all the time, but sometimes.

Would Rina and I ever make it that far? Maybe. It's not *that* insane of an idea.

My mom and dad met in high school, a Catholic school in Bay Ridge, Brooklyn. Their fifteenth wedding anniversary coincided with their twenty-year high school reunion. Yeah, they've had their rough patches. It took my dad injuring his back at this stupid roofing job he'd taken when he couldn't get professor work, and my mom making good on her promise to walk out if he didn't quit, to shake him out of his middle-aged construction worker fantasy. But at the end of the day, they're a pretty good match. They wouldn't be spending all this time together if they weren't.

I glance over to Ammy. She's on her phone, texting some-one, and I wonder who.

There's something about her that makes me want to know *everything* about her.

Something in her face, in her eyes, that reads KEEP AWAY, like the signs on the guy's front yard. She may not have a whole locker full of guns to protect herself like he does, but she has her ways.

"I hope you know I'm not a bad person," I say to her. It's an awkward thing to say, I realize as soon as it's out of my mouth.

Does she think deep down I'm a bad person? Probably not.

But do I care so much that I want to hear her say it anyway? Yes.

She looks up from her phone. "What?"

"I just mean, back in the diner, when I walked away, when I got upset . . ."

She shakes her head. "Noah, it's okay. It doesn't really matter."

"But—"

"Seriously," she says. "Let's just get our car. You don't have to explain anything to me."

I nod at her. I don't know what else to do.

I don't know why it seems to matter *so much.*

Ammy goes back to looking at her phone.

The couple in front of us walks away, eager to get their hands on their economy midsized sedan.

"Here we go," Ammy says. "Fingers crossed."

I step up to the counter, put on my best smile, the same kind I gave the guy who asked his wife for a ride. I may be awkward on the inside, but I try my best to keep it locked up in there, where others can't see.

"We want to rent a car for tonight," I say.

The guy clears his throat. He looks remarkably chipper for the fact that he's stuck inside an Enterprise in an awful storm.

"Do you have a reservation?" he asks perkily.

Ammy takes a short, worried breath, while the other guy behind the counter shakes his head, like he's somehow disappointed in us for daring to come in without a reservation.

I'm worried, too, but I force myself to stay calm for her. "It's okay," I say to her, my voice almost a whisper. "It's going to be okay."

I turn back to the guy. "No," I say. "Is that going to be a problem?"

Luckily, we have the nice guy. He laughs jovially. "Our inventory is a little low, but it should be fine. Give me a sec." He starts typing.

I turn to her, shove my hands in my pockets, and it feels as if everything rides on this moment. It feels *so very important* for us to get a car here. If we don't, what in the world are we going to do? We've missed a train and a bus, walked just about everywhere, and holed up in every place I can think of to stay warm.

Soon, none of the shops will even be open. We don't have any other alternatives. . . .

I imagine Ammy and me, huddled outside the Enterprise office, the awning our only shelter, trying to stay warm.

This is why I don't act without thinking.

This.

Is.

Why.

The guy keeps typing. If the answer was no, he'd have said so already. That's what I'm telling myself, at least.

"Don't worry," I whisper again, and her eyes . . . well, to say they looked worried would be the understatement of the year.

She's trusting me. She's trusting that what I said was right. That it would *all* be all right.

But will it? I wonder. Even if we get the car?

Will it be all right for either of us?

Will I get Rina back?

Will she get whatever in the world it is that she wants?

"Well, we don't have any standard sedans or coupes left," the man says. My heart sinks, and I feel cold and achy all over. Lost. I don't have the guts to look at Ammy, so I grab her hand in mine, squeeze it ever so slightly. Don't let go.

"But," he says. "You're in luck. We do have one car left."

AMMY

IT HAPPENS SO FAST.

We don't stop to ask what the car is or how much it is or any silly details like that. We just turn to each other, and for that moment, it's like we're the only people in the whole wide world. I'm cheering, hooting and hollering, and so is he, so much so that I can barely tell who's even saying what. His hand is still in mine, but then he lets it go, and he opens his arms, and I hook mine on his neck, and then his arms wrap around me as he lifts me up.

The shitty little Enterprise office blurs as he spins me around, and I feel so light, so comfortable, so *right* like this in his arms.

He stops spinning, and I feel almost drunk as our eyes lock on each other's.

Our faces are so close, and I can see a bit of stubble on his chin, the color in his cheeks from hours of adventure that we never signed up for, and yet—here we are.

I can smell a bit of coffee on his breath, mixed with the subtle scent of Tide on his T-shirt, the exact kind my mom always uses—chemical fresh. I can feel the warmth emanating from his body, the two of us a heater in this big blistering world of cold.

And for a second—Lord, I don't even know what will happen.

Because for a second, our eyes still locked together, I'm sure that anything could happen.

And I'm sure of something else, too.

I don't care how messy it is, I don't care about my vow not to date, I don't really care about the consequences at all:

I *want* anything to happen.

I want *him*.

But then the man at the counter clears his throat, and the moment is broken.

We both look over, and Noah finally puts me down, and we start giggling.

And as soon as his arms let me go, I wish so badly that they hadn't.

"Do you want to know what kind of car it is, sir?" the guy asks.

Noah nods as I try to calm my breathing, try to stop the heat rising up to my face. Try to remind myself that it's the middle of winter and romance is the last thing I want right now, especially with a guy who is supposedly on his way to get his girlfriend back.

I try to remind myself that all the crazy feelings running through my head right now—well, they're really just relief at finally being able to get where I need to go, at a bit of shelter from the literal storm.

Because they can't be anything else. They just *can't*.

"It's a Ford Mustang convertible, cherry red," the guy says.

That sends us laughing again.

"One hundred bucks a day, plus an under twenty-five surcharge."

I look at Noah, but he shakes his head, pushing my fears aside, and pulls out his credit card.

I go to fish for cash in my wallet, but he waves his hand. "We can work it out later."

Then he looks at the guy.

"However much it is, we'll take it."

NOAH

I FLIP THE HEAT ONTO HIGH, RUBBING MY HANDS together as I wait for it to warm up.

I adjust the side mirrors and the rearview. My face looks super red.

Is it from the cold? Maybe.

Is it from Ammy? Probably.

Partially, at least.

I was hardly thinking when I picked her up and spun her around. But besides my mind, everything else was going double speed. More alive, more present. My heartbeat, my breathing, the feel of blood in my veins. The feel of *her* in my arms.

I clear my throat, feeling weirdly exposed, like she can

hear my thoughts. "Uh, want to get us hooked up with some tunes?" I ask.

I put the car into reverse and back out as she scans her phone for music. The car moves with a jerk.

"Sorry." I turn briefly to Ammy. "I'm not used to driving such a nice car."

She laughs, but then she goes quiet.

Does she feel weird about the hug? Is she wishing she could just be out of here and never see me again as quickly as possible?

I remember the way she wrapped her arms around my neck. It certainly doesn't seem like it.

But on the other hand, she did call me a stranger.

Slowly, I pull out of the Enterprise parking lot, still getting used to the way the car moves.

"Merge onto US Nine North," the phone lady says. She's a bit late, but I make the turn anyway. I'm paying attention like I never have before, because we may be out of the woods literally, but we're still eighty miles from home, and the snow doesn't look to be stopping any time soon. A detour because I wasn't listening to the phone lady's monotonous voice could prove disastrous.

It's dark out now, the wiper blades working double-time against the storm. I reassure myself that there's no ice yet—at least none that I can see or feel. But there's snow. Lots of it. And I have to be careful.

I keep the phone lady on talking mode, tucked into the cup holder, right where I can hear her. Once we're on the highway, she says we should arrive by seven thirty-five.

Ammy must have missed whatever she's going to, but I could almost make it to see Rina tonight. I wouldn't have the reservations, but I could get flowers, still take her *somewhere*. I could still say all the things I wanted to say.

It could still work.

Maybe.

"How do I do this?" Ammy asks, smashing buttons to no avail as her eyes flit between her phone and the dash.

"I think it's Bluetooth," I say.

"Ooooh," she says. "So *fancy*."

I laugh. This car is much fancier than the old Volvo I sometimes borrow from my dad. "Only the best for you, my dear." I feel awkward as soon as I say it.

But she laughs. A laugh that will be hard to forget.

"Actually, you want me to do it on yours so you can still hear the directions?" she asks.

I nod. "That would be perfect."

Ammy makes fun of about half of the songs on my phone. I'm not afraid to admit it: I can be a pop guy. I like *The Hunger Games*, I dig some Taylor Swift songs. I didn't used to always be that way. Quite frankly, I used to be a snob. But Rina taught me not to be. Rina liked everything: high-brow, lowbrow, middlebrow, what have you. I came to love that about her, as much as I defended my snobbery in the beginning.

I *still* love that about her.

Don't I?

Ammy settles on this synth-y thing Bryson put on my phone for the drive to Lake George. I cringe, but I don't ask her to change it. It's upbeat enough for driving, at least. But it's also a whole album that reminds me of the trip where everything went wrong.

"Music okay?" Ammy asks.

I look at her, and again I think about that hug, only minutes ago. Did she jump into my arms, or did I lift her? For a moment, it was like I wasn't even thinking, the way I spun her around, held her close, the way our eyes locked together.

It felt so . . .

I push it out of my mind. It was *just a hug*.

"It's great," I say.

She turns to me. "Are you okay to drive in this?" she asks.

"Do we have a choice?" I laugh, trying to lighten the mood. But we both know it's true: we don't.

She shakes her head. "Not really."

We're quiet for a moment as the windshield goes white and then clear, white and then clear, with every swish of the blades. As the lead singer of the indie band croons in his uniquely weird and completely annoying voice. As the crest of a hill leads us to another valley with snow-covered trees on either side.

"Should we continue our game of questions?" Ammy asks finally.

I glance at her. She's smiling, more relaxed than I've ever seen her. I look back to the road, and as soon as I do, I feel the car swerve just the slightest bit beneath me. So there is ice, after all. It's okay, I tell myself. We'll be home soon. Well, I'll be home. She'll be . . . who knows?

Ammy rests her feet on the dash and taps her toes to the beat of the song. She's fully embraced the spirit of the red Mustang, even though we've only been in it a few minutes, even though hell would have to freeze over (and at this rate, it could) before we took the top down. "It's perfect for car rides," she says. "I used to play it on lacrosse road trips."

"You play lacrosse?" I ask. There are so many things to learn about this girl. A part of me wants to know every single one, wants to read her like one of her big fat Murakamis, word after word, sentence after sentence, every last page of Ammy.

One of the few other cars on the road zips past me.

I want to go faster, but I'm afraid.

I want to do a lot of things, but I'm afraid.

"*Played*," she corrects me after a moment. And then she doesn't explain further; she just jumps back into the game. "All right, so back to the question of the day . . . why *did* you and Rina break up?"

My hands clench up on the wheel. Her question shakes me out of the thoughts in my head, reminding me exactly what I'm doing here.

"Well?" she asks.

"I don't know," I say.

She crosses her arms. "Well, you have to have *some reason*, don't you?"

I tap my hand on the steering wheel. All of a sudden I

feel guilty, sitting here thinking about our hug back in the Enterprise when I'm supposed to be focused on Rina.

Ammy must sense my discomfort, because she forces a laugh. "Relax," she says. "You don't have to tell me anything you don't want to. I shouldn't be so pushy about things you don't want to talk about. You don't owe me anything."

And the thing is, she's right.

I don't owe her anything.

But at the same time . . .

I kind of wish I did.

I wish she were the one I owed something to.

I shake my head, pushing yet another intrusive thought away.

It *terrifies* me.

Well, it *should* terrify me.

In a small way, at least—

It *thrills* me.

That's the problem with adventures. They open more doors, more possibilities, than they probably should.

AMMY

I SHRUG OUT OF MY COAT, BECAUSE THE HEAT IS RUN-
ning properly now, and it's warm in our tiny little haven from
the cold, otherwise known as a Ford Mustang.

It's still snowing, but I can only see the flakes through
the headlights, and on the windshield—it's too dark to see
anything else.

I run my hands through my hair, feeling the dampness
from all the snow. I must look a mess still, but from the way
Noah looks at me, it's like somehow it doesn't matter.

Noah still seems a little alarmed by my earlier question,
so I decide to ask him something easy, since he very obviously
doesn't want to talk about his ex.

Is it possible that he doesn't want to talk about her because

193

of me, or is it just because his plans are shot as much as mine are?

"What's your favorite childhood memory?" I ask.

Noah takes a while to respond, and the car swerves on ice two more times before he does—I can tell by the way his hands clench up that he feels it, too. But the shifts are small, almost like they're not even there. We're safe. Kind of.

Noah tells me about this Thanksgiving when he was nine or ten. When his cousins from North Carolina were up visiting and they brought this huge deep fryer to cook the turkey. He tells me how his mom and dad decided he could be the "Official Turkey Master" that day. It was the first time in his life he'd ever had so much responsibility. He had an old iPhone without any service that his mom let him play games and stuff on, and he was responsible for timing everything—the marinating, the waiting, the down-to-the-minute instructions for the deep fryer. He even got to calculate the exact cooking time with a formula his mom had found on the internet.

He tells me how his uncle, after one too many Bud Lights, kept on arguing with his parents, claiming that Noah might mess it up, but his parents were insistent—it was Noah's responsibility, and he could handle it. He tells me how that was the day that he really knew his parents believed in him. They'd been saying as much for his whole life, but that was the day he knew. They had his back, as he puts it.

I stare at my hands as he talks, fiddle with the jagged edges of my nails, my trusty old nervous tic. I have this emotion, one that makes me feel guilty and stupid and petty, but one that's still hard to ignore all the same: jealousy.

I get a bit of nail between my thumb and forefinger, peel it until it comes off. I flick it to the floor. Only having to worry about the turkey timer on Thanksgiving seems *lovely*.

"That sounds nice," I say when he's finished.

He laughs. "It was, except the drunk uncle part."

"Even that part sounds kind of nice," I say.

"What do you mean?" he asks, without taking his eyes from the road.

I shrug. "It sounds normal."

"What were your Thanksgivings like?" he asks.

"Fine," I say quickly.

I don't want to tell him about the Thanksgiving when I was eleven, one of the handful of Thanksgivings that was actually on my birthday, when my mom *freaked out* about whether or not we had enough yams and, after a brief yelling match with my dad, spent the rest of the day in bed with the lights off and the door closed. How my dad and I ate at the table alone, how of course there were enough yams, because it's not that hard to get enough yams for three measly people on Thanksgiving. How my slice of pumpkin pie with the candle in it suddenly just looked sad as my dad sang "Happy Birthday" to me alone.

I don't want to tell him how even on the good holidays, I was always afraid something was going to set my mother off. It was the details that stressed her out. All the pressure. Holidays were bad; they always had been. And even when things went off relatively okay, there was still this shadow hanging over them. Tension in the air as you waited for something to go wrong. Eggshells were always a side at our Thanksgivings.

Sometimes, I have a thought that I hate, absolutely, positively *hate*: no wonder my dad left.

But it wasn't like that always. It was only like that sometimes.

And I'd take *sometimes bad* over *always apart*—well, any day.

It wasn't even that bad, I tell myself.

It wasn't even that bad until that last Thanksgiving.

Noah turns the music down. "You okay?"

"Huh?" I ask, startled out of my thoughts for a second. I turn to look at him. He's free of his excess of layers, and I think I may have grown to love his Steelers shirt. He still sports the remnants of the grin he had when talking about his family. You can tell that he loves them.

Why does he have to still love his ex?

"Did I say something to upset you?" he asks, looking over briefly, and his hazel eyes seem almost gray in the darkness, the glow of the dash and the shimmer of falling snow our only light here in the car.

"No," I say.

There's another slip underneath us. Ice, no doubt about it. I watch as Noah's shoulders tense up, as he grips the wheel tighter, and in milliseconds it's over, and we're safe again.

Just a little patch. We're fine, I tell myself. We'll be there

196

soon. The ceremony has already started, and it will be over before I get there, but maybe I'll make it before the reception is over.

Maybe I'll still get a chance to show up for my dad and for Bea and for Kat.

Maybe it will still be a wonderful week.

Who knows? Maybe I'll even stay longer than a week. Maybe they won't ever want me to leave.

Either way, pretty soon, this ridiculous little jaunt will be over.

It will be a story to tell my grandkids, just like Noah said. The time that Grandma got lost in upstate New York with a cute stranger. I'll even exaggerate his looks for the story, I think. I won't even mention his crooked teeth. I may throw in a kiss between us, or two, just for good measure, really jazz up that moment in the rental car office.

Because it's a story, and you can do those things in a story.

Stories don't have consequences. Stories don't hurt others.

Stories are safe.

"So what is *your* favorite childhood memory?" he asks. "I'm still waiting."

Mine isn't hard. I've played this game (or non-game, as Noah likes to call it) before. Dara talked about the first time she went to Orlando, how she threw up on the Tower of Terror but it was still the most fun she'd ever had in her life. Simone went on about the time she and her brother put a fake snake in her dad's toolbox, how he screamed like a girl, and they laughed so hard they had tears in their eyes.

And I told mine. Of course, it was easier then, before the very thought of my dad made me viscerally upset. Oh well.

"The first time my dad and I went hiking," I say, grabbing Noah's phone and flipping to the next song, my favorite.

"Hiking *and* lacrosse," he says. "Quite the athlete."

"You know you sound patronizing when you talk like that," I say.

"Really?" He looks over, ever so briefly.

"You'd never tell a dude who plays one sport and occasionally goes on hikes something like that."

He laughs. "Okay, okay. Fair point. All things considered, I'm surprised you let me carry your suitcase."

"Well, you practically ripped it out of my hands," I argue, laughing.

"Fair point, again," he says.

"Anyway, like I told you, I don't even play lacrosse anymore, so I'm not 'quite the athlete' after all."

"Why not?" he asks.

I laugh to myself. Because divorce is expensive, and so is lacrosse. Because it's yet another thing that my dad took away from me when he left us. Because, really, that first month, I just couldn't bear to go there, pretend I was happy, pretend I gave a shit about catching balls with a dumb net on a stick. I couldn't explain it, not even to Dara and Simone.

"Not important," I say matter-of-factly. "*Anyway*, my

favorite childhood memory . . . so when I was eight, my dad said we should go on a hike. I think he was really desperate to go because he used to go a lot before he met my mom, but she would never go with him. My mom was out shopping or something, and so my dad said he had a present for me, and he gave me my first pair of hiking shoes, which were bright pink, because it was just about all I would wear back then—"

"*You* loved bright pink? That's surprising."

"It was a phase," I say indignantly. "A brief but intense phase. Anyway, we drove two hours to this trail in the Shenandoah Valley, and we played the Beach Boys the whole way because my dad always loved their music, but my mom thought it was cheesy, so he only really played it around me. And we did the six-mile hike like total pros. Without having to stop or anything. At the top of the lookout, we took all these selfies together. It became a monthly tradition."

A tradition that led to him meeting Sophie, I think, but I don't say it. Because eventually, his love of hiking grew bigger than his love of me. Eventually it was all about weeklong REI trips that I couldn't very well join him on while I was in school.

Dara once asked me if I thought it was strange that he took vacations without us. But I defended him, said that my family didn't do anything the normal way.

I was proud of that fact about us—back then.

Back before it screwed everything up.

"Do you still go hiking with him?" Noah asks. The car hits another patch of ice.

I wait until Noah looks calm, until the wheels feel solid beneath us, to answer.

"No, I don't."

NOAH

Ammy's face betrays her fear of the ice on the road. She bites her lip, and her face goes white.

Quite frankly, I'm worried, too, though I'm trying not to show it. It's only sixty more miles. We'll be there soon as long as I focus and stay calm enough to handle whatever slickness this highway throws my way. Of course, it's hard to stay calm when she tucks her hair behind her ears with both hands. Or says something I know there's so much story behind. Or when she laughs, the bubbly sound filling the car like champagne in a glass.

"All right," I say. "Next question, please."

She turns to me. "Are you sure you're okay? Driving in this?"

"I'm fine," I assure her. I don't want her to worry.

"Okay," she says reluctantly, but she doesn't ask me a question. She looks straight ahead, nervous.

After a few minutes, after the croony song has switched to another croony song, I clear my throat. I want to know what's really going on with her, and this is probably our last chance. I don't know *why* I need to know everything about this girl who I will likely never see again in my life, but I do. I decide to take my dad's advice. Don't ask for something if you aren't ready to give something in return.

"I'll offer you a trade," I say.

She looks over. "What do you mean?"

I keep my eyes on the road ahead, on the ten or so feet of road I can see in the light from my brights. "I'll tell you what happened with Rina, what *really* happened with Rina, if you tell me why you're here."

She's silent for a moment, and I'm afraid I've upset her. But then finally: "Who goes first?"

I grip my hands tighter on the wheel, bracing for any ice patches. I keep my eyes on the yellow lines in front of me, flicking my brights off temporarily as another car approaches. "I'll go first. As a display of confidence." I shoot her a smile. "To show that I trust you."

She nods, not looking away. I have to. I'm driving.

I decide to tell her the truth. Even though it's embarrassing. And makes me feel foolish. Even though if I hadn't hooked up with that girl three days later I probably wouldn't be here.

I walked away from that cliff and went straight back to the room. I came out for dinner, but I was quieter than normal. She knew something was up. I waited until after dinner, when Rina came in, asking what was wrong. It was the last night of our trip together, and we should have been happy—she would have been, if not for me.

When I told Bryson what she'd said to Cassie, he insisted that I not let it go. *She's gonna keep pulling this shit until you stand up to her,* he told me. He was like Rina in his way, always pushing me to be bolder. Just a different kind of bold. Not adventurous, but confident. Demanding, even.

At first I told her it was fine, but she kept pushing, kept asking.

Then it came out, all at once. Like the fireworks we'd seen over the lake a couple of nights before. *Explosive.*

I listed everything she'd ever said that had made me unhappy. She began to cry at my raised voice; she asked me how in the world I could get so mad at her over something so stupid. I stormed out of the room, spent the night on the couch.

The next day, we didn't speak. We drove back to Hudson in silence.

She came over to my house that night. We stood in my parents' backyard and yelled at each other. She told me I'd been way out of line for starting such a huge fight on the last night of the trip, for "blindsiding" her.

I told her that she'd been "out of line" for the last two and a half years, the way she kept trying to change me. Make me someone different from who I was.

I spat her words right back at her. "No one wants to be with a guy who's scared and worried about the whole entire world."

"Well, I definitely don't want to be with you the way you're acting right now," she yelled.

"Good!" I said. "That's settled, then."

Her anger disappeared from her face instantly. Replaced with sadness. Shock.

How could you even say that over something as stupid as this?

You can't be serious. You're not actually serious.

Is Bryson putting you up to this?

Don't turn around, Noah. Don't leave me like this.

Stop!

But I didn't listen. I walked away, left her standing there crying in my parents' backyard.

I tell Ammy how it might not have been over. I might have backtracked. But I hooked up with that girl three days later.

I'd never hooked up with anyone else besides Rina.

I tell her how guilty I felt, how I couldn't go back to her after that.

"Wow," Ammy says as soon as I'm done.

"I know," I say. "The whole thing was so dumb. Ridiculous."

I brace my hands on the wheel, waiting for her to say what I know she'll say. You broke up with the love of your life because she teased you about not jumping off a cliff?

You left someone for *that*?

She's silent, looking straight ahead.

She's judging me, I know.

I deserve it. It was awful to break up with Rina like that. To blindside her. To hook up with another girl right away, ensuring we couldn't go back to what we'd had.

When Ammy looks at me, her eyes aren't judgy at all. They look almost . . . understanding?

"I don't get it," she says finally.

I shake my head, flicking my eyes back to the road, which is straight, at least, for now. "What do you mean, you don't get it?"

I turn to see Ammy shrug, tugging at the cuffs of her sweater so they cover more of her hands. She keeps her eyes locked on them as she speaks. "It's just that if she was always treating you like that, why do you want to get back with her anyway?"

It's shocking, to hear her say it like that. It's not what I was expecting . . . at all. This whole time I've just been thinking about how I screwed it all up. But . . .

But . . .

I feel another patch of ice, and I grip the wheel.

I realize in an instant that I don't have an answer for her question.

Not when she puts it like that.

AMMY

I FIDDLE WITH THE EDGE OF MY SWEATER, TUGGING at an errant piece of yarn.

I'm surprised I had the nerve to say that to him, to come out with it, just like that.

But what's most surprising—or least surprising, since both of our feelings seem to change by the minute—is that he doesn't have an answer.

And it's only now, with the silence hanging between us, all thick and dense and present, that I realize just how badly I wanted one.

I tug at the yarn again, and two knit loops unravel. It's crazy how easy it is to undo something that's been knit together, if only you pull in the right place.

206

For the last hour or so, I've been telling myself that this was all in my head. I knew it was ill advised, and I knew what romance does to people, and I knew, most of all, that this was all a bad idea. But it didn't matter anyway, because I always had the fact that he was completely taken with somebody else to fall back on.

And I still do, I guess.

And yet he still hasn't answered.

I can't help but think about how he lifted me up in the Enterprise office and spun me around, how for those brief, wonderful moments, I thought that maybe, just maybe, it was me he wanted, not her.

I hoped it was true.

It was a tiny hope, as small as the snowflakes spinning in the air around us, but a hope just the same. One I hadn't realized I had until now.

But does that make it all okay?

He's going to tell another girl he cares about her, that he wishes they were still together. Does that make *me* the other woman this time?

Because if that's the case, I couldn't stand it.

I know it's different—that Noah's not married, that the girl isn't even aware that he's coming to surprise her tonight, that we're teenagers, not old people with families and stuff—but still, he told me that she's the one for him. He's been telling me this entire trip that he regrets breaking up with her.

I'm rationalizing, and I know this, but I want it to be the truth.

Because I want him to be right for *me*.

As much as I've been telling myself otherwise, as much as I've been reminding myself of my vow, sitting here in the car with him, it's hard to listen to anything but my heart.

And he *still* hasn't answered.

I don't know how to put it all into words.

Don't pick her! Pick me!

It's all ridiculous. All sappy. All everything I wanted to avoid.

So I stare straight ahead. So I begin picking at the tiny bit of leftover nail polish on my thumb. So I'm silent and still.

But suddenly, none of that matters.

I recognize the familiar feeling of ice beneath the car, see Noah's fists clench, like they do every time the car hits a patch; we swerve, and he says: "I don't know how to answer that."

And I want to ask, what in the world does that mean?

I want to make him clarify. Make him tell me whatever is going on in the deepest part of his heart. But I can't. I don't have time.

"Damn it," he says. The car is still moving. Noah turns the wheel, but it's like the car has a mind of its own. I feel a bumping, and my whole body begins to bounce. Just like that, the car swerves out of its lane, and it keeps on swerving.

I turn to Noah. His hands are still on the wheel, but his face looks terrified now, and I don't even know what order it all happens, but we're still moving, on the edge of the road, toward the shoulder, the ice carrying us where it wants us to go. I brace my hands on the dash and Noah swears again, and then he slams on the brakes and . . .

We spin.

One, two, three times maybe. I don't even know.

The world, the darkness, the storm is all around us, and we are spinning frantically, and my blood is pumping, and my breathing is so fast I'm scared I'm going to have a full-on panic attack, just like my mom, and Lord knows what will happen now. If I'll ever make it home at all. If I'll see my dad or my mom or Kat or Bea or Dara or Simone or even Sophie—if I'll see any of them ever again. And all I can think is that I don't care anymore. I don't care about being mad. I don't care about last Thanksgiving. I don't care that my dad left and built a new family without us. I don't care if it was my fault or his or my mom's or anyone's.

I just want to see them. All of them.

I just want another chance to love them.

I want another chance to forgive myself, to forgive *everyone*.

Noah's hands grasp the wheel desperately, and I move one hand to his thigh, the other to the side of the door, bracing myself.

And then—finally—the spinning slows.

We can see again. The road and the trees and the fluorescent lights flanking the highway in the distance.

And then we finally come to a stop.

NOAH

I can't believe it.

I seriously can't believe it.

My heart is racing so fast it's scary, but the world is going on like nothing happened, the snow still falling, the lit-up signs on the other side of the highway glowing, the wind outside the car whirring.

The car is turned around, off in the grass next to the shoulder but facing the wrong way, like a toddler dropped us haphazardly on the toy road set at his preschool.

Ammy's hand is in mine. I grabbed it as soon as the car stopped, without even thinking. I can feel her pulse. It's fast and furious. Like the car was only a minute ago.

I turn to look at her, and she's sitting rigidly straight, her eyes locked ahead. Shocked.

I find my voice before she does. "Are you okay?" I ask.

She doesn't answer, only breathes in and out, in and out, her breaths labored . . . heavy, yet short.

My hand is still in hers. I don't let it go. I couldn't let it go, even if I wanted to, which I don't, because she's holding on to it so tight.

I give it a squeeze and ask again, "Are you okay?"

That jolts her out of it. She turns, and her eyes are huge and doe-like, as if she's an animal lost in the woods in one of those fairy tales my grandma used to read to me.

"I think so," she says finally.

All that could have happened, it terrifies me.

Damn adventures. We could have gotten hurt. Worse, we could have . . .

I can't think of it, because it's the polar opposite of everything I want.

I want to protect her. So badly.

I want to make sure she never gets hurt.

"Are you?" she asks, her voice shaking.

"I think so, too."

Her hand squeezes mine back. Then she returns to staring through the window. "Just sit a second. Just don't talk. I'm okay."

I glance down at my legs and then over at her. No blood. No bruises. No nothing. My shoulders hurt a little from where they slammed back against the seat, but in the grand scheme of things, we both seem okay. No one but the two of us will ever know what it felt like, what it meant.

We're okay.

We're just scared out of our minds, that's all.

"I've been driving for two years in the winters here, and nothing like that has ever happened to me," I say.

"I thought I told you not to talk," Ammy says, but she squeezes my hand again.

She's still staring straight ahead.

"I'm really sorry. I had no idea that was going to happen. I never would have driven if I thought that . . . well, I'm so sorry. About everything. I could never get over it if I caused something to happen to you."

My eyes are wet. I brush the tears away with the back of my hand, the hand that's not holding hers, hoping she doesn't notice.

Knowing that even if she did, she wouldn't care. She's cool like that. She's not one to judge.

"You really suck at not talking," she says.

I laugh harder, and more tears come. I wipe them away. "I know."

She lets go of my hand and turns to me. She leans forward and runs a thumb along the bottom of my eyelid.

I feel a chill run through me, a tingling all over. Like waking up after a long dream.

I look at Ammy, and I want so badly to do something I know, very much, that I shouldn't.

But then her hand drops from my face and she leans back in her seat.

Relief. Calm. *Disappointment.*

"We can't keep driving in this," she says.

"I know," I say. Even though we've only gone just over twenty-five miles, and we still have fifty-five to go.

Then she points through the window, at the neon lights on the other side of the highway.

All I can do is nod.

It's a Super 8. Quite possibly the worst of all the motel chains. A crappy motel, for us and us alone. I can't help it . . . the thought of that drives me wild.

I pull out slowly, the gravel and snow on the side of the road crunching beneath the wheels of the car.

My heart beating wildly once again.

It takes us fifteen full minutes to get there. We have to get back on the road, take the next exit, and wind around to the other side of the highway. I'm so damn nervous—about crashing the car? About spending the night with her?—that I don't dare go above fifteen miles per hour.

Finally, we pull into the parking lot, which is mainly empty. That means vacancy; it has to mean vacancy.

I park the car as close as I can to the front.

"I'll handle this," I say.

Ammy puts a hand on my shoulder as she unclicks her seat belt. "No. I'll come with you."

We walk up to the awning and approach a set of double glass doors that don't look like they've been cleaned very recently. The door opens, and at first glance, it looks like no one's inside. I start to worry, but Ammy walks up to the desk and dings a bell like she owns the joint.

As we wait, I contemplate the prospect of us setting up camp on the crappy couch in the lobby if no one shows. I'm convinced that somehow no one will show, even though it's not even seven o'clock. It's been that kind of a day.

But finally, a guy our age approaches.

"Help you?" he asks. He's got curly hair, scruffy stubble, and a weak chin.

I breathe deeply, preparing. Ammy looked up the Motel 6 policy on her phone while we drove. Most locations will let you in if you're only eighteen. Some require you to be twenty-one. I pray that this is the former. "We'd like a room for tonight, please."

The guy starts typing on the computer. I sigh, relieved.

"Single or double?" he asks.

"Double!" Ammy says before I can join her.

"Two full beds it is," he says. "ID?"

I retrieve my wallet. Push it over to him.

The moment of truth . . .

He picks it up, looks at it for a minute.

"So here's the thing . . . ," he says.

Crap. Damn it. Balls.

Ammy jerks her head up. She's thinking the same thing I am.

"I'm from Hudson, too. Went to Hudson High. You?"

My heart bursts with joy. He probably just wants to reminisce; he looks like the kind of guy for whom high school was the highlight of life.

"Nah," I lie. "Private school."

"Aww, man," he says. "I love catching up about the good old days."

Bingo.

"Breakfast starts at seven. Checkout is at eleven. Enjoy!"

He gives me the keys, and I turn to Ammy. Her eyes are full of so many things . . . exhaustion and, of course, relief.

But there's something else in there, too. Excitement?

When I left this morning, I had no idea I'd be spending the night with another girl.

And I had no idea just how thrilled that would make me.

AMMY

THERE'S A HUGE UPTICK IN MY PULSE AS SOON AS WE walk into the room.

My eyes go straight to the beds, with ugly mauve floral-patterned coverlets that look like they came from an old lady's yard sale, but oh so close together, only a couple of feet between them.

Only a couple of feet between him and me.

It doesn't disappoint me, this fact.

If I'm being totally honest, that is.

For a crazy second, I almost wish that there hadn't been a room with two beds available. That there had only been one. . . .

I'm being nuts. I force myself to stop and take a deep breath.

But Noah shuts the door behind us, and I feel a tiny electric shock shoot through my body as it fully sinks in that I'm in a motel room. With a boy. Someone who I only met eight hours ago. Someone who's already so deep under my skin I know I'm not going to be able to get him out.

"Which bed do you want?" I ask him.

Noah comes up next to me, and I can feel his presence all over me. It's so big and imposing, here in this tiny motel room. He gives me a pat on the back, and my skin seems to come alive where he touches it. "Your pick, Mrs. Adler."

I turn to him, try to stay composed. *Cool.* He's got a stupid grin on. "You know I would *never* take a dude's name," I say. "*Ever.* I'm Ammy West until the day I die."

He chuckles. "It was a joke."

My narrowed eyebrows don't move an inch. He throws his hands up. "All right, all right, fair enough—don't take my last name." He winks. "I wouldn't either if my name was so cool."

He smiles, and I pause, realizing that I hadn't told him my full name until now.

That now he could look me up on Facebook, message me, talk to me, tell me all his secrets, long after tonight.

But if he's thinking that, he doesn't say it. "So I take it that means you *don't* want to pretend marry me?"

I shake my head, but I feel my face getting hot all over. I

hope it's not turning red. "I'll pass."

Needing an excuse to look away, I set my suitcase on the bed closest to the window. I pull off my gloves, tossing them on top of my suitcase, and sit down. The comforter is as scratchy as it is ugly, like sandpaper against the palms of my hands. The bed creaks as I plop down, doing justice to the cheap motel room cliché.

"I'll take this one," I say, my face fully composed now.

He tosses his bag on the other side, plops down himself. "Well, that leaves this one for me." He grins. He's enjoying this, our little charade.

And I am, too.

I look around. A beat-up, puke-brown shade is drawn, and the carpet is this distracting teal that I think I've only seen before in the Crayola crayon box. There's a print of a bad painting of a lake on the opposite wall, over a flat-screen TV that looks to be the only modern upgrade in decades. The walls are expired-milk white, and the lights are somehow too bright and not bright enough at the same time, one of the lampshades tilted haphazardly like someone tossed it on while they were drunk.

Noah leans forward, putting his hands on his knees, and looks at me. "Well, it's not exactly a quaint ski lodge, but it will have to do."

I smirk. "I know; here I thought the Catskills were supposed to be *charming*. That's what my dad is always saying, at least."

"We're not in the Catskills," he says, laughing. "Hudson

is closer to the Berkshires, if anything."

My dad was always going on about the magic of the Catskills, where he met Sophie. I guess I got them mixed up. It's hard to keep up with facts when you're learning that your family is falling apart. "Whatever," I say quickly.

Noah sits up a little straighter. "Do you need to . . . uh . . . tell anyone you're here?"

I take a quick short breath, and then I look over to my bag like it's an alarm or something. "Oh shit."

"Forgot?"

I hop off the bed, rush to my purse, and pull out my phone without even answering. There are three texts from Kat.

Girl, what's going on? I'm worried about you!

Are you going to make any of the party?

Lemme know you're OK, ok?

I type back as fast as I can.

Looooooooooooooong story, but the train broke down and this guy

and I tried to rent a car, we hit ice, and now we're in a motel

She doesn't say anything back, so I send her one more text.

I'm sorry to miss everything but don't worry about me, hopefully

home tomorrow.

And then, because I can't help myself, I open the muted conversation with my mom.

Is it over?

What was it like?

I guess you're not talking to me now?

I tap out of the conversation, because there's nothing to say to her.

When I put my phone down, I see that Noah's staring at me, leaning back on his elbows, grinning.

His smile pushes the bullshit one-sided convo with my mom right where it needs to go—away. His smile gets my heart beating quickly again. His smile makes me want to jump right into that bed with him.

"So you still won't tell me?" he asks.

"Tell you what?" I sit back down on the bed. *My* bed. The safe zone. The zone where I don't lose my mind wondering if he's going to touch me again.

"Why you're here. I mean, we *did* have sort of a deal, and I *did* go first, and whatever's going on, it's probably not *your* fault, unlike with me, since I got into this whole mess due to not being able to jump off a cliff . . ." His voice trails off.

I force myself to laugh, to lighten the mood if anything. But inside, I'm pissed. At this stupid girl who would try and make him feel like he needed to be anyone else but himself. Someone who would pick at him, year after year, day after day, and then be shocked when he flipped out.

I have a sudden, awful thought.

Is that how my dad thought, after that last Thanksgiving together?

Was it just too much?

Was he right?

I stand up as soon as the thought hits me, because it's suffocating, and the room is too small, and Noah is too, well, *here*, and I'm afraid if I stay I'll do something crazy.

Like wrap my arms around him and tell him I'll never make fun of him for backing off a cliff, tell him that cliff jumping is insanely stupid anyway.

Like ask him if he'd leave me, too. If one day I'll become as bad as my mom and push him away, just like she did with my dad.

Lord, Ammy, get ahold of yourself.

"I'm going to get some ice," I blurt out, fast as I can. "And—er—some snacks and stuff."

Noah stands up as well. "Do you want me to come with you?"

I shake my head, fish in my bag, and pull out the first few crumpled dollar bills I can find, and then without looking him in the eyes, I head out the door.

ACCORDING TO THE fire exit map, the ice machine is all the way down on the other side of the motel. I follow the desolate balcony to the end. The highway is relatively silent, and the lack of sound makes it hard to focus on anything but the fact that it's downright *freezing*—I should have brought a coat.

The snow is still falling—it might have slowed a little bit, but it's hard to tell in the dark—and I lean over the balcony, looking for our Mustang. It's already got a blanket of white over it, and I can only hope that tomorrow we'll be able to get out of here at a reasonable time.

And then at the same time, I don't.

I take in the views around me, the confetti-like sprinkling

of flakes, the darkness and the stillness on the highway. We're in a snow globe—Noah and I, in this motel—and it may be crazy, but I don't want to get out. I want to stay right here.

I imagine a world where I don't have to go to my dad's and walk the fine line of trying to be part of his family and wanting nothing to do with it, where I don't have to eventually return to my mom and deal with the fallout of betraying her like I did.

Where I don't have to do anything but cuddle up with Noah and stay warm.

I keep on walking, past 203, 204, 205, 206.

Maybe this feeling has nothing to do with my mom or my dad or Sophie, after all. Maybe it's just that the idea of holing up in a shitty motel room with Noah for weeks on end is the most appealing thing I could think of right about now.

Maybe this is exactly what I want.

Who knows, maybe it's even what I need.

The ice machine looks like it's older than I am—by a lot, probably. I lift up the lid and dig around with the black plastic bucket I grabbed from the room. I'm not even sure why I need ice—it's cold enough without it, and room-temperature water wouldn't be the worst thing in the world right now, but ever since I was a kid, the first thing I used to do in hotel rooms was go to get the ice. It was my special duty, like Noah and the turkey timer.

We used to go to Asheville in North Carolina, once or twice a year. We'd stay at the Sheraton downtown. In a room with two big queen beds, one of which I got entirely to myself—the benefit of being an only child, I suppose. In the winters, we'd go to the Biltmore, see the Christmas decorations my mom was always so wild about. It was magical, those trips, and my mom planned the whole thing—they'd never have happened without her. We'd get the special edition Christmas ornament to add to our collection, the tree full and heavy with our yearly bounty. In the summers, we'd walk around, have brunch, go to the art shops. Whenever we'd get in, the first thing I would do was find the ice machine and perform my duty. My mom would make a big show of plopping a bottle of white wine in the bucket like we were super fancy, even though the standard hotel ice bucket hardly had space for a few cubes of ice *and* a bottle of wine.

When I was younger, my parents would hire a sitter for Saturday night. They'd get all dressed up and go out to a fancy restaurant, while the sitter and I ordered room service. Later, when I was twelve or so, I got to stay in on my own, rent a movie, and order as much food as I wanted.

I won't ever do that again, I realize. Maybe I'll go with just my mom, or maybe I'll have kids of my own one day and drag them along, but I probably won't. Because the memory is ruined now. Like scar tissue, there always, but painful and puffy—not to be poked at too much.

I get ten or so cubes into my bucket, but the rest is stuck together, a big old block you'd need one of those old-time soda-shop picks to get through, not that I've ever been to a soda shop that had that sort of thing, or a soda shop at all, for that matter, but I've seen enough horror movies to know that, at some point, that was a thing.

I slide the door shut and head back to the stairwell. I have eight dollars and seventy-five cents in change. I settle on three bags of Cheetos—because one can never have enough Cheetos, especially when junk food is your entire dinner— two bags of pretzels, two Cokes, and a pack of Skittles. My fingers are practically numb as I feed each crumpled bill in, but miraculously, the machine takes every last dollar, and the occasionally evil spiral dispensers don't steal a single item from me. I tug at the hem of my sweater, making a basket of sorts to hold all the goodies, and I head back to the room.

Maybe—just maybe—it will all turn out great, I tell myself.

Maybe my dad will appreciate the gesture of me at least trying to come up for the faux wedding. Maybe we'll have a wonderful week, the five of us, like our own little nuclear family. Maybe I'll call my mom and apologize and we'll do something clichéd and mother–daughter-y when I get back, like get mani-pedis together or something.

Maybe I'll stay longer. Maybe a week will turn into a month and my fake nuclear family will become my actual one.

Maybe Kat and I will grow close, and we'll spend the next five months carting Bea to practice and eating at the fancy brunch spot in downtown Hudson on Sophie's dime, and flirting with boys down at Claverack Creek.

Or maybe even the cute stranger I spent a night with wherever we are now will become something else.

Maybe *we* will become something else.

I don't know what will happen tomorrow—I don't know how any of this will work out. I don't know what Noah is thinking right now.

But I know this—at least we have tonight.

NOAH

AMMY'S CHEEKS ARE STRAIGHT-UP PINK WHEN SHE walks in. She's got a sweater full of snacks, an ice bucket hooked on her arm, and her hands are frigid white.

"You were gone forever," I say. "I was starting to get worried." I take the ice bucket from her hands. "Good thing we have ice after the day we've had!"

She shoots me a look.

"Sorry—bad joke. Thanks for getting everything."

She pours the array of snacks onto the bed. "It's a habit of mine," she says, giving me a hint of her Ammy smile. "And by the way, it takes forever to feed crumpled dollar bills into a janky vending machine. Shouldn't they have

226

invented an app for that or something?"

"An app that flattens your crinkled dollar bills?" I ask.

She puts a hand on her hip. "No, where you just wave your phone in front of the machine and everything you want comes out without you having to pay."

"It's called iCrappyMotelSnacks. It's on the horizon."

She laughs rather loudly at my horrible joke. It makes me feel warm all over.

She waves her hand across the bed. "I did good, though, didn't I?"

I don't bother with the snacks for a moment. "You should have worn a jacket," I say.

"Thank you, Captain Obvious."

I don't like the idea of her being cold and uncomfortable. And I'm still worried her feet will get frostnip. I rush to my bed, pull back the comforter, and tug at the fleecy blanket underneath. After a few pulls, it comes out.

Ammy raises an eyebrow. "Is that really necessary?"

I don't bother to answer. Instead, I kick the remaining linens into a pile and walk up to her, wrapping the blanket around her shoulders.

"What is this, my cape?" she asks.

"Captain Obvious is nothing without his lesser-known counterpart, Queen Snark."

Ammy smirks but her eyes are kind, and I can tell she thinks it's funny, at least a little.

She takes her hands and wraps them in the corners of

the blanket, pulling it tight beneath her chin. I rub my hands up and down her arms, trying to warm her up. "That any better?"

Her mouth breaks into a slightly off-kilter smile, and a piece of hair falls in front of her face. There are snowflakes on it, snowflakes melting right in front of my eyes.

"Yeah," she says, her eyes on mine. My hands stop moving up and down. They rest on her shoulders for the smallest of seconds.

She doesn't drop her gaze.

What would it be like to kiss her?

What would it be like to kiss that adorable smirk right off her face?

It's too much. I drop my hands, take a couple of steps back. Clear my throat. And my head.

"Do you want to play cards?" I ask quickly.

She laughs. It sounds a little forced, or am I imagining that?

"You brought cards?" She pulls the blanket tighter and sits on her bed.

"Yeah," I say. "Never leave home without them!"

Everything I'm saying sounds awkward, and my face goes red. I head to my bed and unzip the front pocket of my messenger bag, eager to escape her gaze for a moment. I dig through the gum, receipts, and a folded-up piece of paper where I've jotted down my poem for Rina.

Rina.

What the hell am I doing? I shake my head, reach into a

different pocket to get the cards.

Our adventure is getting to me. We've been together for who knows how many hours now, we've been through what seems like hell and back, we've talked and talked and had to rely on each other . . . of *course* I'd be feeling all the feels, as Rina's little sister always used to say.

This isn't real. It's nothing more than me having watched one too many romantic comedies in Rina's company. It's situational. I don't know this girl. She won't even tell me *why* she's here.

If anything happened tonight, it would ruin everything with Rina.

Rina never liked my jokes. So much that eventually I stopped telling them.

Rina, who never liked a lot of things about me.

Ammy's words ring in my head:

Why do you want to get back with her?

It's too much to figure out, right here in this moment, so I fish for those damn cards like my life depends on it.

My hands land on the cards as Ammy starts in on the junk food. I take them out: a hole-punched deck my grandparents got me in Atlantic City. My grandma Jen was so good at blackjack, half the time she'd *make* money when she went there.

I don't care what we play, I just need a distraction. Some time to get my head in order.

Before I hooked up with Bryson's cousin, I didn't think. I wasn't kind to her—or myself. I need to think now.

Ammy means something to me, after what we've been through. I can't use her to help me figure out whether I should be with Rina or not. I already know that if I kiss her, it will mean a whole hell of a lot.

I turn around, walk back to the bed, and sit down next to her.

The cards shuffle easily as my eyes survey the goods: pretzels, Skittles, soda, and . . .

"You got three bags of Cheetos?" I ask.

She bites her lip and scoots back on the bed, leaning against the headboard, the blanket still wrapped around her. "Too much?"

"No," I say. "It's just . . ."

"What?" she asks. "You're not allergic, are you? There's not any gluten, it's just corn. Not that gluten is a real allergy, but . . ."

I shake my head.

"Oh shit, you don't have celiac, do you? I guess it *is* an allergy if you have celiac. But no, you ate two sandwiches today. I saw you. . . ."

I laugh. "It's nothing."

She cocks her head to the side in that way she has of making me not care about anything besides telling her everything on my mind. "Come on," she says. "What?"

"My mom has this dumb story about Cheetos, that's all," I say.

She pops a Cheeto into her mouth. "Go on. . . ."

I hesitate, feeling silly. It's not a particularly interesting story. And it's weird that it means so much to me right now.

Ammy shakes the bag like a bootleg maraca. She leans back, and her head hits a crappy painting of a pier. She scoots down, readjusting, her short hair fanning out so it looks like a dark seashell. "Come on," she says, unaware I'm sitting over here writing poetry about her hair. "I want to hear."

I breathe deeply, preparing. Even though it worked out, it still hurts to talk about. "My parents split up last year. Well, technically they got separated . . ."

Ammy stops midbite and sits up straighter against the fake wooden headboard, careful not to hit her head again. "I didn't know your parents were split up. I thought you said—"

"They're not," I say quickly, as it seems to upset her. "Wait, are yours?"

She looks down, staring into the crinkly foil bag as if there's an answer in there. It says everything.

"Anyway," I say, and she looks back up at me. "Remember I said they were on a 'renewing their love' cruise?"

She laughs and seems to relax, now that the spotlight is once again off her. "I just thought that was because they were old."

I laugh, too. "Give me some Cheetos," I say. She does. I pop one into my mouth and wipe the orange flecks onto my jeans. "They separated because my dad was out of work as a professor. He was on a tenure-track but something happened with the head of his department. Anyway, he started doing this job that could hurt his back and really should have been done by a teenager. I'm not sure if that was all of it, but when he got hurt doing the job, I think that was the breaking point for her. My parents have a weird relationship with money—we seem to either have it and are spending it all the time, like with this cruise, or we don't have it at all. And my dad was offered this gig at a community college, but he said a formerly tenure-track professor would never teach at a community college, especially the one in question—so he took this job instead. She got really pissed that he was risking his health to save his pride."

Ammy nods. "That makes sense, I guess."

"My dad's not in the best shape," I say. "Trust me, if you'd seen him up there laying roof, you would have said the same thing. Anyway, so a couple of months ago, my mom tells me that my dad quit the roofing job and took the community college one, and that they're getting back together, and I'm happy, I really am, but I don't know, I'd been pretty upset about their separation, and I worried they were doing it for me. My parents are the kind of people who *would* do something like that for me, so I asked her if it's what she really wanted."

Ammy nods, leans a little bit closer, puts the bag down.

What's *your* story? I want to ask her. I want to abandon this one and hear hers.

"So what did she say?" Ammy asks.

I smile. "She said that there was this one night when they were first dating, and they were supposed to go to a nice restaurant in Hudson, but something went wrong with the reservation, so by the time they got it sorted all the restaurants were closed. They went to a deli and got an extra-large bag of Cheetos and two sodas, and they sat in my dad's car by the train station—my mom had come all the way up from the city for the date—and they shared their dinner while waiting for the eleven o'clock train so she could go home."

"And?" Ammy says. "So?"

I smile. "So my mom said she'd been unhappy with my dad, and he was being an idiot about the roofing job, but she said that to this day there was no one else on earth she'd rather share a bag of Cheetos with in a crappy car while waiting at the train station."

Ammy raises an eyebrow. "So, what? I remind you of your mom? Eww," she says, laughing.

"No, not at all. It's just, I saw the Cheetos, and I thought about that story, and I thought about what she said, and I don't know, I thought about how much fun I've had with you today, even though it's been a nightmare, too. . . ." My voice trails off, and I look down at my hands.

"I don't know," I say finally, my eyes still locked on my hands. "I said it was a stupid story. I don't know why I even told you."

When I look up, Ammy's staring back at me. Her smile is everything.

Everything I ever wanted.

In one person.

In this motel room.

Sitting across from me.

"It's not stupid," she says. "It's not stupid at all."

AMMY

"MAYBE WE SHOULD PLAY CARDS," I SAY.

Noah is staring at me, and somehow we're sitting closer on the bed than we were when he started his story, and the only thing that really separates us is an ever-dwindling pile of vending machine goodies, and my heart is beating super-duper fast now, and I swear if I don't do something else, he's going to feel it pounding, vibrating right through the springs of the lumpy mattress beneath us.

And then what?

He looks as relieved—and as disappointed?—as I am. He pushes the snacks aside and pulls out the deck of cards. Am I crazy, or are his hands shaking, just a little?

He starts to shuffle. A real bravado sort of shuffle, like

you'd see in a casino or something. My mom was always trying to show me how to shuffle all fancy like that. She used to
try and teach me all kinds of card games, too, but I wouldn't
have it. I'd rather go hiking with my dad. I'd rather be outside
than cooped up, as she preferred, playing cards and complet-
ing puzzles. If she was going out, it was to go antiquing, to
find more things to fill her nest inside. She was always working to make our house so beautiful, but I never really cared.

"What should we play?" he asks. "Gin? Rummy? Strip
poker?"

I roll my eyes. "Please."

He raises a hand. "I kid, I kid," he says again, just like he
did earlier in front of the 7-Eleven. I still find it funny. And
adorable. I meet his eyes. His grin is wide, and I can see his
imperfect teeth. Perfectly imperfect, I think to myself.

Lord. I have to stop.

"How about Go Fish?" I ask. One bag of Cheetos is officially finished. I open another.

He raises an eyebrow and runs a hand up and down his
exposed arms, tugging at the Steelers shirt I hated initially
and now pretty much just adore. "Are you cold?" I ask. "Do
you want my blanket?"

He ignores me. "Go Fish is a game for five-year-olds," he
says. "You don't know anything else?"

I sigh, thinking of all those times my mom implored me
to do something she liked. Why was I so against it? It was
like this unwritten rule in our house—Mom would screw up,
so Dad and I would do our thing. We loved her, of course,

but—well, sometimes it was just easier without her around. Weekends were more fun with just the two of us. Even the antiquing trips dwindled near the end, the one thing that had brought us all together, a little mix of both worlds.

Maybe that's why it was suddenly so easy to decide to come up here for the fake wedding. Call Dara for the ride, tell Kat I'd be there in time. Maybe I stopped being Team Mom a long time ago.

"I don't think I have the energy to learn something new after the day we've had," I say, digging into the Cheetos once again. "Come on. Deal 'em out."

He doesn't argue; he just shoots us each seven cards. I grab them and start to organize. I've got three queens, and I decide that that's not a bad start.

"Do you have a queen?" I ask.

He smirks. "I don't know, do I?"

"Very funny," I say, reaching out a hand. "Hand it over."

Outside, the wind whips hard, rattling the glass.

He hands me the queen. "Good thing we stopped here," he says.

I take it from him, our fingertips brushing. Does he notice it as much as I do?

I put my book of queens down. Triumph.

"Any twos?" I ask.

He shakes his head smugly. "Go fish."

I grab one out of the pond and arrange it in my small fan of cards. "Your turn."

He pulls up the scratchy comforter around him, dragging

it halfway off the bed. He looks goofy, like a kid, but he's not a kid—and I'm not, either. We're two almost-adults in a motel room, alone. If this were the 1950s, they wouldn't even be allowed to show this on network TV. "So you never told me what your biggest regret is," he says. "I told you mine."

I tilt my head and take a deep breath. "I'm pretty sure that's not an acceptable question in the game."

He sets his cards down for a moment. Outside, I hear the crackling of falling icicles. "So? Let's go back to Questions."

"You said it wasn't even a game," I protest. "You said you wanted to play cards."

He scoots in a little closer. "I agreed to go first," he says. "It's not my fault I ran off the road before you had your turn." He smiles jokingly.

I scoot back, bump my head on the shitty painting again. I rub the back of it with my hand. "So which do you want to know?" I ask finally. "My biggest regret or why I'm here?"

He shrugs. "I have a feeling, given your reticence to tell me, that they have something to do with each other. Mine did."

I take a deep breath, but that's when my phone buzzes.

I pick it up. It's Kat.

LOL wut? Are you serious? You're missing the wedding to shack up with a guy? Girl, are you making this up?

I type back.

I know, I suck, but it's not my fault. And it's not like that. He's a nice guy. Goes to Hunter. We just got thrown into this weird situation together. Hey, you were the one who was always telling me to be

more adventurous, right?

I can see that she's typing something, but then she stops.

"So do you have any threes?" Noah asks.

I look at the phone again, but there's nothing more from her, so I put it down. I pick up my cards. "No threes," I say.

He raises an eyebrow.

"Really," I assure him.

He draws a card, and I watch as he organizes it, as he runs a hand through his shaggy hair, as he cuddles tighter beneath the comforter. I check my phone again, but there's nothing more from Kat.

I put my cards down and force myself to calm my breathing.

Something about hearing that his parents were separated, hearing the words actually come out of his mouth, makes it easier. Because that's what they don't show you on TV shows and movies about divorce: the gray area. In those, the kids either don't give a shit at all or totally lose their shit. But there's this whole big in-between. It's so hard even to say it out loud—my parents, the people I love more than anything, the people who are my *family*—aren't together anymore.

My family isn't my family anymore.

And then when you add the fact that my dad has found a new family, that I'm leaving my mom on one of the hardest days of her life to celebrate his premature, divorce-papers-aren't-even-signed-yet union, well—it makes me sound awful.

It makes me feel awful.

Maybe it's the fact that he knows how hard it is. That it's

already partially happened to him. It's different at this age, when you're an almost-adult yourself.

Dara says she can hardly even *remember* her parents' divorce. "Give it time, and it won't feel like *that* big of a deal," she was always saying to me.

But it is a big deal. It's the *whole* deal. Maybe it's because I know he'll understand me now.

Or maybe it's because I know he's the kind of person who would at least try to understand anything.

I take another deep breath, then go. "My parents split up, too," I say. "But they aren't getting back together."

Noah sets his cards down. "I'm sorry. That sucks."

I shake my head. "It's not that, really. Or maybe it is. I don't know. It happened almost a year ago. I've moved on. I mean, I've adapted. But, well—" Lord, this is hard.

"What?" he asks.

I shake my head. "It's embarrassing."

Noah tilts his head to the side. "Everything's embarrassing when you really think about it. It's okay."

"My dad left us. The usual story, you know, except for that it wasn't with a woman at work or whatever, it was with a freaking *yoga instructor* he met on an REI trip, if you can believe it."

Noah's eyebrows scrunch up for a second.

"What?" I ask. "What is it?"

He shakes his head vehemently. "Nothing. Keep going."

I cross my arms, wanting to get through this stupid story as quickly as possible. "See, the thing is, I came up to Hudson for ten days last summer. I met my new family. I even kind of liked them—well, besides my stepmom."

Noah shrugs out of the comforter and leans back on his palms.

I don't say anything for a moment, and he scoots closer. "What happened?" he asks. "You can tell me."

I realize I've been unconsciously picking at my nails, and I force myself to stop. "I don't know what happened—really, I don't. See, my mom was always anxious. But . . . I guess after my dad left, she just kind of unraveled . . ."

He nods, encouraging me.

I see a flash of her screaming at me the last time I suggested that she log off of Facebook for a minute.

So now you're pretending that none of this ever happened, just like your dad?

"She became, like, obsessed with his new life. Following it all on Facebook. She even found one of my stepsister's Instagram accounts."

Noah offers a weak laugh. "We've all tried to stalk our exes at some point, I guess."

I shake my head. "With her, it was obsessive. And she kept trying to get me involved, too. I would tell her I didn't want to spend my afternoon that way, but she wouldn't listen. And then when the wedding invite came—"

"The wedding invite?"

I sigh. "My dad's girlfriend—she's this New Agey person, and so she has this idea that she wants to make their relationship valid in the eyes of some spirit nymph or something, so she decided to have a commitment ceremony. She can't have a wedding because my parents aren't even fully divorced yet."

"How'd your mom like that?" Noah asks sarcastically.

I shrug. "How do you think? The Facebook stalking became even worse. It was suddenly all she ever wanted to talk about—no asking how my school day was or where I wanted to go to college or any of that normal stuff—all the stuff I'd found annoying before, but I started to kind of miss it. Even the way she talked about everything was circular, just going on and on around the same topics. *How does she think she can do this? Does she know we aren't even divorced yet? How can he let this happen?* That kind of thing. And then every time she'd see something about the wedding, she'd lose it. She had four panic attacks in a month. And I was the one who had to take care of her. If I even suggested she shut down all her social media accounts and take a break, she'd just yell at me."

Noah shakes his head, too. "That must have been hard for you to watch."

My eyes start to water. "It was. I just wanted it to stop. It was like a roller coaster. I was always just waiting for her to freak out again, for her to see something that set her off. She had this whole stupid thing planned for today. We were going to watch *Gilmore Girls* and a bunch of sad movies and 'be there for each other,' which really meant just bitch about my dad. Last night, when I told her I didn't really want to, she flipped out, and I got so mad. Suddenly it was like I wanted to come to their stupid commitment ceremony. I wanted to be part of the family that, even if they were all tools who had no problem with breaking up marriages, at least it felt like they were sane. Normal." I feel the first tears start, and I wipe them away. "But now I just feel like I've taken his side. Like I'm abandoning her, too. And it was all for nothing. Because I didn't even make it to the wedding."

Noah waits a second, to see if I have anything more to say, but when I don't speak, he does. "Man," he says. "I'm sorry. I'm so incredibly sorry. That's awful. It's so sad."

"Tell me about it," I say, trying to force a laugh, but it comes out as a stifled sob instead. Noah leans closer, but I hold up my hand. "No," I say. "I'm okay. I just need a tissue."

He's up in seconds, jetting over to the shitty vanity by the bathroom. He pulls the whole box of tissues out of the countertop, the metal door that once held them in falling to the floor with a clang.

"Here," he says, pushing the box at me. I take two and wipe the bottom of my eyes. My mascara leaves black streaks on the tissues.

"So that's your biggest regret?" he asks. "Leaving your mom for this wedding?"

I shake my head. "No, it's not. That's not it at all."

It wasn't the first time my birthday had fallen on Thanksgiving—it was the third, in fact—but I was turning seventeen this time around. It felt special.

And of course, it wasn't the first time my mom had stressed out over a holiday—had caused a scene, if you will—

but, again, this time was somehow special.

I'd been asking for a Kindle for the last two months. As an avid reader, I'd at first been reluctant to embrace the e-reader thing—you know, the romance of paper and all that—but then I learned that you could get library books, and that books before the 1920s were free, and suddenly, I wanted that bookish little gadget like nothing I'd ever wanted before. I could take it on camping and hiking trips with my dad. I could even tuck it in my backpack on days that I had to lug my huge calculus book around and didn't want to weigh the bag down with *Madame Bovary* or whatever.

My parents were never huge on gifts. It wasn't my mom or my dad being weird about it—it's just that they were always kind of thrifty. It was about the thought more than the dollar amount. I can't remember a single time in my life I got anything worth more than forty or fifty dollars or so. But I wanted that Kindle. And not the cheap one, either. The nice one, the one that looked white like real pages, the one that let you read at night, perfect for the times I slept over at Simone's but fell asleep long after either she or Dara did—the hundred-dollar-plus price tag was, of course, out of my limit.

But I launched my campaign nevertheless. Explained how it was educational, really, and I could probably use it in a couple of years at college. And how I wouldn't be hassling them to drive me to the library all the time, and I wouldn't have to cruise the bargain bin outside of the used bookshop for classics—I'd have them for free.

I reminded them that it wasn't just my birthday—it was

Thanksgiving, too. And sure, you didn't usually get *presents* for Thanksgiving, but hey, it was two holidays. If we were ever going to go above and beyond our normal gifting limits, this was the time.

I may have even reminded them that as an only child, they'd already saved buckets of money on presents over the years.

I delivered a persuasive argument.

I must have, because I got it.

My dad looked so happy that morning. My mom did, too. I was in pj's watching the parade, as I always did on Thanksgiving, and Snoopy was floating down Sixth Avenue when my parents came in.

"Ready for presents?" my mom asked. She was already dressed. In black capri pants and this beige silk top that my dad had had his boss get her when he went to Paris. My dad always did things like that. Things to make her feel special. Her hair was pulled up into a topknot that made it easy for her to cook but also looked incredibly chic. My dad was still in pj's—flannel pants and a Carolina Panthers T-shirt. You could tell just by the way he looked at her, even in moments like this, that he loved her. That he thought she was beautiful.

Of course, I didn't care about that, then. Right then, all I was focusing on was somehow hiding the inevitable disappointment on my face when I didn't get the Kindle.

"Sure," I said, turning the volume of the parade down

just a touch and sitting up straighter on the couch, crossing my legs.

My mom pulled a box from behind her back. "From both of us," she said.

It was small, book-shaped, about five by seven inches. I looked at my mom, then to my dad, and then I reached for it eagerly.

After the Kindle was opened, after I'd loaded up the entire Jane Austen, Henry James, and Thomas Hardy collections, after I'd figured out how to set up library books and all that, my mom pulled me aside.

"I know holidays haven't always been perfect," she said to me. "But today's going to be different. From now on, everything is going to be different. We're going to have a perfect Thanksgiving and a perfect birthday. You deserve it."

I should have said that there was no such thing as perfect. I should have said that *perfect* didn't matter one bit to me. Maybe things would have been different.

We had enough yams that time. That wasn't the problem. And my mom was trying. She really was. She had the turkey in the oven—it was almost done—and a bunch of dishes laid out and ready to go in as soon as it was out. Green bean casserole (my favorite). Yams and marshmallows. Macaroni and cheese for my dad. We'd have leftovers for weeks.

There were twenty minutes left on the turkey, and she told me to keep an eye on the mashed potatoes while she went up to do her makeup.

My dad was setting the dining room table. Pouring wine. I was supposed to stir the potatoes so they wouldn't burn. She was afraid if we took them off the heat they'd get tough and sticky and she'd have to add a ton more butter, so she had the burner on low, and I was on stir duty.

It was the first time she'd done potatoes that weren't straight out of a box, and so she was being particular. I understood.

The only thing was, stirring wasn't exactly *thrilling*. And I had my brand-new Kindle, and I'd downloaded *The Return of the Native* by Hardy, and—well—I don't remember what happened, but all of a sudden, it smelled like smoke, and my mom was bolting into the room, eyeliner on one eye, none on the other, screaming.

"How could you be so ungrateful? After all I do for you? After your dad and I got you that stupid expensive thing, and I ask you to do *one* thing so our dinner isn't *ruined* and you can't even do that!"

Immediately, my dad was in the room, but that didn't stop her. There were tears in her eyes, and her face was red.

"All I want is one *fucking* holiday where everything doesn't go to shit. Is that too much to ask?"

"I'm sorry," I stammered, tossing the Kindle onto the counter, flipping the burner off, trying to salvage the potatoes, feeling my own eyes well up. "I'm sorry. I guess I got caught up reading."

She stormed in front of me, grabbed the Kindle. My dad was yelling, too, now, but she wasn't listening. "You ask us for this expensive toy, and *this* is how you repay us. I'm returning this."

"No," I said. "You can't. It's mine."

I tried to grab it back, out of her hands.

But she wouldn't let go. She pulled back, and then I pulled back, and then I don't know quite how it happened, but I must have lessened my grip because it went flying out of her hands, landing against the wall. It left a subtle dent, chipped eggshell paint.

I think that was it for my dad. I think that's when he officially gave up. He signed up for the REI trip the next day. Two weeks in Patagonia at the beginning of March. I had school, so I was obviously out. He weakly offered for my mom to come, knowing there was no way in hell she'd be backpacking for two weeks. When he wasn't working, he spent the next three months planning the trip, stocking up on gear, chatting with other attendees on their trip's Facebook group. He didn't even see how much my mom was trying to get better. I just don't think he really cared anymore.

I try to tell myself that maybe it wasn't my fault. I do.

It's impossible to deny it: if I hadn't put so much pressure on her—if I hadn't asked for that stupid, pointless gift—well, then maybe he wouldn't have taken that trip; maybe he wouldn't have met Sophie. Maybe my family would still be my family.

Maybe I wouldn't be here after all.

NOAH

WE'RE SITTING SO CLOSE OUR KNEES ARE PRACTI-cally touching. It's hard not to lean in and hold her after everything she's just said.

She was right. It's not a sob story. No cancer. No car acci-dent. No abuse.

But I can tell it's tearing her apart.

It would tear me apart, too.

"That's my biggest regret," Ammy says finally. "All right?"

I shake my head, looking at her. Her eyes aren't wet or teary anymore. They're sad, empty. Lost. I wish harder than anything that she'd never had to go through that. That she could have been dealt different cards.

I felt so guilty even contemplating Ammy having frostnip.

So awful breaking up with Rina, hooking up with another girl. To think that you did something, no matter how irrational it may seem, that could cause your parents to split up. It must be awful.

"You know it's not your fault, right?" I ask Ammy.

She shrugs. She pulls the blanket up higher, so it's just past her chin, her small mouth and wide eyes poking out. "That's what everyone has to say. Because I'm the kid and she's the parent, and all that. And I'm allowed to mess up and she's not, and *blah blah blah*. But if I hadn't been such a brat—if I hadn't put *so much pressure* on her by asking for the Kindle—even if I'd just paid attention to the mashed potatoes like I was supposed to, it would never have happened, and my dad would still be with us."

"He wouldn't, though. It would have been something else. It was the—"

"—straw that broke the camel's back. I *know*. I'm not an idiot. I can read internet advice, too. My stepsister said the same thing. But still. She might have gotten better. She *was* getting better, until he left. After Thanksgiving, she doubled up her therapy sessions, and she tried a new antidepressant, and meanwhile he booked the stupid trip where he met my stepmom. If it all hadn't happened at that exact time, they would have missed each other, they would never have even met . . ."

"But it's not your fault," I say again. "Really, it isn't."

Her eyes catch mine, sharp for a second. Inquisitive. "Well, then why did it happen when it did?"

249

I look down at my hands, rub the comforter between my fingers, pick at one of the errant threads. "Maybe it just wasn't right. Like it was a long time coming."

She looks at me, her eyes cutting for the first time. "That's easy to say, Mr. My Parents Got Back Together After All."

I laugh weakly, then go back to picking at the comforter. I wish I could touch her. Hold her. Make it all go away.

I sigh. "I'm sorry. I really am."

I finally catch her eye again. "I know everyone says they're sorry, but I'm not just saying it. I'm sorry you had to go through that. I'm sorry you've been living all this time thinking it was your fault when it wasn't."

She stares at me a moment, then seems to believe I'm genuine. "Thanks," she says. "It sucks. And it sucks that I left her today of all days. That's why I didn't want to tell you. Well, it's part of why, at least. I just felt so guilty for hopping on a train and going to celebrate my dad's new fake marriage when my mom was, like, literally falling apart."

"*Figuratively*," I say.

She manages a weak laugh. "Usually that bugs me, too, but I'm too upset to give a shit right now."

I look at Ammy. I know I can't convince her. Not in one night. Or a few words. I know what guilt's like, and how what-ifs feel. They're always there, waiting for you. Not easy to fight on your own.

Sometimes it takes meeting a stranger on a train to get the courage you need to finally stop asking yourself . . . *what if.*

I cross my arms, smirk. "Well, I guess now I understand why you despise Kindles so much."

Ammy's face brightens and she laughs out loud. "I guess that makes my earlier argument null, huh?" she says.

I shrug. "I'll give you a pass."

She reaches in for another Cheeto and sips on her soda. "You know, my dad ordered me another one that night, but I made him return it. I told him that I didn't really like it anyway, that it wasn't really for me after all. I lied so hard that I think I convinced myself." She smiles.

"You can always borrow mine," I say.

It hits me so hard, what I haven't let myself feel until now. She doesn't live here. Not in Hudson. Not in New York. Not even close. I've known that the whole time, but now it feels heartbreaking.

Like we only have so much time together.

We should make the most of it.

She shakes her head. I wonder if she's thinking the same thing I am. "I'm pretty set in my ways now."

"I guess I'll have to mail you the Hunger Games trilogy, then," I say, trying to make it all a big funny joke, the fact that I've found someone who understands me who lives so far away. "Plus whatever other super-commercial book you'll judge without reading."

"Hey," she says. "Not nice." She picks up the cards. "All right. It's my turn. Do you have any jacks?"

I hand her my jacks.

"I had this crazy thought on the train," she says. Our

fingers brush against each other, and my skin comes alive where it touches hers.

"What's that?" I ask.

"I don't know, I just thought—what if I could stay longer than a week; what if I didn't have to go back to Virginia? What if my dad's family just became my new family?"

I cock my head to the side, try to still the beating of my heart, try to keep it all casual. "Hey, you never know. Maybe we'll end up being neighbors."

She's smiling when she looks up. In fact, she's almost glowing.

"One thing at a time," she says. "Now give me all your fours."

AMMY

WE REACH THE END OF THE GAME, AND NOAH WINS, miraculously.

It's now past eight, quickly approaching full-on night. I don't think I've ever even been alone in the presence of one guy this long—much less in a motel room.

I remember suddenly what Kat said, the second weekend I was there. There was a party she wanted to go to. It required sneaking out, riding six to a five-person car, lying to Sophie and my dad. I wasn't even planning on drinking—my dad sometimes let me have a glass of wine at dinner, and so I knew what good stuff tasted like, and I had no desire to pound cheap beer in the woods—but still, the rebellion was too much for me. I hadn't ever done anything like that before.

"You only get tonight once, Ammy," she'd said. "You'll *literally* never get it again. Do you really think that in fifty years you'll regret going to some sweet party in the woods? Our parents do whatever they want, even if it breaks up a marriage—why shouldn't we? You spend way too much time worrying about other people. Sometimes, you have to just *do something.*"

The party had been fun. Kat had been right. One hundred percent right.

You only get tonight once.

And this *tonight* is in a motel room, no less.

The thought is electrifying and scary and anxiety-inducing all at the same time. It makes my heart race and my palms sweat and my lips feel all tingly.

I look at him. He's packing the cards back into the box, so close that our knees are touching, two points of heat in a cold room.

A cold world.

The snow is still falling continuously—I can see it through the tiny space of window that the shade doesn't quite cover up. I don't even want to think about what would have happened if we had kept driving.

I look at his eyes, and he catches mine, too. He has to feel this excitement, this pulse in the air.

He *has* to.

"It's cold in here, huh?" I say.

Noah gets up, sending a wave of disappointment though my body, his knees no longer touching mine, and goes over to the heater. "It's set to eighty-two," he says. "I have a feeling that's an exaggeration, though." He kicks the heater, and it jangles like it's a hundred years old. Then he pulls the shade up, looking out. It's super dark, but the parking lot lights illuminate a blanket of shiny white, covering everything, every move, every step, every track. It feels like protection, like no one can see us, like it's just us together.

It's beautiful.

Noah pulls the shade down and comes back to the bed, sitting down to face me. His knees return to their original position, but now they feel somehow even closer. He looks up and catches my eye. He doesn't look away.

I feel like I can't breathe. Like my heart is going to explode and the papers tomorrow will all say that an eighteen-year-old girl died of excitement at spending her first night in a motel room with a guy.

"You want some blanket?" I ask.

He shakes his head. "I have this." He starts to lift the comforter again.

I shrug an arm out of the blanket. "That isn't a blanket. That's a shitty-ass comforter."

He laughs, but he doesn't reach for it.

My heart goes once again into furiously beating territory, but I suddenly feel bold. I think about what I told him, the way his face betrayed not even a hint of negativity—no judgment, no embarrassment, no discomfort—only kindness.

"Come on," I say. "Have some."

I don't wait for him to move. I do it instead. Maybe it's

the storm, or the fact that we've been together for almost nine hours now, or the way his eyes got all concerned when I told him everything, like all he wanted in the whole wide world was to make everything better. Or maybe it's simpler—maybe I just *like* him. Who knows? Maybe he even likes me, too.

He has to, I tell myself. I can feel it.

Maybe he knows that his ex was all wrong for him. Maybe he feels what I feel.

Maybe nothing even matters but this moment. Right here. Right now.

I push the blanket over to him and wrap him up, too.

He looks startled for a second, but then his shoulders relax as he pulls it tighter around him—the two of us, together, in our own little cocoon, protected from the weather, from families and exes, from things that don't matter—or at least things that don't matter right now.

My heart pounds. My breathing gets short. But it's not because I'm panicked or anxious this time—or at least, it's a different kind of panic, a delicious kind of panic.

He stops trying to put the cards together and instead flicks them off the bed, and they fall to the floor, scattering around like the snow outside.

Then he leans closer, so close that our faces are only inches apart, so close that I can practically taste his breath, drink in the smell of him. "Did you think this morning that you'd be sharing a motel room with a stranger?" he asks, an eyebrow raised. Then he lifts his hand to my face and tucks a lock of hair behind my ears.

"Ammy, sweet and fair," he adds.

My skin feels like it's caught fire, hot and tingly all at once.

My phone buzzes.

We both look over in its direction.

It buzzes again.

"Uh, do you need to get that?" he asks.

I shake my head. "It's probably just Kat."

Immediately, he pulls back an inch or so, and his hand falls from my face. "Kat?" he asks.

"My stepsister," I say, reaching my hand up to his cheek, rough and stubbly and perfect. Pulling him close. "Just ignore it."

NOAH

SHE TELLS ME TO IGNORE IT, SO I DO.

I lean in, because I'm afraid if I don't do something now, I'll regret it. I'm afraid I'll wish forever I'd done something different.

I've learned to hate regrets. And I've had so many of them lately.

My lips touch hers, softly at first. She doesn't pull back. I lean in farther, pressing against her. She leans back on the bed, and our whole bodies are touching now. I can feel every kiss down to my toes.

Her body is soft and welcoming. It fits so perfectly with mine.

Her lips, her cheeks, her tongue are warm. Warmer than

258

the blanket that's wrapped around us.

She rolls on top of me, and my hands find the back of her head, holding it. I run my fingers through her hair, finding the silkiness of the skin on the back of her neck, the heat emanating from beneath her shirt.

Kissing her feels like coming alive. Bold and energetic. Hot and raw.

We roll over again. Now I'm on top, and her hands reach around my neck, and it's exciting, thrilling, familiar, but like nothing else all at the same time.

She tugs at my hair ever so slightly, pulling me somehow closer to her.

All I can think is that this is right.

This is different from how it's ever been before. More real.

More present.

I want to dive into each kiss and drink her up. I want this moment to last forever and ever and ever. I never want to leave this crappy motel room. I never want the storm to stop.

I just want to stay here. Like this.

I pull back for air. Her face is flushed. Her breathing is heavy.

I smile. Her eyes are welcoming. Her short hair is a mess, all over the place. She looks so perfect wrapped up in her blanket.

We are so perfect wrapped up in our blanket.

Together.

"Wow," she says.

I nod. "Wow."

And the truth is so clear. Clearer than it's ever been.

No matter what I thought before, or why I'm here in the first place, or all the things that led us to this point . . . I'm entirely, completely, *absolutely* crazy about this girl.

AMMY

HE STARES AT ME LIKE I'M A MOVIE STAR OR SOME-
thing.

He stares at me like I'm the most wonderful thing he's
ever seen in the whole world.

No one has ever looked at me that way.

I lean in, give him a light peck on the lips. "You definitely
didn't think you'd be here tonight, did you?"

I can see tiny freckles around his eyes. Little flecks of
blondish red in his otherwise dark eyebrows. I can see that his
hairline is jagged like the side of a mountain and his stubble
is prominent enough that he could probably grow a decent
beard if he tried.

I can see that his eyelashes are thicker than mine and his

eyes look green up close.

I can see that he cares about me.

"Never," he says. "But I'm glad I am."

He lowers his lips to mine again, and I'm back on that roller coaster again.

He is urgent and strong and patient and soft.

I have never—*ever*—been kissed like this before.

And I never—*ever*—want these kisses to stop.

But they do. Of course they do. Eventually he pulls back, and he looks at me again, and he says the most perfect thing in the world, like he studied how to talk to a girl once, like he read a manual on this sort of thing, chapter eleven of *How to Win a Nerdy Girl's Heart*.

"You are like a book I want to read forever."

It's cheesy, I know. But he is cheesy.

And it makes my heart do all the cheesy things I didn't know my heart could do. Flutter. Race. Soar. I finally understand what Simone meant when she said all those times that her soon-to-be girlfriend gave her butterflies.

AFTER MINUTES OR hours, it's hard to even tell right now, Noah pulls back. "You know what? We need dessert."

I look at the clock and realize two hours have passed. We both laugh. He kisses me on the forehead and leaps off the bed. "I'm going to brave the cold to make a trip to the vending machine. Get my lady some dessert."

I roll my eyes. "You really need to stop embarrassing yourself."

He laughs and kisses me again.

When he's back, when we have two Honey Buns between us, we turn on the TV and alternate between the weather and an old eighties movie that I think I watched with my mom once, and I feel so . . .

Safe.

And I realize that I haven't felt this safe, this comforted, in a really long time.

I think about telling him that, but I'm pretty sure he already knows.

Because I'm pretty sure he feels the same way.

NOAH

I DON'T KNOW WHEN WE DRIFTED OFF, BUT I WAKE TO the sound of an infomercial on TV.

The first thing I see when I open my eyes is Ammy. She's only inches away from me, with her eyes shut, a peaceful look on her face. She's snoring, but it's a small snore, adorable and quiet.

We're on top of the covers, fully clothed, empty Honey Bun wrappers between us. The nightstand light is on, but there's no light coming in from the curtains. It has to be pretty early.

I grab the remote and flick off the TV.

I seriously have to pee.

I sit up in bed, and she must be a light sleeper, because she stirs.

There are so many things I don't know about her.

So many things I want to know about her.

Her eyes flutter open. "What time is it?" she asks.

I glance at the clock on the nightstand. "Five. Go back to sleep."

She smiles groggily. "It's weird waking up and seeing you."

"It's nice, isn't it?"

She nods.

"Okay, I really have to pee, though."

I lean in and give her a peck, and then I head to the bathroom.

Once I'm done, I make sure to put the seat down—I want to make at least a semi-good impression in this matter—and turn on the water to wash my hands.

The lights in the bathroom are fluorescent. In the bright light, my face looks pale and my eyes look red. Probably from the dusty comforter that the motels never clean, according to the internet.

A thought races back to me, like when you wake up and it takes you a second to remember the awful thing you've done, like the day after I broke up with Rina.

What Ammy said, just moments before the kiss.

It's probably just Kat.

It *can't* be, I think. It would be too uncanny. Too strange.

My grandmother is always going on about the world being a small place, but I was always way more logical about it. I always knew about confirmation bias. She would go about her day ignoring all the times that there were no coincidences. She asked the checkout girl at the supermarket if she knew me at Hunter, only to get a pert no. All the times the world proved it's really not that small at all. But then one thing would happen, like when her neighbor in Jersey turned out to be my old kindergarten teacher, and it was proof that the world was small after all.

But it's not.

Not this small.

We are going to about the same place.

We're the same age, too.

But come on. It's a big train. I got on at Penn Station, for Chrissakes.

It can't be.

I finish drying my hands, and before I open the door, I decide to let it go.

It can't be. It really can't.

AMMY

5:03 A.M.

I STRETCH OUT ON THE BED, LUXURIATING ON THE rock-hard mattress, the scratchy linens, and gaze at the flecks of the popcorn ceiling, completely relaxed. Every muscle in my body feels both alive and calm at the same time.

I lift my fingers to my lips, almost checking to make sure that last night really happened.

But it did. It all happened. And I don't care about my stupid vow and everything I told myself I believed about romance.

I don't care about any of it at all, because I only care about this.

I feel good. *This* feels good. Better than anything has in a really long time.

I try to imagine this morning and what it will bring. The two of us finishing the drive, finally getting to where we need to go, in a different place completely from where we were when we started, and I'm not only talking about geography.

How much time do we have left together? I wonder.

Will he want to see me again?

That's when the door opens, and the smile on his face answers my question. He crosses the room in a few quick strides and jumps into the bed, moves to kiss me again.

I lean back, hold a hand between our faces.

"Do you have a mint or something? I've got morning breath." I know this whole waking up next to a boy thing is romantic and all, but I can't exactly get in the mood when I can still taste the Cheetos from last night.

He smiles. "I don't care about that."

I smirk. "I do."

"There're Altoids in there," he says, pointing to his messenger bag, which is leaning against the opposite bed, from another time—another world—where we weren't exactly planning on sleeping next to each other.

Or maybe we were.

Even then, maybe we were.

I lean over, not even bothering to get out of bed, and Noah gives me a flirty smack on my butt.

"Hurry," he says.

"Relax," I call over my shoulder.

I support myself with one hand on the floor, and with the other, I unzip the front pocket.

I dip my hand in and immediately feel the smooth tin.

But as I pull the pocket farther open, I forget about mints, about my breath, about everything.

Because there, among the slick receipts and folded-up sheets of paper, my eyes catch on something . . . that can't be.

Something . . . *insane.*

My heart races, and I squeeze my eyes shut and then I open them again, hoping to make it disappear, but it doesn't work.

It's still there.

She's still there.

I set another hand on the floor, launch myself out of bed, pull out the photo, and stare at it.

"What?" Noah asks. "What's up?"

There she is. Real. In front of me. On a glossy Polaroid image, with a hot-pink feather boa around her neck and a top hat on her head.

Laughing.

Smirking.

Goofing around.

With him.

Is this some kind of sick, insane joke?

I stare at her, willing her to disappear. My hands begin to shake.

I turn around slowly, the room already beginning to spin, the world already different, like it's shifted on its axis—all in a millisecond.

I feel almost like I might throw up or I might fall down,

but when I see him, those feelings go away.

I feel like I might scream instead.

He looks up at me, and his smile fades as soon as he sees my face.

"What happened?" he asks. "Are you okay?"

And then his eyes catch the strip in my hand.

And he knows.

NOAH

"Are you fucking with me?" she asks. Her face is red, and the way she's standing above me, fuming, it's like she's a giant.

I feel like I felt all those times that Rina told me I had to do this or that. I feel small. Helpless.

But it's not the same, I know. It's not the same at all. This time, Ammy is right.

I stand up, fear invading my whole body, from my head right on down.

I glance quickly at the blanket, the blanket that held us together not that long ago but what now seems forever ago, crumpled on the bed.

"What happened?" I ask again.

I already know. I don't want to believe it, but I know.

She steps closer. Raises her voice. "Are you fucking with me?" she asks again, the photo strip clutched in her hand.

Her eyes are starting to well. *Damn it.*

"No," I say, shaking my head and walking around the bed to be close to her again.

I want to hold her. I want to tell her that it was all a big mistake.

I'm afraid I won't ever be able to hold her again.

She takes a step back, creating more space between us.

"I should have known," she says, more to herself than to me. "I should have known shit like this wouldn't work out."

I look around, at our little motel room, our little retreat. All of a sudden it feels more like a prison.

"What are you, an insane person? A sadist? I don't get it."

I step closer and put a hand on her shoulder. "Just let me explain. Please?" My voice cracks.

She shrugs my hand off and pushes the strip of photos in my face.

I don't even have to look at them to know what they are.

Rina sent me one last message after we broke up.

Cassie told me about Bryson's cousin. I've blocked you everywhere. Don't ever talk to me again.

Sure enough, she was on lockdown. She didn't even come up on my Facebook results. I was blocked. Her Instagram and Snapchat and Twitter, all private. She deleted every photo—every moment—we ever had.

But the worst was I went onto my own networks and saw

that every last remnant of us . . . it was gone, too.

We'd borrowed each other's computers frequently enough that she knew my password: *rinarina103*.

Her nickname, and the anniversary of our first date.

She'd managed to delete every photo, every status, every *everything* we'd had together. She'd erased us completely.

When I told Bryson, he'd said it was proof that she was vindictive, that she wasn't right for me anyway. But I knew the truth, even then. It was proof that she was hurting. It was proof I'd done something awful by not ever telling her how what she did bothered me, by letting it all build up until I was breaking up with her on my senior trip, throwing it all away in a flash.

Maybe that's why I'm here after all.

I knew deep down she'd never take me back.

I knew it wouldn't be good for either of us if she did.

Perhaps I just needed to apologize, to tell her how much she meant to me, to let her know I was sorry.

I let my eyes focus on the photos in Ammy's hand. They're from my dad's forty-fifth birthday party my junior year. He and my mom had splurged for a photo booth, pulling out all the stops.

I dropped my phone in a toilet not two weeks after the breakup, and I'd never been good about backing up my stuff. That photo is the only thing I have left from years of loving her.

Ammy must see it all in my face. "So you knew?"

I shake my head. I didn't. Until five minutes ago, I didn't

think it was possible.

"No," I argue. "I had no idea. Promise." It's the truth. How was I supposed to know that such a wild thing could happen to us? How was I supposed to know that the world really is that small? Even after the clues, after I saw those socks, after she talked about her stepmom teaching yoga, her stepsister named Kat, even still . . . how was I supposed to know it was *my* Katrina she was talking about? What are the odds, anyway? Most Kats are Katherines. And plenty of people teach yoga—it's *the Hudson Valley*, for Chrissakes.

Ammy tosses the photo strip out of her hands, lets it flutter to the ground. Rina stares up at us, smiling.

There's nothing but anger in Ammy's eyes. That's the thing about big eyes. They're so wonderful when they're happy, so terrifying when they're not.

"Just calm down," I say. "I didn't know. Not really."

"Don't tell me to calm down," she says. "Unless I'm wrong, unless this is your freaking cousin or something, and this was snapped at a family reunion, I have every right to not be calm."

"Ammy . . ."

She shakes her head, backing away from me like I'm fire, or I'm poison, or both. Like my sheer presence has the ability to destroy her.

This time it isn't a mechanical failure that's hurting her. It isn't her messed-up family or her fears about the future.

It's me.

"Don't 'Ammy' me," she snaps. "Just say it. How *in the*

world do you know my stepsister? I want the whole truth. No bullshit."

I take a deep breath. I don't want to say it, but I have no choice.

I can hardly believe it myself.

"She's my ex."

AMMY

I SIT DOWN ON THE BED, CRUNCHING A HONEY BUN wrapper beneath me in the process, scooch back against the headboard, and glare at Noah.

The feeling of nausea has gone, and all I have is anger—sharp, jagged, seething anger. He's taken a seat on the opposite bed, and he's staring at his feet.

I knew Kat had an ex, but she never wanted to talk about it. And I didn't want to press her. I was only there for ten days. We became close, but not that close. Not enough to push her on things she didn't want to talk about.

"When did you guys break up?" I ask.

"In the summer."

"No, but what was the date?"

"June eleventh," Noah says, rattling it off quickly. He's thought about it a lot. "Why?"

"My dad moved to Hudson at the end of June. You broke her heart right before all this shit happened. Did you even know that?"

Noah shakes his head. "I did a summer program before the school year started. I was hardly in town at all."

"You didn't, like, see it on Facebook or something?"

He shakes his head again. "She blocked me on there. And all her other stuff she set to private after the breakup."

He's not lying. Bea's stuff is mostly all public—it's where my mom gets about half her info about the family—but Kat's is not. I had to get approval from her on everything. I'd thought it was kind of weird for a wannabe actress to be private everywhere, but I thought it was just her way. Kat's unique. Whatever she does, it somehow seems cool.

"Where were you in August?" I ask. "Were you back in Hudson then?"

His eyes lift to the ceiling, like he's thinking, and then land back on mine. "For the first few weeks, yeah. Why?"

It's crazy to me that he was in Hudson when I was in Hudson. That we could have run into him in town—or at Target—and Kat could have pulled me aside and said "That's my ex" and "He's the worst" and "He dumped me totally out of nowhere and then hooked up with our friend's cousin three days later" and then I would have seen him approach me on the train, and I would have said "This seat's taken," and I would have texted Kat: *Girl, you won't believe who I just saw on the train. . . .*

But none of that happened. No hints on social media. No late-night gossip sessions about her ex. No accidental run-ins. The normal order of things wasn't followed.

And now here we are.

I know it should be different. I know that it would be better for Kat, for everyone, probably, if I'd known Noah's name, face—anything.

But at the same time, this tiny, awful part of me is glad that I didn't. Glad that I had last night.

I instantly feel sick.

"Did you know last night?" I ask, my voice no longer a yell. I'm exhausted suddenly. Spent.

He stands up, moving toward my bed, but I shake my head, making it clear that that's not okay. Not now. Not with all that I know. I point back to his bed. He sits down again.

"I didn't know until just now," he says. "I didn't know until I saw you holding that photo."

"Right," I say, staring him in the eye, daring him to look at me. "Then why do you look about a million times less shocked than me?"

Noah looks down again and presses his hands onto his knees, so hard his knuckles turn white. In another world, I would have wanted to help him. Manage the anxiety, ease the pain. But we're not in that world anymore. We're in this one.

Believe me, I'd give *anything* to be able to go back to the world of last night. Just like I'd give anything to go back to the world before my dad left. Or the world before that Thanks-giving. Or any of the worlds that were easier than this one, the one I'm in right now. In a shitty motel room with a boy I thought I cared about—a boy I did care about.

A boy I'm not supposed to care about. *At all.*

He looks up from the floor and back at me. "How could *I* know?" he asks, his voice pained. "How did you *not* know? Didn't she ever tell you my name? We only broke up a couple of months before you came to visit."

"She didn't say anything more than that she had an ex and didn't want to talk about him," I say. "Maybe she talked about you to Bea, I don't know. But not to me."

From the look on his face, I can see that he's been operat-ing under the idea that even if she didn't talk *to* him, he still meant enough to her to talk *about* him. I can see how much it hurts him, and it makes me feel bad.

I shake my head viciously, because he can't have it both ways. He can't be all sad about her and all into me at the same time. "You looked at me weird last night when I said her name," I say, staring at him. "You knew. You knew the truth, and you kissed me anyway. You let us have last night, even though you knew."

He shakes his head. "I thought it was a coincidence."

"Really?"

"There were two other Kats in our year alone," he says. "You didn't even tell me how old she was."

"And how many of them had moms who were yoga instructors?" I ask.

"I thought it was a coincidence," he says again. "Even if there was a second where I thought maybe it wasn't a coincidence, I *wanted* it to be one. I don't regret it. Even now. I don't."

"I do," I snap.

Noah's face falls. He shakes his head.

And then another thing occurs to me, something that's been bugging me. "Why in the world did you go on calling her Rina?"

NOAH

5:16 A.M.

AMMY STARES AT ME, WAITING FOR AN ANSWER.

"It's a nickname," I say. "I made it up, I guess. I'm the only one who ever called her that."

She sighs, and I pull the comforter up around me. I don't have a blanket on this bed. Mine, *ours*, is on hers. I stare at it for a second, wishing we could go back to before.

"You have to believe me," I say. "I didn't know. Not really."

"But you thought, *maybe*," she says. "I saw it in your eyes. And you kissed me anyway."

The space between the beds is like a strange wall between us now. "Because I wanted to. Didn't you?"

She ignores the question. "Just like you *wanted* to break up with Kat for barely any reason," she snaps. "Just like you

281

wanted to hook up with some girl and make it impossible to fix things?"

My chest aches. She's right. Goddamn it, she's right.

There's something else, too. Something she's forgetting.

"You said you didn't even know why I wanted to get back with her."

She crosses her arms. "Well, that was when I didn't know it was Kat."

I catch her eye. "What do you want me to say?"

"Nothing." She lies on the bed, like she's all of a sudden run out of energy. She stares at the ceiling, like there are some kind of answers up there. She looks exhausted.

"Maybe you should try and go back to sleep," I say. "It's too early to drive back. It's not even light out."

She doesn't say anything. She just flips off the light that we left on last night, grabs the blanket, pulls it tight over her, and turns, her back to me.

I stare at the ceiling, too, but after however many minutes of debating, I decide I can't sleep in my jeans, so I get up to head to the bathroom. As I do, I step on a bag of half-eaten Cheetos. It crumples loudly beneath my weight. "Sorry," I say.

She doesn't say anything back. I curse myself for telling her that stupid Cheetos story. And for somehow falling for the one girl in the world I really shouldn't be with.

I grab my backpack and take it into the bathroom, retrieve a pair of basketball shorts and a plain white tee. Change my clothes and splash water on my face.

Then I walk back to the bed and slip under the covers.

What would have happened if I hadn't offered her those Altoids? How much longer would it have gone on? I would have continued to think it was all just a coincidence. I didn't want to see it any other way. I didn't want to say, "Your stepsister is named Kat? Really? What's her last name?"

I didn't want to open Pandora's box.

Would we have gotten all the way to Rina's house? Maybe.

Would we have made out all morning? Probably.

Would I have begged her to give me her phone number and hang out with me the rest of the week? Definitely.

Would my heart have begun to race as I pulled the red Mustang up to Cortland Road?

Would I have told myself, even then, that it was all just a big coincidence?

Until I literally watched my ex walk out the front door and hug the girl I had, in one day, completely fallen for?

Yes, yes, and yes.

Would I have hurt Rina even more than I did before?

Have I already?

I wish we could pause and rewind. Go back to minutes ago, before she saw the photo, before my look gave me away. I wish we could have just been us. I wish we could have figured out what "us" meant without having to deal with all of this.

It's not fair. It's not fucking fair.

I know what I should do. What I'm *supposed* to do. I should drop Ammy off tomorrow, a couple blocks away, so

Then I walk back to the bed and slip under the covers.

What would have happened if I hadn't offered her those Altoids? How much longer would it have gone on? I would have continued to think it was all just a coincidence. I didn't want to see it any other way. I didn't want to say, "Your stepsister is named Kat? Really? What's her last name?"

I didn't want to open Pandora's box.

Would we have gotten all the way to Rina's house? Maybe.

Would we have made out all morning? Probably.

Would I have begged her to give me her phone number and hang out with me the rest of the week? Definitely.

Would my heart have begun to race as I pulled the red Mustang up to Cortland Road?

Would I have told myself, even then, that it was all just a big coincidence?

Until I literally watched my ex walk out the front door and hug the girl I had, in one day, completely fallen for?

Yes, yes, and yes.

Would I have hurt Rina even more than I did before?

Have I already?

I wish we could pause and rewind. Go back to minutes ago, before she saw the photo, before my look gave me away. I wish we could have just been us. I wish we could have figured out what "us" meant without having to deal with all of this.

It's not fair. It's not fucking fair.

I know what I should do. What I'm *supposed* to do. I should drop Ammy off tomorrow, a couple blocks away, so

Rina and Bea and everyone else never see me.

I should tell her it was great getting to know her but, for obvious reasons, we should never talk again.

I should tell her not to tell Rina, that it would only hurt her further. I should tell her to play down any stories about the stranger she met on the train, the stranger that Rina has already at least partially heard about—I've seen Ammy texting.

I know I should do all these things.

I owe it to the girl I loved for so long. The girl whose heart I broke, even if I didn't mean to, even if our relationship was far from perfect.

Even so, at the same time . . .

I don't want to do any of this.

I want to kiss Ammy again. I want to do more. I want to show her Hunter's campus in the city and get bagels the size of our heads. I want to watch bad movies with her. I want to take her to my favorite breakfast spot in Williamsburg, find out how she likes her eggs or if she even likes eggs at all. I want to argue with her about what would be faster—the subway or Citi Bike—and I want to know about her life, too. I want to go to Virginia, meet her mom, meet her friends. I want to ask her why she doesn't play lacrosse anymore. I want to know whether she calls it a remote control, like my dad, or a clicker, like my mom.

I want to tell her none of this matters, that we can find a way to work it out.

"Ammy," I say.

Immediately, I hear her breathing stop, as if she's holding it, playing dead. She's not asleep. I knew she wouldn't be.

"Ammy," I say again.

There's nothing. Her breathing resumes. She doesn't say a word.

AMMY

"AMMY?" HE SAYS FOR THE THIRD TIME.

Of course I'm not asleep, given that we only stopped arguing about ten minutes ago, but I'm exhausted.

Because I let myself feel something. I let myself break my own rule. And look what happened—I betrayed my new sister.

Yeah, I didn't know it, but I did it just the same. What if she ever found out? How crushed would she be? I spent the night with the guy who broke her heart so bad she deleted him from her whole life. So bad that she never even spoke to him again.

Even if he didn't mean to hurt her, even if all is fair in love and war or whatever, still. He was hers.

286

It's against the stepsister code.

Even the fake stepsister code.

My friendship with Kat is the only good thing to ever come out of my dad's betrayal.

It doesn't matter that we only spent ten days together, because those ten days mattered to me.

I'd always said that Dara and Simone were like sisters to me, but with Kat, it was different.

On my second night there, there was a knock on my door, just as I was reading and about to drift off to sleep. It was Kat. She came in, complained about Bea's snoring—they were doubling up so I could have my own room for the week—and she asked if she could sleep in my room instead. She grabbed a pillow from the bed and plopped down on the small couch in the corner. "Want to watch some *Friends* reruns or something?"

I actually hated *Friends*, but I didn't tell her that. I booted up my laptop and we picked one out on Netflix. She crawled into bed with me, and I propped the tiny screen in front of us. The show took on a new hilarity with Kat. Something about the way she laughed like crazy made Courteney Cox and Jennifer Aniston just a tad less annoying. We ended up watching four episodes and passing out sometime after 2:00 a.m.

It's not like we were besties. It's not like we shared every secret of our lives with each other or anything. It's not like we even ever hung out more than those ten days. But after I left, when I went back to school, we kept in touch. Texted each other stupid things and complained about our parents.

The usual. She wasn't my sister; she wasn't even my proper stepsister—she still isn't, because my dad and Sophie's ceremony carries all of zero legal weight—but I had a feeling that she could be.

And now I've screwed that up.

For a second, I remember what it was like to kiss Noah, how intense and addictive it felt to have his body on top of mine, skin on skin. I can still feel my hands in his hair, on his scalp, pulling him toward me. The memory sends an electric shock all the way through me, makes the tips of my fingers tingle and my stomach churn. My mind knows the truth, but it's like my body hasn't figured out how to catch up.

My skin suddenly feels fiery, and as I listen to him breathe—obviously not asleep, either—it's like I crave him. Part of me wants to crawl into bed, cuddle up to him, hold him tight, kiss him again, take everything off, feel what he's like beneath the Steelers jersey. Part of me doesn't want to stop until we're one.

Part of me thinks that none of this is fair. That Kat had him already, that clearly their relationship wasn't that good anyway. That maybe this is my chance to have something real.

That everyone else is fine with hurting others to get what they want.

Why can't I be, too?

I shake my head vigorously. I pull the covers up higher, as if I can protect myself, as if I can trap my stupid body with a mind of its own underneath all the layers.

I focus on the sound of the wind outside, the quietness around us—there can't be many cars on the road right now, if any.

"Ammy," he says again, and his voice sounds raw.

But I can't.

Because if I let myself give him even the tiniest of openings, who knows what will happen?

Then I really might just betray her.

PART THREE

HOMECOMING

NOAH

THE LIGHT SEEPS THROUGH THE WINDOW.

It's after seven, and I still haven't had any luck falling back asleep.

Frustrated, I toss my Kindle aside and turn toward Ammy.

She's on her side, facing me. She's kicked most of the comforters and blankets away, just as I have. Either the heat started working a lot better, or it's not as cold out now that the sun has risen. Her legs are bent, and her body is curled up into a little ball. One hand is underneath her pillow, and the other is flung overhead like someone tossed a doll and it didn't quite land right.

By my count, and her light snoring, I'd guess she fell asleep somewhere around six.

I might as well just accept it. I'm not going to sleep any more today.

I turn away, kick back the remaining linens, get out of bed. My phone's almost dead, and when I touch hers, it's black and turned off. Between the making out and the fighting, neither of us managed to plug in our phones last night or this morning.

I dig in my bag for my charger, grab an extra one, too, then plug in both mine and hers.

Then I load up the maps on mine. It's still fifty-five miles to Hudson, about an hour, assuming the roads are okay to drive.

I grab my jacket and creep to the other side of the room, skipping my shoes because hiking boots sound like too much of a pain to try and get on, then turn the handle.

The open door floods the room with light. I don't want to wake Ammy, so I step out immediately, blinking my eyes to adjust, trying to ignore the icy chill of the concrete balcony on my bare feet.

I pull the door almost shut so a big gust of cold air doesn't snake into the room, but I don't shut it all the way. The key is somewhere in my wallet, which is somewhere in the jeans I left in the bathroom. I don't want to go back in there and risk stepping on another bag of junk food, waking her again.

I peer over the edge of the balcony. I can't see the highway, because there are too many trees, but I can see the road we drove in on, and it looks much clearer already. There are snowdrifts on the side, but it's mostly asphalt and slush; the snow isn't falling anymore. The storm is finally over.

Looks like those fifty-five miles won't be so bad after all.

The knowledge is comforting and scary all at once. I know it's going to be awkward, every single minute of the last leg of our trip, but at the same time, I don't want it to end.

I bounce from one foot to the other as the cold starts to get to me. Just as I'm about to head back in, there's a strong gust of wind and an unmistakable . . .

Click.

I whip around to confirm.

Damn it.

I jiggle the handle. Nothing happens. It's locked. And even bootleg motels have good locks. I can't even try the credit card trick, because all I have on me is a pair of athletic shorts, a cotton tee that's feeling increasingly thin by the moment, and a winter coat with disappointingly empty pockets.

There's a sliver of space where the shade doesn't cover the window, and I peek through. Ammy is still asleep. I lift my hand to the window and briefly think about knocking on it, waking her up, but I know she's exhausted. I know she needs sleep.

So I drop my hand to my side. After all we've been through, the least I can do is let her sleep.

I STEP THROUGH the sliding glass doors into the lobby, my feet already freezing from walking the length of the balcony, down the stairs, along the sidewalk, and into here.

The smell of pancakes and bacon meets me. My stomach rumbles.

I step up to the desk, put on my most convincing smile for the older woman behind it. I think of what my public speaking professor said last semester: *Dress for how you'd like to be perceived.* Nothing I can do about that now, though.

I go for it anyway.

"Hi," I say.

"Did you forget something?" she asks, nodding to my feet. "You know, technically we're not supposed to serve anyone without shoes."

I want to make a joke about how I'd expect nothing less from the über-discerning Super 8, but I refrain.

"I'm so sorry." I glance at the plastic name tag affixed to her stiff polo shirt. "Angela. It's just that I got locked out of my room, and I was wondering if I *there was any way* I could get another key?"

She looks at me, her eyes daring me to explain why I was outside without shoes in the first place, but she starts typing on the computer.

"Room number?"

"Two oh one," I say.

She types some more. "Looks like you already received your two complimentary copies," she says. "Extra keys are five dollars."

"Fine," I say, reaching into my pocket almost on autopilot.

Damn it again.

"I don't have my wallet," I say. "It's locked in my room. Can I charge it to the room?"

She nods. "Just need an ID to put it on your room charge."

I sigh loudly. "But I don't have an ID. It's all in my wallet. Everything's in the room. Don't you get it?" I feel my voice rising, but I try to calm down.

"I'm sorry, sir," she says. "And there's no need for that tone."

I clear my throat. "Can't you make an exception? I can come right back down with five dollars. I promise. You don't even want to know about the last twenty-four hours I've had. I'm desperate," I say, feeling my eyes on the edge of tears. Being embarrassed but not caring at all.

The lady just stares at me, completely unsympathetic.

"*Please?*"

AMMY

I SEE AN ALERT ON MY PHONE AS SOON AS I WAKE UP.

It's plugged in. Noah must have done it.

I look over at Noah's side of the room. His bed is empty, like he's only just gotten out of it, and the bathroom door is open, so it's not like he's in there.

He probably went down to get coffee or something.

I pick up the phone. It's quarter after seven. There are two messages from Kat. I go into my messages to read them, already feeling raw and exposed, like this phone is a two-way mirror, and if I even click on her name, she'll be able to see what's happened, know what we've done.

But I do anyway. Both are from last night, around midnight.

298

Hunter, LOL, watch out for Hunter guys. My douchey ex goes there

And then five minutes later.

But you must tell me if anything goes down . . . I want all the deets!

My heart sinks. I feel so dirty, like I've done something so wrong. What in the world am I going to tell her? There's no way out of this but to lie. I don't like liars, and I hate that my dad lied to my mom—and me—for so long.

But I have to lie to Kat, because anything else would be wrong.

I imagine the conversation playing out, her coming to the door, wrapping me in a bony Kat hug, dragging me into my room, closing the door, and demanding all the details. She'll want to hear all about my night with a stranger.

And I'll have to lie: "Oh, nothing. It wasn't like that. We just got stuck is all. Now tell me—how was the wedding? What did I miss?"

It will sound as fake as my dad and Sophie's fake wedding. But she'll believe me, because she's Kat. She's loyal, at least until you fall from her graces. She's made it clear in the short time I've known her that she trusts me.

I don't want to lose her loyalty.

I should probably let her know when I'm coming back, but I can't do that until I find Noah. I head to the bathroom and quickly brush my teeth. Then I grab my sneakers and pull them on without messing with the laces—for once in the last twenty-four hours, they're dry. I don't bother changing out of my clothes from last night. All I want to do is find Noah so I can know when we're getting home and when this will all be over.

I grab my key from the nightstand and head to the door.

But I open it to see Noah standing there, no shoes, no proper clothing—nothing but shorts and a T-shirt and his stupid jacket.

His chin is shaking from the cold, and he bites his lip as if in pain. His eyes are puffy, like he's been crying or something.

"Jesus, what *happened* to you?"

NOAH

My adventure of the last fifteen minutes was completely pointless.

I step closer, and Ammy moves to let me in the room. I feel relief as soon as my feet hit the crappy carpet. It may not be plush and luxurious, but at least it's not concrete. I sit down on my bed cross-legged and pull the blanket over my legs, trying to warm them up.

"Are you okay?" she asks. "You look awful."

I laugh weakly. I hold up the little white piece of plastic that's caused me so much drama. "I forgot my key."

Ammy shakes her head and sits down opposite me. "Why did you go outside without shoes?"

I shrug and look down at my feet, unable to meet her gaze I'm so embarrassed.

"I just stepped out on the balcony to check to see if there was still snow on the road and if driving was going to be a problem. I had the door cracked open, but it got windy, and it blew shut, and then I had to go downstairs, and because it's a Super 8, they charge you for extra keys, but I didn't have any money, and the lady would only charge it to the room if I had an ID, and I looked like a creep with no shoes anyway, so it's not like she really had much motivation to help me, and so I went into the breakfast area, and I just asked a bunch of people until this older man took pity on me and gave me five dollars. That's how I got the key." I sigh. "So now we have three. In case you need an extra."

I look up, and her lips are pressed into a thin line. I'm sure this whole story has made her even angrier.

She starts laughing.

"I know," I say. "The whole thing is pathetic." I gesture around the room. "All of this is pathetic. I'm sorry."

"No." She stops laughing, but it looks like it takes some effort. "Just, why didn't you, you know, knock on the window? I would have let you in. I'm not *evil*."

I shrug. "I didn't want to wake you up. I figured we'd already been through enough. I didn't think depriving you of REM sleep was the best idea."

She laughs again, but then she stops, looks at me, her eyes quiet, thoughtful. "That's sweet," she says.

I think for a second that we could fix this, but then she looks down.

I do, too, rubbing at my feet through the blanket. They're starting to feel a bit better. So I've got that going for me, at least.

"Noah," she says, and I look up immediately, hoping against hope that she's thinking what I'm thinking, that we can find a way through this.

"Er, you want to get breakfast?" she asks. "Turns out Cheetos and Honey Buns don't exactly make the most filling dinner."

It's not what I wanted to hear, but I'll take it.

"Yeah," I say. "I do."

AMMY

7:28 A.M.

It smells like pancakes as soon as we get in the door. The older woman at the desk eyes Noah up and down. "I see you've elected to wear shoes this time," she says, mild disdain in her voice.

Noah smiles sheepishly. "I did."

"Come on," I say, following the smell of grilled sugar and butter to the dining area. "Ignore her."

There are a few trays lined up against the wall. Not-so-fresh fruit in a basket in the corner. Fake, dairy-less creamers in a variety of flavors next to tall pots of coffee. A waffle maker in the corner. It's not the downtown Asheville Sheraton continental breakfast, that's for sure, but it's not so bad for a cheap motel, all things considered. I step up to the end of the table and grab a plate.

Noah ignores the buffet, making a beeline for a table at the other end of the room, pulling out some money and handing it to an older guy who looks to be on his second plate of undercooked bacon. I can hear his embarrassed "sorry and thanks" from across the room.

Poor guy, I think.

And then not—not poor guy at all. Noah is reckless, with his relationships, with Kat, with his train trips, with me. It's not surprising that he'd recklessly step out into the winter cold without so much as a room key in his hand.

But he means well, the other part of me, the devil on my shoulder, argues. He only suggested we leave the train because he could see how upset I was. He only broke up with Kat because he knew it wasn't right. He only kissed me because he felt exactly what I did, that there was something special, different, between us.

In my AP English class this year, Mrs. Everett assigned us Plato's *Symposium*. Explained that our use of the term *platonic* is completely misguided, and that a platonic romance is actually one in which you find your other half, that Plato's story tells of how everyone was divided and went looking around for the other piece to complete them.

Though Dara and Simone couldn't have cared less, I found it fascinating. First, that we were all going around using the term completely incorrectly. Smart people, too.

But second—well, that someone as smart as freaking Plato could believe that such a love exists. That he could subscribe to something so cheesy, so obviously fake. Two halves searching the earth for each other? Please. Those lofty, stupid ideas were likely responsible for all the evil shit in the world, like my dad leaving my mom, like Sophie believing it was okay to just break up a marriage because she met a guy she thought was cute on an REI trip.

Like everyone who's ever said "love will find a way," "love is all you need," or "love is the answer" and meant it unironically. Because love isn't the answer, a lot of the time. At least not romantic love. Sometimes, the other kind—the loyal kind—is what really matters.

And yet—

When Noah was on top of me, when we kissed for hours, I couldn't help it. I thought of those words: platonic love.

And I thought—who knows? Maybe Plato was onto something?

NOAH

AMMY USES THE SUPER 8 WAFFLE IRON TO MAKE A waffle for both of us, while I load up on eggs, bacon, orange slices, a muffin, and a bowl of Cheerios.

I take a seat about as far from the old guy who lent me money as possible, and I dig into my Cheerios.

After a few minutes of waffle cooking, Ammy joins me.

She carefully forks half a piping-hot waffle onto my plate. There's no room, so she plops it on top of my eggs.

She tries to take a bite, but as soon as she raises it to her lips, she puts it right back down. "Too hot," she says.

"Want some eggs instead?" I ask.

"I'm okay," she says. She takes a sip of coffee.

She looks pensive, intellectual, all of a sudden.

307

"Random question for you."

I take another spoonful of Cheerios. Nothing feels right between us now, like where everything was easy before, it's now all off. "What's that?" I ask cautiously.

She stares at me for a second, like she's not sure whether she wants to ask. Then she touches her waffle with one finger but doesn't start cutting it or anything. Finally she opens her mouth to speak. "What do you think about platonic relationships?" she asks.

I put my spoon down. Raise an eyebrow.

On one hand, she could be hinting at the fact that there will be nothing between us, *ever*, if I understand *platonic* to mean what everyone else thinks it means.

On the other?

She reads Murakami. She knows I'm a comparative lit major. She's exactly the kind of person who *would* know what Plato really meant.

I take a sip of coffee, biding my time, wondering what in the hell she wants me to say. A half hour ago, I was only hoping to get us both where we're going without any more fighting.

But now?

Between the way she looked at me when I came into the room, with kindness in her eyes, and the way she looks now, asking me this strange, leading question . . . I don't know.

I put my coffee down. "I think it's real, especially when you meet the right person, someone you just click with, you know, right away . . ." My voice drifts off.

She stares at me a second, and in her eyes I know it for sure: she knows exactly what Plato meant.

She hesitates, and it's like she's standing on the edge of some sort of precipice in her mind, waiting to make a decision.

After a second or sixty—I can hardly tell—she drops her gaze. Cuts at her waffle quickly, like she's trying to destroy it, break it apart.

"Got enough food?" she asks without looking at me.

I'm a little surprised by the quick change of subject, but I smile, cock my head to the side. "I'm kind of a nervous eater," I say.

"What's there to be nervous about?" she asks, looking at me straight again.

She doesn't wait for me to answer. "Seriously," she says. "We only have—what?—a couple of hours left together, tops. And then we're never going to see each other again. And neither of us is ever going to tell Kat about anything. So why are you nervous?"

My face falls, and I shove a spoonful of Cheerios into my mouth. Then another. And another.

When I'm done scarfing them down, Ammy looks me in the eye.

"Did you think that just because I felt bad for you being stuck out in the cold I was going to be okay with betraying Kat?"

I shake my head.

"Or that just because you read Plato's *Symposium*, I'm

going to, like, want to date you in secret or something?"

Of course I didn't.

Did I?

"I just—"

Ammy puts her fork down. "You just thought if you did one sweet thing for me, if you said the right words— whatever—that I'd forget about that tiny little fact that you and I are a completely horrible idea?"

"No, really, I—"

Ammy pushes her chair back. "You know what? I'm not hungry."

She stands up quickly.

I get up to follow her, but she turns around and looks at me, glaring. "Don't follow me, okay? We're not in a movie. It's not cute."

Then she stomps out of the room, and I'm left staring at my huge plate of food and trying to avoid the pity-filled looks from everyone around me.

I take another spoonful of Cheerios, but they're somehow already soggy.

AMMY

I TURN AROUND TO CHECK THE BALCONY ONCE I GET
to the room. Noah hasn't tried to follow me. After the look I
gave him, I'm not sure who would.

I'm assuming he has a key, that I haven't forced him out
into the cold again. At least he has shoes, I remind myself. I'm
not a totally horrible person, because he has shoes.

I slip the key in the slot so hard and fast that nothing happens. I do it again. And again. And again. I stomp my foot
and let out an audible sigh. Luckily, there's no one around.
No one to see me being a child and throwing a tantrum over
a computerized key entry system.

I push the card in again, slowly this time. I swear it's like
the CIA up in here.

311

My eyes begin to water, but after a pause that seems almost endless, the little light flashes green and beeps. I turn the knob and push the door open.

The room is a mess, and the second I walk in, I get a flash of last night. Of Noah on top of me. The weight of his body. His lips.

I shake my head, pushing it away, focusing on the feeling, the confusion, the insanity, of seeing those photos of him and Kat in his bag.

I pull my suitcase up onto the bed and start to arrange it. It's a mess of books, clothes, my dirty socks from when I changed them in the art museum, the ticket from the train ride, an errant Skittles wrapper, and a bunch of playing cards that Noah swept off the bed last night.

I start with the cards, even though they're his. Something about having his stuff all mixed into mine really bothers me. Only serves to remind me that our lives were already stupidly intertwined before he even sat down next to me.

Reminds me that the worst coincidence in the world is stealing the only thing that's given me happiness in a while.

I pick them up, one by one, trying to calm my nerves. My thoughts. Everything. I should never have asked Noah that stupid question. As soon as he said his stupid answer, about finding the right person and that platonic love really is possible and all that bullshit, I got mad.

I got mad because he said the right thing.

The thing that I could only dream of someone saying about me.

I got mad because I was afraid that if I didn't get mad, I would do something stupid.

Even after knowing everything I did, I was tempted to be like my dad. Throw everything—family, loyalty, all of it—away, just because I had some swoony feelings.

When I'm done with my bag, I zip it up, then head to the bathroom to collect my toothbrush and toothpaste.

I stare at myself in the mirror. I don't have any makeup on, and my eyes are puffy from not enough sleep. My hair is a mess. I haven't washed it, which means I haven't dried it and straightened it and all that jazz, so it's starting to wave, frizz, rebel, and become its natural self. Normally, I wouldn't be caught dead in front of a cute guy like this.

I hear the beep of the door unlocking. It must be him.

Stop it, Ammy, I think. You've got to stop this.

I toss the toothpaste in the bag, tuck my hair behind my ears, wipe any tiny remains of mascara from under my lids with the tip of my finger.

Then I head out.

He's standing there, just in front of the door, looking awkward, like we're playing that silly game everyone used to play as kids where the ground is lava, and if you touch it, you die.

I hang by the bathroom door, as if I'm afraid to get too close, too.

"Is it okay I came up?" he asks. "I'm done with breakfast, so . . ."

"Fine," I say, looking away immediately, over to his backpack in the corner. "Are you ready to go?"

He nods. "Five minutes."

"Cool," I say, as calm, cold, and unemotional as I can muster. "I'm going to check out. Just meet me downstairs when you're ready."

I cross the room, toss my toiletry bag into my suitcase, zip it up again, and grab my key on the nightstand. I grab the pack of cards, too.

"These are yours," I say, chucking them onto the bed.

"Thanks. Do you need help carrying your stuff?"

"No," I say brusquely, avoiding his eyes.

"Okay, then," he says. He shifts his weight from foot to foot, nervously, but I just grab my suitcase, toss on my coat, and push past him.

In seconds, I'm out the door.

I pause, listening to the door shut behind me, taking a deep breath of the fresh winter air. It's like, for a second, all the bad stuff is locked away, in that room. Like we can leave it there, like you'd leave a glove on a ski slope or a new book on the seat of a train. You'd remember it, miss it, maybe, but it would be gone. No way for it to come back and haunt you. Because there would be no real way to get what was missing back.

I walk down the balcony slowly. The sun is higher in the sky now, and the brightness is welcome after the dark of the motel room. The air feels good now that there's not a biting wind—crisp, but not too cold. The lack of snow is refreshing.

I pause at the top of the stairs, roll my suitcase just up to the ledge and then stop.

I let myself do it, just for a second.

I imagine turning around, abandoning my suitcase, shoving the plastic card in and out however many times it takes to get the door unlocked, swinging it open, seeing his face, his eyes, his body, the whole essence of Noah, running up to him, wrapping my arms around him, and kissing him until we fall back onto the bed.

It sends a warmth, a heat, through my body, a contrast against the chill around me.

I turn for a second and stare at the door.

But then I turn back around, grab my suitcase, lift it up, and start down the stairs.

NOAH

8:06 A.M.

WE PULL OUT OF THE PARKING LOT IN SILENCE. There are fifty-five miles left on the drive, just over an hour. She'll be home, to Rina's, by nine fifteen. I know she's missed everything that she wanted to be there for. But at least she'll be there.

It's weird how even if I hadn't met this girl, I was destined to fail from the beginning. I somehow managed to decide to profess my love for Rina on the day her mom was getting married.

The roads are slushy, last night's blanket of white tainted with dirt and grime and exhaust. It reminds me how beautiful things can change.

The phone lady doles out directions. She's the only one talking in the car.

It's silent for a few miles before I can't take it anymore.

"Maybe some music?" I ask. "If that's okay?"

I laugh to myself, remembering my demeanor just the night before: "Want to get us hooked up with some tunes?" I was so happy then; there was so much promise.

I wanted to be with Ammy then, that much was already clear. I was telling myself that I still owed everything to Rina, but I knew that wasn't how it was going to turn out.

She did, too.

We were taking our time, enjoying step after step to the inevitable destination. I knew it when we hugged in the Enterprise, when we got in the car, when we stepped into that motel room, when I sat down on her bed, when we pretended, for however long, to care about Go Fish.

"What do you want to listen to?" she asks. Her voice is as monotone as the phone lady's. Not angry. Not excited. Just . . . empty.

I shrug. "Maybe something off of yours? Whatever you want."

"Okay," she says. She fishes her phone out of her bag and begins to flick through her songs.

She's going through her library, the car weirdly quiet without music, when I hear a rumble.

She keeps flicking, but then it goes again.

"Is that your stomach?" I ask, almost laughing, but

knowing full well that I don't have the luxury of laughing with her. Not anymore.

She shrugs and chooses a song. It's slow and sad. *Subtle, Ammy,* I want to say. Very subtle. I imagine a world, an alternate universe, where everything is okay and this is just the beginning. Years from now, we'll be joking about how we first met, and we'll finish each other's sentences, telling how I walked onto her train, how everything went wrong, how we almost lost each other, and then when we get to the part about this car ride, I'll tease her for playing this song. For being so obvious about it.

It would be a good part of the story, the part where we would laugh about how it almost didn't work out. How if either of us were a touch more proud or stubborn or lazy, it never would have happened.

But we're glad, so glad, in this alternate universe. Because it did work out. It's still working out.

That's when I'd slip my hand in hers, and I'd ask if she needed more wine, and I'd leave her to mingle with the other professors and professors' spouses while I refilled our drinks at the elaborate oak bar at the speakeasy-style establishment of the annual faculty Christmas party.

Her stomach rumbles again, shaking me out of my reverie. My silly, pointless reverie.

"Do you want to stop and get something?" I ask.

She shrugs. "What's the point?"

I grip the wheel tighter as we go right through a pile of

slush that the sun hasn't yet seen fit to destroy. "We have over an hour left, and that's without traffic. It's still technically part of winter break for a lot of people, so you never know. Plus, a lot of people probably got stuck last night like we did. Who knows how many people will be on the road? If you want to eat something, you should."

She sighs. "I should have just eaten at the motel. It was stupid. Waste food and waste money just to make a point."

The road opens up and so does the valley, and with the sun shining down on us it's really quite beautiful. I should savor these moments, even though she'll never have me. I'll still remember that time that I really, truly was inspired by a girl. Cared about her like she was a part of myself. I know it's only been a day. But when you know, you know, my mom always says. Like with the Cheetos outside the train station.

She knew then, and I know now.

Of course, it doesn't fix a damn thing, because everything is already way too messed up.

Still.

I *know*.

"It was a good point, at least," I offer.

She scoffs. "Yeah," she says. "Right."

I glance over at her, but she looks straight ahead. Avoiding me. "It was. Maybe I was getting a little ahead of myself. And I did think you were just going to put it all behind you because I did something that wasn't even that nice or special. All I did was not wake you up."

She crosses her arms. "It was nice," she says. "That's not the point."

"What's the point, then?" I ask.

She sighs. "The point is that even though you did something nice—even though you *are* nice—it's still not okay, because she's my family."

I take a deep breath. "I know."

Up ahead, I see a highway sign adorned with those signature golden arches. "I'm going to stop up there," I say. "Get you something to eat."

She just shrugs. "Okay," she says. "Whatever you want. It doesn't matter anyway."

I'm not sure if she's talking about the food or us or what, but I take the exit anyway, because if there's any way we can figure this out, if there's any way at all . . .

Well, damn it, I have to try.

AMMY

WE PULL UP TO THE DRIVE-IN WINDOW, AND A MUF-fled but somehow still very loud voice calls out through the black box. "Welcome to McDonald's, can I take your order?"

I look at him. "Egg McMuffin and hash browns."

Noah rattles off my order, plus a sausage biscuit, and we pull around.

"You're eating *again*?" I ask.

He just turns to me and shrugs.

"Right," I say. "Nervous eater."

He nods. "It's true."

I look out the window. "I'm sorry I was so bitchy about that, back in the motel."

"You weren't bitchy," he says as we follow a shitty old

Toyota in front of us, taking our spot in front of the window.

"I know I was," I say. "It's okay."

A girl about our age hands us our orders, and Noah pulls ahead, rolling into a spot.

I unwrap mine on my lap. Then I just stare at it. My stomach was rumbling a minute ago, but now it's hard to focus on eating, sitting here in the car like this with him.

Noah bites into his. I seriously don't even understand how he's eating right now.

"Not hungry after all?" he asks.

I pick a tiny piece off of my hash browns and pop it into my mouth. It's too greasy, too salty. I lift the sandwich to my mouth but put it down before I can take a bite. I turn to Noah. He's somehow already polished off his sandwich. "I know I should eat, but it's hard."

"Want me to help you with that?" he asks with a smile.

I manage a small smile back.

"Will you be honest with me?" I ask.

He doesn't look away, doesn't pause, doesn't flit his eyes around the car—nothing. "Yes."

"Did you know when you saw me on the train?" I ask.

He shakes his head. "No."

I believe him.

"What about when I said that my stepmom taught yoga?"

His eyes look away for a second, then back at me. "I thought, that's funny, Rina's mom teaches yoga, too. But a lot of people teach yoga in Hudson. And in Woodstock, which is only like forty minutes away. It wouldn't be that nuts."

"You could have asked me," I say. "You could have asked me what her last name was."

He stares at me. "You could have asked me what Rina's last name was, too. You could have asked to see a picture. I could have asked what the house looked like, or the exact address you were going to. I could have picked up your phone and saw that you were texting a girl named Kat. But I didn't. You didn't. I had no reason to think that something so weird would be true. I had no reason to ask questions, because in my mind, you and Rina were worlds apart."

I look back at my sandwich, then back at him.

"Okay, so you promised to be honest, right?"

He nods.

"Whatever I ask."

He nods again.

I take a deep breath. Here goes. "What did you think when I told you my stepsister was named Kat?"

He closes his eyes briefly. Opens them again. I can tell it's difficult for him. I can see traces of guilt on his face as he speaks. "I hoped it was a coincidence."

"But you thought . . ."

"I thought I didn't really care about anything else besides the fact that I wanted to kiss you."

I look away, embarrassed. And hurt. And excited, all at the same time. Because I was worth it—even with all the guilt he must feel about betraying Kat, even though the prospect of us actually being together is null and void, even with all that—he wanted me so badly that he didn't care.

And it makes me feel vibrant. Alive.

And horrible just the same.

I turn to look at him, and he's staring at me, lips parted like he's got something to say.

"What are you thinking now?" I ask. I'm hoping and praying he'll say one thing and hoping and praying at the same time that he'll say the complete opposite.

"I'm thinking I don't really care about anything else besides the fact that I want to kiss you."

And that's what finally gets me to take a bite of my sandwich.

Because I don't know what on earth I'm supposed to say to that.

NOAH

I PULL OUT OF THE PARKING LOT AS SHE FINISHES her sandwich.

Should I have said anything about wanting to kiss her? Of course not.

I know that Good Noah would have kept his mouth shut.

Good Noah would probably never have kissed her in the first place, if there was even an ounce of worry about her being related to Kat.

Good Noah wouldn't have exploded at Rina without ever once telling her before how much her trying to change him hurt him.

Or kissed a girl three days later and made the breakup hurt her as badly as it did.

325

Or any of the thousands of steps that have led me here.

That's the problem. I *am* here.

I pull back onto the highway, meet a vision of sky and trees and mountains in the distance. More of the slush has melted, and though there is still white on the ground and in the trees, it's almost hard to believe the storm happened. Just hours ago, we were spinning off the road, holding on to each other, *literally*, for dear life. It's hard to believe I might never see this person I shared this crazy experience with again.

We have fifty miles to go.

I can't help it that the air in the car feels electric, that I *do* want to kiss her again. I glance over at Ammy. She's finished her sandwich and is rolling up the paper, stuffing it in the bag, tucking it into the side door compartment.

Even now, without makeup, with the tiniest bit of ketchup from her hash browns on the corner of her lip, she looks more beautiful than anyone I've ever seen.

Even the way she crumples McDonald's wrappers looks adorable to me.

"I'm sorry," I say. "For saying that before."

She looks at me, but there isn't anger in her eyes anymore. At least I don't think there is. She just looks . . . tired. "You don't have to keep apologizing," she says. "It doesn't change things. It doesn't make it better. And I don't want you to feel guilty. There's no point."

"Can I ask you a question?"

She nods.

"And you promise to answer honestly?"

She purses her lips for a second, as if debating whether she really does want to be honest with me. "All right," she says. "Go ahead."

I pick up speed, feel the growl of the Mustang's engine, marvel, for the smallest of seconds, that I'm driving a Mustang with a beautiful girl through one of the most scenic parts of my home state. I wish I could pull over, take her hand, ask her to come with me and make a snow angel. Our clothes would get wet, and we'd find an adorable café in one of the millions of adorable little towns up here, and we'd get hot chocolates or vanilla lattes, and we'd laugh about how we'd pretended to be kids only moments ago. And then we'd go back to my parents' basement, and no one would be home, and we'd kiss until our lips hurt. And we'd order pizza from the best place in town, and we'd watch *The Godfather: Part II*—my favorite, which I'm assuming she also loves because she's cool like that—and we wouldn't care if it started snowing again, because we'd have each other, and that would be enough. . . .

Ammy clears her throat. "Um, do you have a question?"

I hesitate for a second, but screw it, I want to know. "All right, if I wasn't Rina's—sorry, Kat's—ex, would you want to see me again?"

She whips her head toward me. "What is the point of that question?"

I sigh. "I don't know," I say. "If the answer is no, then I'll feel a lot better."

She looks back ahead of her and shrugs. "I don't know

what to tell you," she says.

"You said you'd be honest."

She looks at me, with her doe eyes and her small mouth and all of the features of her perfect, beautiful face. I want to draw them. I want to learn how to draw just so I can draw her.

"The honest answer isn't going to make you feel any better."

AMMY

KAT IS TEXTING ME, AND EVERY SINGLE MESSAGE IS painful, hits a new nerve.

Are you on the road? When do you get here?

I know you missed the wedding, but I can't wait to see you!

I wanna hear about your night with a stranger . . . get it grrrrrrrl

I turn to Noah. "What time do you think we'll get there?"

He glances down at the clock on the dash. "Nine forty-five, I think. We're only about twenty-five miles away. Is that okay?"

I nod. "I need to let Kat know."

Her name hangs in the air between us, accusatory and sad.

Noah shakes his head. "I would never intentionally hurt her, you know."

I bite my lip. "Yeah, me either."

But it doesn't change the fact that our very presence here would hurt her if she knew about it.

It doesn't change the fact that I have no choice but to lie to my stepsister. To my friend.

I text Kat the ETA and assure her that nothing happened with the guy, marvel at how the lies have already begun—and I'm trying to do the right thing, I really am.

But it's hard to know what in the world the "right" thing is now.

I check for more messages from my mom, but thankfully, there's nothing, so I put my phone away and stare out the window. It's beautiful out. The sun is shining, glinting off the snowcapped trees, like we're driving through some kind of painting or something. There isn't a billboard in sight, unlike the highways in Virginia—no fast food joints or cheap diesel fuel. It's just us and the trees.

I let myself pretend, for a minute, that Noah never dated Kat, that he's just a guy I met, maybe my first year of college, or at my summer job, or through friends, or whatever. I pretend it's our first road trip. That we're nervous about taking our relationship to that next level. The one where you don't just go on dates here and there, you don't just make out while pretending to play video games, you actually travel together. Go somewhere, just the two of you.

"It is such a gorgeous day," I'd say, and I'd reach for his hand.

Noah would probably say something cheesy, and I'd roll my eyes. But then all he'd need to do is squeeze my hand, and that would tell me everything. That he's glad we're here together, that he's looking forward to whatever the future brings.

I shake my head. That's not why we're here. And pretending won't change it. Pretending won't fix a thing.

"I know you never meant to hurt her," I say, finally getting the nerve to put into words what's been kicking around in my head since I found out the truth.

"Thanks," he says, laughing weakly. "You don't sound very convinced, though."

I take a deep breath, pause.

He turns to me. "What is it?"

"I'm trying to find the right words. Hold on."

He smiles. "I like that about you. That you care about finding the right words."

I feel the now familiar, delicious feeling—that of being appreciated, and not just being appreciated, but being appreciated by someone I truly, genuinely, like. I ignore it.

"It's just that sometimes even if you don't mean to hurt people, you do."

I think about my dad, and for the first time ever I feel the strangest thing—a flash of empathy.

Maybe he never wanted to hurt my mom or me at all. Not really.

"I know," Noah says. "That's what's so hard for me."

"What do you mean?" I ask.

He takes a deep breath and flicks on his blinker, pulling into the right lane behind a minivan that can't be going too much over sixty, almost like he has to slow the car down to have this conversation.

"Hurting people. I don't like it at all."

I turn to face him. "No one likes it."

He shakes his head. "I know. Of course. I don't mean that you do like it, even if you are a little snarkier than I am." He looks over and gives me a half smile. "But I *really* don't like it. I don't like arguing. Or confrontation. It makes me feel uncomfortable. I think maybe that's why I never told Rina how much she was hurting me by cutting me down all the time. I was afraid it was like I was calling her a bad girlfriend or something, and she wasn't. Really, she wasn't."

He takes a deep breath, but he doesn't stop talking. "Maybe that's why I wanted to come back here. I thought I wanted her back, I did, but now I think I just wanted to say I was sorry. It all happened so fast that I never really got a chance to do that."

He sighs. "She might have taken me back, that's the scary part. I'd have missed her last night because she'd have been at the wedding, but I'd have found her today. And she might have said yes. It would have been bad. I would have hurt her even more. We're not good for each other anymore. Who knows? Maybe we never really were. I wanted to make it work, but in the end, we weren't right. She wanted me to be different. She deserves to be with someone who's exactly what she wants. It was good that I met you, in that way. It was so we didn't put each other through that."

His words cut at me, because he's suddenly so raw, and he's sharing so much of himself with me, and if it were in any other setting or situation, it would make me feel absolute *elation*.

But not like this.

"I wish you would have figured that out with someone else," I say. "Someone at Hunter, whatever. Not me."

He shakes his head. "No, you don't."

"I do," I say.

But that's what kills me. I don't.

After all this, I don't.

I think about my dad. Was he doing the right thing after all? Does Sophie make him happier than my mom ever could? Would he and my mom have split up even if Sophie had never come into the picture?

Of course he should have figured it out on his own. He shouldn't have done what he did and broken us apart.

But what if, in some strange, crazy way, it was what was supposed to happen?

If it hadn't, I'd never have seen him as happy as he seems to be now.

I'd never have even come up here.

I'd never have met Noah.

Still, I think about my mom, about the masses of texts I could barely stand to read, and suddenly it doesn't matter.

Because sometimes, it doesn't matter if you're happier in the end. It doesn't matter if it was the right thing for you.

Because actions hurt people. They hurt my mom.

And if Noah and I ever did anything, they'd hurt Kat.

And I don't like that. I don't like that at all.

NOAH

I DON'T KNOW HOW MANY TIMES I'VE DRIVEN DOWN Cortland Road.

Hundreds, if not thousands, in all the years of me and Rina. We've made out in my car, parked in front of her house. Argued in the yard. Driven down this street in good moods and bad. Everything in between.

It is weird and odd and unnerving to be driving down this road with Ammy.

I drive past the house Bryson and Rina and I egged once, before we felt so bad that we cleaned it up immediately. The street where Rina's friend Jessica used to live, before she moved to Florida.

The house that is supposed to have the nicest pool, that

335

Bryson was always trying to get us to sneak into, because they were city people who were only there half the time. We never did, because we were too scared.

There are so many memories on this street. Ones that are supposed to be over. I'm supposed to be moving on from this.

Yet here I am, driving down Cortland Road again.

What memories does this street already hold for Ammy? The nervousness of meeting a new family. The judgy, uppity tone of Rina's mom. The return from a swim in Claverack Creek, clothes wet and skin burned.

"In point two miles, your destination will be on the left."

There's no time left. Ammy's been quiet since she told me that I was wrong, that she wasn't glad she met me. Her silence is proof enough that she meant it.

We had our moment—one night that I'll remember for a long, long time—but it's over. I'll never see Ammy again. I'll never speak to Rina again, even as friends, for fear of lying or hurting her any worse.

I'll never drive down Cortland Road after this.

"Maybe you should stop a couple of blocks away," Ammy says. "I don't want Kat to come out and see you."

"That's what I was going to do," I say. I go another block, then I pull over in front of the big red monstrosity of a house that Rina's mom always hated. I put the car into park, let the engine idle.

I wish there was something else to say.

I wish there was *anything* to say.

Ammy unclicks her seat belt, then stares straight ahead.

"I would help you carry your suitcase," I say, "but I guess that would defeat the whole point."

She laughs. It's forced. "You just couldn't let me go without trying to carry my suitcase one more time, could you?"

I laugh weakly.

She reaches for the door.

I want to stop her, so badly. I want to reach over and kiss her again, but I know it's wrong.

I want to find a way for us to be . . . *something*.

The problem is—I have no idea how.

AMMY

MY HAND SHAKES AS I REACH FOR THE DOOR.

I'm not kidding, it freaking shakes.

And my heart beats fast.

And my face feels hot.

And my body feels all prickly and raw.

"Can you open the trunk?" I ask.

"Sure," Noah says, and he reaches down and pulls the lever.

I shrug into my coat and finally get the nerve to open the door.

Noah gets out on his side, too.

The tiny trunk is open, and Noah pulls out my bag and pushes it toward me. I grab the handle, laugh to myself about how crazy it was to drag the suitcase over open, snowy fields—only yesterday.

I wish that there was an opportunity for Noah to carry my suitcase again. Even though the whole idea is totally anti-feminist and annoying.

I look up at Noah. "Well, thanks," I say. "For getting me home."

He nods, closes his eyes, and opens them again.

"Don't forget to tell your grandkids about our little adventure," I say.

His mouth forms the smallest of smiles. "You too."

"Well, this is it, I guess," I say. The wind blows through the branches above us, and snow falls from the twigs, like it's a storm again, just for a moment. Just for us.

Noah steps forward, almost like he's going to hug me, but I'm afraid of what will happen if he does, so I take a step back.

"Good luck at Hunter," I say. "And let me know how much I owe you for the car and motel and everything. Er, message me on Facebook or something. But don't friend me. Because, uh—"

He shakes his head. "I got it. I won't."

And I turn around, drag my suitcase up and over the curb, and walk away as quickly as I can.

I don't look back, because I know if I do that, every ounce of reserve will be lost.

I know that if I do, I'll make a mistake.

NOAH

She doesn't look back.

Not even once.

She lugs her suitcase down the road, one step after the next, and I pray that she turns around, runs back, like they do in the movies.

I could stop her.

Run after her, reach out and touch her, hope that she feels the same way as I do.

Then what?

We would make out, right in front of Rina's house?

A car whips past me, and on the other side of the road, a guy shovels his driveway, and I feel small. Other people are

340

going on, about their days, recovering from the storm, drinking their coffee, reading the *New York Times*.

Ammy and I are just a blip on the radar.

A non-blip, because Ammy and I will *never* be anything.

She's almost out of sight. She still doesn't turn back.

Another man comes out with a shovel in hand. A woman with a bucket of salt.

A car goes by.

Ammy turns, vanishes out of sight, behind a clump of trees.

It's over.

I shut the trunk, shuffle into the road, around the side of the car, open the door, get inside. I feel like I'm on autopilot, like a door has shut forever.

I know it's the right thing to do for Rina. I know she deserves not to be hurt anymore. This is the last time for me on this street—and that's how it should be.

I load Facebook and find Ammy. It's an unusual first name, so it's not hard. The photo is a close-up of her face. She's got bright red lipstick on, and she looks beautiful. My thumb hovers over the friend button even though I said I wouldn't. I wish I could, but I know I can't.

It feels wrong, I think, as I stare at her profile.

It took a train breakdown and a missed bus and a trek through the snow and so many little adventures for me to learn, but I finally got to know what it was like to be with the person who brings out the best in you.

Now I'm supposed to just walk away from that? It doesn't feel right.

Nothing about it feels right at all.

AMMY

I DRAG MY SUITCASE ACROSS THE GRASS IN FRONT OF the farmhouse.

The gravel drive isn't exactly suited to a rolling suitcase, and I don't want to make a lot of noise, because I can't bear the thought of Kat coming out right now, hugging me, asking me for all the details—everything.

I just want to go in quietly, put my suitcase down, take a deep breath, and mentally unpack all that happened. I stare at the beautiful white house, at the porch with the rickety steps and the red door. At the hanging "NAMASTE" wooden sign that Sophie bought in Woodstock.

I stop at the steps.

343

I imagine my dad inside, talking over breakfast about the ceremony with Sophie.

He's happy, I realize. I knew it when I came here last summer.

I *hated* him for it. It was so unfair, when he'd hurt us so badly.

But the thing is, I hated my mom for being unhappy, too. I hated her for letting him break her like he did. I hated her for expecting me to fix everything by listening to her constantly.

I just wanted her to be a mom. I just wanted her to take care of me.

And maybe that's why I'm here, after all. Maybe it's not about the ceremony or any of that. Maybe it's just that I know that my dad is in a better place to be a parent right now than she is.

Maybe, after everything, that's really what I needed.

I'm about to open the door and go in when my phone rings.

I check it. It's my mom. My heart begins to race.

I want to ignore her, do what I've been doing for the last twenty-four hours, text her that I'm okay but that I don't want to talk.

But I don't.

She might not be perfect, she might have hurt me, too, just like he did. But she's still my mom, even if she hasn't been acting like much of one these last few months.

"Hey," I say.

I brace myself for the yelling, for the rush of anxiety, for the reprimands about me going. For everything.

"Ammy," she says. "You answered. You're at Dad's?"

This time it's not a lie. "Yeah."

I can hear her breath catch. I can hear that it's hard for her, imagining me up here, with them, playing at family when she's not invited.

"I don't want to ask you about the ceremony," she says. "And I'm sorry I did last night. I know it will only make me upset." She takes a deep breath. "I just wanted to say that I'm sorry for yelling at you." I hear her voice waver, but she doesn't stop talking. "I'm sorry for everything since he left. I called my therapist this morning, and I'm going to start getting help again. I know I can't rely on just you anymore. You have every right to be in your father's life. I'm sorry, sweetie. I really am."

I feel tears on my cheeks, taste salt on my lips. My voice cracks even more than hers did. "It's okay, Mom."

There's something so painful about your parents apologizing to you. Something that cuts you to your core. Because you're supposed to be the one who messes up, not them.

But sometimes that's not how it goes. Not with mine. Not with Noah's. Not with Kat's.

Even parents are human. Even parents make mistakes.

"I know you're just doing what you need to do. I want you to know that. And that I love you. And that I never want anything with your dad to come between us. Okay?"

I nod, wiping the tears away. "Okay. I'm sorry I abandoned you. I'm sorry Dad did, too."

She sighs. "You didn't do anything wrong. And your dad, well, he's not perfect, but I'm not, either. I'm trying to forgive him. I really am. I'm trying to be as strong as you are."

And that's what really gets me. That's what makes the tears stream as I'm standing out on the porch. I wipe them away.

"I love you so much, Mom," I say.

"I love you, too, baby. Be safe up there. Call me tomorrow, okay?"

"Okay."

She says bye and I love you again, and then she hangs up.

I stand there, staring at my phone.

And then I look back at where I walked from.

He's probably long gone. He's probably halfway to his house by now.

And even if he isn't, I shouldn't.

But there's this thing that kills me.

It's that if my mom can forgive my dad, if she can at least try, then, I don't know, maybe anything is possible.

Maybe when you're lucky enough to meet someone who makes you feel like this, well, maybe it means something. Maybe you're not just supposed to throw it away. Maybe you're supposed to chase it, like I chased that stupid bus. Maybe you're supposed to chase it until you're out of breath.

Still, I made it clear enough in the car that we should

never see each other again.

It's the right thing to do.

It's the only thing to do.

So I turn back around, grab my suitcase, and take the first step.

NOAH

I CLOSE FACEBOOK AND THEN MESS WITH MY PHONE, trying to find something to listen to. I settle on Taylor Swift, the poppiest album I have. I need something to cheer me up. To distract me. Sad indie music is certainly not going to do it.

I'm connecting it to the Bluetooth when I hear a knock on the window.

I turn, and I can hardly breathe.

It's Ammy, standing there, like I hoped she would be. Like I imagined.

Except I'm not imagining it. It's real.

I roll down the window.

"Did you forget something?" I ask nervously.

She shakes her head. "Can I get in?"

I nod.

She opens the door and gets inside. Her eyes are a little red, but she looks happier than I've seen her this whole time. She looks, in some strange way, relieved.

"Nice music choice," she says.

I smile. "I had to drown my sorrows with pop."

She laughs.

I turn it down.

"I wanted to change my answer," she says.

I raise an eyebrow. "Your answer for what?"

"My biggest regret," she says. There's a smile on her lips.

"Okay. . . ."

She takes a deep breath. "My biggest regret is walking away from you."

My heart starts beating faster. It somehow becomes even more difficult to breathe normally.

She smiles at me. "I guess it's not really a regret, because I just fixed it. But it would have been my biggest regret if I hadn't," she says. "And I don't want that."

I don't know what to say, and she laughs. "All of this sounded a lot more eloquent and less cheesy in my head."

I laugh, too, but deep down, my heart is soaring, threatening to beat so hard it could send the Mustang shaking. "I don't want that, either."

She reaches out, hands me a receipt.

"What's this?" I ask.

"It's my number," she says. "I would type it into your phone, but like I said, paper is better than digital. Call me sometime."

She leans forward and kisses me, ever so lightly, on the lips.

And then she opens the door and walks away.

EPILOGUE

AMMY

11:02 A.M.

THE TRAIN STILL DOESN'T FEEL ROMANTIC, BUT maybe that's because I've done it four or five times now.

The journey from Bard isn't long—just a ten-minute ride to the Rhinecliff station and then a little under two hours on the Amtrak. Of course, nothing is long compared to last year's journey, that's for sure. Now every time I do this ride, it feels easy.

My bag is tucked neatly in the overhead bin. It's smaller, but still has wheels. My dad got me new luggage for graduation. My old one wasn't exactly in the best shape when I arrived at his door last January. My punched ticket is tucked into the seat ahead of me.

I stare out the window. The sun is shining brightly, and

the trees are getting fuller every day. Spring is beautiful here. It's what I learned last year when I came up for my spring break—and again for two weeks in May, after graduation. My mom didn't argue with me those times. I think she almost enjoyed the time on her own. It's funny—after last January, something was different. Like, without being angry at my dad anymore—without it consuming her all the time, at least—she finally had the space to get better.

I'm not saying everything magically changed. She still has anxiety attacks every couple of months. She still has days she needs to take Ativan. But it's okay. We get through it.

She even managed to back my decision to go to college at Bard so I could spend more time with my dad and Sophie and Kat and Bea.

She didn't like it at first, but she accepted it eventually.

My phone died this morning, so I dig around for my backup charger in my purse and plug it in, because everyone seems to freak out now if I'm not communicative when I'm traveling, even somewhere that's not that far at all. It takes a minute, but it finally comes to life. There are two new texts.

I open my mom's first.

Be careful in the Big Apple. Keep your Mace on you! Let me know when you get to Kat's!

I laugh. My mom is always calling it "the Big Apple." I don't have the heart to tell her that she sounds ridiculous.

The next one is from Kat.

So turns out Joey has to pick up a shift at the diner tonight, so it's just us, girlie!

I smile, because I know what a wild girls' night in New York will be like with Kat. A double bottle of wine and *Friends* reruns in her NYU dorm room. She'll tell me all about Joey, even though I've met him three times now and heard about him ad nauseam since they met at freshman orientation. She'll tell me about their plans. And they have a lot of them.

She's happy, and it makes me happy.

I shoot my mom back an **I'll be okay, don't worry** text and then assure Kat that I'm so excited for a night of wine and girl talk in her dorm room.

My last visit, just after the holidays, flashes into my mind. Joey was working, and it was just us again, and there was this bar near Washington Square Park that was really chill with IDs. She and I split a pitcher of beer, and she was telling me all about Joey and how much she loved him, and I just couldn't do it anymore. I couldn't keep the secret.

And so I told her.

Everything. How I met Noah on the train. How I never meant to hurt her. How we kissed that night we spent together, how we shared a bed, but that was it. And how, yes, we still texted sometimes. But nothing else. Because we both cared about her. We both didn't want to hurt her.

She asked me what we texted about, and I told her the truth. How he told me about his comp-lit classes, about a party on Ninety-Third Street, about his dad's new job at a different university. How I was seriously pondering studying journalism, even though the degree sounded about as useful as a comp-lit one.

I had to take an earlier train back to Bard the next morning. She didn't talk to me for two weeks.

But then she did.

And when she did, she gave me a gift—a big one. She forgave me. She forgave us.

She didn't have to do it, but she did. Because she cares about me as much as I care about her.

I'm about to put my phone away and pull out a book when I get another text.

I can't help but laugh, because it's a stupid nickname. It's too long, too ridiculous.

But he likes it, so I can't really object.

Can't wait to see you, Ammy, sweet and fair.